Forgotten Ghosts

Forgotten Ghosts

Eric R. Asher

Print Edition

Edited by Laura Matheson
Cover typography by Indie Solutions by Murphy Rae
Cover design ©Phatpuppyart.com – Claudia McKinney

~

Tamales or chimichangas? Is it a plot clue?
Foreshadowing? No, I'm hungry.

~

CHAPTER ONE

THE OCEAN CALMED as we made our seat among the hexagonal structures of Giant's Causeway. Nixie unwrapped her arm from around my waist and snatched the blue and white cardboard box from my grip.

"Of all the food we could get here," I said, "you really wanted a Crave Case?"

"It'll be some time before I'm back in Saint Charles," Nixie said as she popped the box open, and the very foreign scent of White Castle cheeseburgers mingled with the salt of the surrounding ocean. "In fact, I suspect Finn McCool himself would rather enjoy these sandwiches, if they were only a bit larger."

A slow smile pulled at the corners of my lips. I took a slider from Nixie and turned my attention back to the shoreline. The causeway had become one of my favorite places to visit. A surreal landscape where you could almost imagine yourself in an alien world. Perhaps not as alien as the Abyss itself, but a more welcoming land, with far more hope than the darkness had.

"It's quiet here." I took a deep breath and sighed.

"The ocean is quite loud," Nixie said. "Did I damage you?" She raised an eyebrow and leaned forward, one side of her mouth lifting ever so slightly.

I barked out a short laugh. "I mean the dead. They're quiet here. It's not like the constant roar back home, especially on the battlefields." I rubbed at my back and grimaced. "But that wasn't the most comfortable place I've ever had sex."

Nixie raised an eyebrow. "You were on top almost the entire time."

"I'm not as squishy as you," I said, grumbling.

"Are you calling me fat?" she asked with a sly grin.

I snorted a laugh. "I'm not … why would you even … I'm just saying I need pants."

A slow smile crawled across Nixie's face. "Sam was right. You look flustered."

I froze. "She told you to say that?"

Silence.

"Stupid vampire," I muttered. My sister had always been a master of the guilt trip.

Nixie snarfed down a slider before snapping up another one and leaning back with a satisfied growl. "Someone in Faerie needs to learn how to make these."

"You just need to visit more often," I said.

Nixie looked up from her sandwich and gave me a small, sad smile. "It's only been six months since the death of Lewena. We defeated her forces in Saint Charles. It was a battle won, but not the war. We have to press our advantage."

At that moment, the feeling of things being normal again evaporated. "I know. Nudd and Hern are still in Falias. And still a threat."

Nixie nodded.

"How are the other water witches? Lewena's witches, I mean?"

Nixie chewed her sandwich, pondering that question as the shadows of two distant tourists wandered the edge of the causeway far above us.

I started looking for my pants in earnest.

"Some have joined us," Nixie said. "And some of those I trust. But it is a slow process, the aftermath of any battle. Some will harbor resentment for us, for me, until I am dead or dethroned. But some of them will value peace above vengeance. Some will want their children and their families safe from the war Nudd wants so badly. I'm trying to keep them all too busy to get into trouble."

A wave peaked high and crashed onto the causeway. A spray of cold, salty water reached us, just enough to remind us it was there. I studied Nixie, the subtle crease in her brow, and wondered how much influence she actually had over the nearby waters. Some stories said the water witches could control the oceans, and I'd certainly seen them control bodies of water before, but the seas themselves were vast, and sometimes terrible. The ocean was a beautiful, deadly thing.

Nixie hesitated. "We're making due. What about Sam and Foster? And Frank? They're still consulting with the military, I assume?"

I nodded. "They're good. Frank's friendship with Sergeant Park paid off. Or I should say, First Sergeant Park, now."

"Not to mention your actions in Saint Charles," Nixie said. "The support you gave Casper's squad, and that her squad gave our allies in return, was no small thing."

Casper and her people had proven themselves invaluable. It had been a risk, giving them the arms Mike had forged that could kill undines. But it was a risk with great reward. Casper had struck a deadly blow against Lewena, and she had saved my ass in the process. But that had turned Casper into the new poster child for the military, and she hated every minute of it. They'd rolled out banners around the base, and even a few billboards in Saint Charles. She didn't like being a face for recruiters and propaganda.

The crashing waves drew my attention once more. There was something calming about the ocean, or perhaps it was more the silence in my head. It held a great many mysteries, even from the water witches themselves.

"You remember me telling you about that video?"

"The propaganda idea?" Nixie looked up from her newly unboxed slider.

"Yeah that one," I said. "It's been making the rounds. From what Park says, a good portion of the military has seen it now. They've added a few things to it, like the details on how to strike down a dark-touched. But the basics are still the same."

Nixie frowned and swallowed. "I'm still unsure how to feel about this. Training humans to recognize us, and in some cases even how to kill us. And we know we have enemies among their ranks."

"We have allies among the ranks, too," I said. "I only hope that proves more important than the former."

Nixie exhaled slowly. "Time will tell. It always does."

We ate in silence for a while, watching the waters and listening to the cry of nearby birds. I took down seven or eight of the sliders from the Crave Case, and Nixie inhaled the rest. Something squawked over the rolling waves of the ocean. At first I thought it was only another bird, but as it grew closer, I could make out words and something else. Concern.

"My queen," a voice shouted.

It drew our attention as fast as a battle cry would have.

"Euphemia," Nixie said. "What is it?"

The water witch sprinted across the columns of Giant's Causeway. As I watched her graceful movements across those steps, I wondered how much truth there was to the legend of Finn McCool, and whether a giant had in fact once lived here. Or perhaps still did. And then I remembered I still didn't have pants on. It was about then I saw the sly grin on Nixie's face and she lifted the damp denim out of a pool behind her. I snatched my pants back and hurried to pull them up before sitting my wet ass back down beside Nixie.

"There's been an incident back in the States," Euphemia said, and the absence of jabs about our lack of clothing said worlds.

My back stiffened, and I leaned forward.

"How bad?" Nixie asked as she magicked armor back onto her body with a wave of her hand. "Casualties?"

Euphemia shook her head. "Nothing so dire as that. At least not yet. Have you checked your phone today? I was not sure if you would've already heard the news."

I looked around at the beauty above and below us and frowned. "Why in the world would I look at my phone here?"

"Because humanity is addicted to them," Euphemia said.

I gave a sideways nod of my head. "Fair point. So, what is it?"

"Search for the phrase 'Saint Louis dragon.' I believe it will tell you most of what you need to know."

"There is no need for games," Nixie said glancing from me to Euphemia. "What has happened?"

But I'd unlocked my phone before Nixie finished asking the question. I'd already typed the phrase in and stared at the impossible image on top of the results. It had been posted by what amounted to little more than a tabloid, but I'd seen dragons. And I had little doubt of what I was looking at.

I cursed and looked up at Euphemia. "Did they attack? What happened?"

As the words left my lips, I stared at the silhouette of the dragon gliding through the Arch before my eyes roved down into the article itself. There were no human casualties, but the dragon had been seen fighting with a group of Fae. With such a delicate balance between the military and the Fae, I didn't like the idea of anyone trotting out a dragon.

"Goddess," Nixie said, pulling my phone closer to her. "That's not Drake."

"No," Euphemia said. "It's not. Can you think of no one else?"

"Can't be," I whispered. I zoomed in as close as I could, and at the base of his neck, was a lump just large enough to be a young teenage girl. "Vicky?" My mouth felt dry, and a terrible dread climbed its way up my throat.

Nixie looked from the phone screen to me and back again. "Shit. She's a risk, Damian. She's a risk to you, to me, to all of us."

"What? I mean, she shouldn't have flown a dragon into Saint Louis …"

"No, Damian, you'd do anything to save that child. Too many people know it. She's a weakness. *Your* weakness. If she won't stay hidden, we have to act. Now."

CHAPTER TWO

I GRIMACED AND turned off the do not disturb settings on my phone. The roll call of notifications felt like it was cursing my own carelessness. But I'd needed to get away. Nixie and I hadn't had much time lately. Between keeping our alliances together, trying to integrate the water witches that had been loyal to Lewena into the society of witches who had struck down their queen, and launching some of our more underhanded campaigns, time had become precious indeed.

Nixie leaned over and studied the rather intimidating list of missed calls and text messages. "I can see why Euphemia thought we might have already heard. Is that a different Foster?" She pointed to a rather irritated text message.

"No, that's our Foster."

"And he carries a phone?" Euphemia asked, stepping closer to Nixie. "No device like that can transition with him."

I nodded. "He's with First Sergeant Park today. Sam's carrying it for him."

"I hope their training went better than last week," Nixie said, referring to an unfortunate incident where Foster had accidentally impaled one of the privates when he'd failed to follow directions.

"Let's hope." I copied and pasted the same response to half a dozen concerned text messages. *We saw it. Will be in touch.*

"Hugh is still in Kansas City," Euphemia said. "The witch coven has gone to meet the pack. I am unsure if they were invited, or if this move is of their own volition, but they continue to hunt the dark-touched."

"And the blood mages?" Nixie asked.

"Elizabeth would likely follow Ashley if she suspected danger," Euphemia said. "I haven't been able to reach her or Cornelius, which likely means they're already there."

"Ashley can take care of herself," I said. "Woman could probably kill more people in one strike than the three of us."

Euphemia nodded. "And you have yet to see what the blood mages are truly capable of."

I frowned at her. I'd seen enough of their power, and I couldn't stifle the shiver that rolled down my spine as I remembered the creature they'd summoned from the shadow realm.

"What about the other wolves?" I asked. "Dell and Caroline aren't stationed far from the southeastern edges of Falias."

"They are charged with the protection of the armory at Antietam," Euphemia said.

Nixie glanced between us. "The Utukku are more than capable. Be sure they're aware we may need the Irish Brigade. I am certain Wahya would not miss a chance to sink his claws into the allies of Gwynn Ap Nudd."

I rubbed my chin. "We could ask Caroline outright, see if they'll stay closer to Falias."

"The Obsidian Inn would shelter them," Euphemia said.

"See to it," Nixie said.

Euphemia gave an informal nod of her head. I liked that, seeing the witches in a more casual exchange. The rituals of Fae were not so unlike those I'd read about in history books, formal ceremonies that almost felt designed to cause discomfort and remind those who served that they were less. To say I didn't like it would be a bit of an understatement.

"What of Graybeard and the vampires?" Nixie asked as she turned to me.

I rubbed my palms together. "As far as I know they haven't killed each other."

Euphemia chuckled.

"That was just rotten luck," Nixie said. "Zola turning up that little tidbit in the archives. No one could have foreseen that. I wouldn't think Vik would hold a grudge that long."

"A vampire can hold the grudge of his sire and his sire's sire," Euphemia muttered. "They can be most trying. Look at Camazotz if you need further evidence."

I smiled and looked at Nixie. "I have little doubt they'll be able to put aside their differences to help Sam."

"But what exactly happened?" Nixie asked. "How did Graybeard, mortal at the time, plunder a ship full of vampires?"

"He hasn't told me yet," I said, "but you better believe I'm working on him." I leaned forward and looked up at Euphemia. "Speaking of the Obsidian Inn, have you heard from Aideen and Angus?"

"Yes," she said with a nod. "Training is going well. Angus is well versed in, shall we say, less-civilized methods of combat."

"Isn't pretty much every Fae?"

"Brutal combat, yes," Nixie said. "But his more devious tactics are beyond what even I would have deployed in our darkest hour."

Euphemia blew out a breath. "I am afraid the darkness

grows bolder every hour, my queen. It may be that the time for more civilized warring has passed."

Nixie grimaced, and it sent a chill down my spine. I'd seen how merciless the Fae could be. What in the ever-loving hell were they holding back?

"Angus won't rest until Hern and his entire legacy are buried," Euphemia said.

"At what cost?" Nixie whispered, running her fingers through her hair.

I already knew the answer to that question: "Any."

The three of us sat in silence for a time, watching the water crash below us as ravens soared above. One, a monstrous bird with slightly off, diamond-shaped tail feathers, swooped low, circling as it went.

"Morrigan," Nixie said, frowning at the bird.

The raven cawed back twice before speaking. "We must leave, Euphemia. Your message has been delivered, now come."

Euphemia looked to Nixie, and only when her queen nodded did the water witch take her leave.

"No judgmental observations today?" I asked. "Just going to be an angry bird in the sky?"

I could have sworn the raven glared at me before rocketing over the cliff and vanishing on the other side.

"Good hearing," I said.

"She is not the best being to torment," Nixie said. "She could kill either of us."

I smiled, watching the sky where the bird had vanished.

Nixie frowned and turned to the horizon. She still wasn't too happy about what the Morrigan had done to me at the Obsidian Inn. Essentially, had I failed her test, I would have died. A small, slightly mad part of me wondered if the Morrigan would have survived Nixie's response. Being we weren't dead, I hoped that was a grudge I'd never see play out.

"Go," Nixie said. "I must meet with Ward and the Old Man. They're journeying to Faerie, and I fear the timing could not be much worse with the unrest across the realm."

More of the Fae wanted to come live in the new Falias. I couldn't be sure how humanity would respond to that, but I had a pretty good list of concerns.

"I fear a civil war between the Fae, Damian. And that I cannot abide. The world may not survive it."

I stood up and brushed my pants off before holding my hand out to Nixie. "Sounds like we need to get back to work."

She leaned forward and kissed me, and I smiled as I felt that soft warmth before she pulled away. "Be careful."

I nodded as I fished Gaia's hand out of my backpack. "I just need to drop by and see Park and Casper to make sure they don't go shooting at dragons. The kid picked a rotten time to stop hiding." I turned to go, but Nixie grabbed my arm.

"Did you speak to Zola?"

I nodded. "She's at the cabin. I'm heading that way after I talk to the military."

"Good."

"Any word from our agents?" I asked.

Nixie looked out at the ocean and hesitated for a moment before shaking her head. "Not yet. It's been almost a week, and I'm starting to get somewhat concerned."

"Does Euphemia know?" I asked. There weren't many people who did. And only those in Nixie's deepest confidence knew about the agent who had slipped into Gwynn Ap Nudd's ranks.

"No," she said. "Not even Euphemia. Once we have something we can act on, or perhaps I should say *if* we have something, I'll tell her immediately. Right now, it is only you, Morrigan, Sam, and Foster."

"It was a lucky thing, meeting those three."

Nixie nodded, though she didn't say their names, names I'd come to know well in the past few months. Liam, Lochlan, and Enda. They were a family of Fae that we more or less accidentally rescued from the ruins of Falias. They'd been hurt by Nudd and Lewena in the past, and it hadn't taken much convincing to get them to help Nixie's cause.

Nixie stepped away, but I followed her and wrapped my arms around her. Her armor was cold beneath my fingers, but Nixie's lips were soft and warm, and the salty taste of the sea lingered as she leaned into me. I gave her the best smile I could muster as we drew apart.

Nixie adjusted the sword at her waist as I laced my fingers into Gaia's and stepped into the darkness. The stars of the Abyss tilted around me as the warm glow of Gaia's form slowly took shape to my right.

"How may I assist you?" Gaia asked.

"So formal," I said. "What's the occasion?"

When Gaia didn't respond, I looked up at her. There was a small shadowed crease in her golden brow.

"I suppose it is simply an old habit. I have tried to leave the old compulsions behind, as you requested, but I cannot fully abandon them."

I smiled at the Titan, letting the smooth cadence of her voice wash over me, providing a warmth that the Abyss lacked in every way. "Don't worry about it."

"Where may I take you?" she asked as we walked the dimly illuminated path.

"I need to get to Sergeant Park, First Sergeant Park, I mean," I said. "There's a dragon in Saint Louis. And I don't want him taking a shot at it."

"A dragon?" Gaia frowned as we strode along the path. "That is most unusual."

I shook my head. "You're telling me. I thought Vicky would stay hidden longer. I never dreamed she'd take Jasper out. I'm worried."

My own words struck me. I was worried. I was very worried. Most days I felt like the war was going well. Lewena had fallen, and it had been months since we had a conflict with Hern or Nudd or even the dark-touched.

"Your thoughts are troubled, young one."

"It just feels like the calm before the shitstorm," I muttered.

"I am not familiar with this term. Shit … storm."

I glanced up at the Old God and chuckled. "It's almost worth it just to hear you say it."

Something glistened near the path beside me. I mistook it for one of the massive Leviathan tentacles we sometimes crossed in the Abyss. But a closer look showed something different. It was like thousands of rubbery gray worms slowly rising and wriggling in a giant ball, only the ball had form. It ended in some semblance of a hand, and I followed that mass up into the shadows, somewhat disturbed to see that the writhing appendage continued up into an arm. I suspected there was much more lurking in the darkness.

Even as I watched, the gray rubber worms cracked open at

the ends, revealing countless thorn-like teeth in their eyeless faces. I'd seen something like it before on a nature show. They looked like lampreys. The creature blossomed with countless fanged mouths as it leaned toward us in an impossibly slow strike.

"What the hell is that?" I asked.

Gaia turned her head toward the shadowed mass, even as it faded behind us in the strange time-space of the Abyss. "Some things do not have names, Damian Vesik. And some things never should."

A distant groan that sounded more like a thunderclap half a state away echoed through the starry darkness. I couldn't stifle a shiver.

Gaia's stride slowed. "We are here, when you are ready."

I nodded.

"Be safe. There are things in the darkness you cannot see."

And with that reassuring message, Gaia released my hand.

CHAPTER THREE

I WAS ALWAYS a bit concerned when Gaia was dropping me off at a military facility. It seemed likely that if I appeared in the wrong spot, I'd probably be deflecting bullets, or just be catching one in the back of the head and that would be that. I've always been an optimistic person.

In this case, though, Gaia had returned to one of her favorite delivery methods. As the Abyss disintegrated, a cinderblock wall appeared right in front of my nose and didn't have the courtesy to stop. I turned my head at the last second, and my cheek smacked into the wall before the rest of my body thumped into it as well. I cursed and frantically felt my nose to make sure it wasn't broken. Foster could heal it in a snap, most of the fairies could, but it hurt like a bitch.

"Fucking A," a surprisingly unsurprised voice said behind me.

I sighed in relief as I grew sure the cartilage of my nose was intact before raising my hands away from any threat I might have concealed about my person. My backpack grazed the cinderblock wall as I turned, and I smiled when I saw Casper standing in the hallway with a sheaf of papers.

"Why don't you just use the front door like a normal person?"

"I was in Ireland. I didn't really have that choice."

Casper blinked.

I paused, waiting to see if she would say anything. When she didn't, I asked, "Is Park around?"

"Ireland?" Casper said.

I nodded. "That's where I was. But now I need First Sergeant Park."

Casper narrowed her eyes. "That's a nice travel plan. You'll have to show me how to do that one day."

"I'm not sure how well that would work," I said. "And it would be a pretty bad way to die. Or I suppose, more accurately, die over centuries, maybe millennia?"

Casper's curiosity vanished. "Let me grab the First Sergeant."

"That would be great. I don't want you shooting the dragon."

Casper hesitated beneath the bright fluorescent light that washed out her already pale skin. Both her eyebrows climbed a little bit higher. "It certainly doesn't get boring here," she said, and vanished down the hallway.

She poked her head back around the corner. "Are you coming? I'll just take you to his office. It's probably simpler."

I hurried down the hall and joined her. She'd become something of a celebrity among the water witches. I don't think she realized that herself, as the witches tended not to mingle with humans very much. Or at least they tended to avoid non-magic-using humans, those we called commoners. While Nixie had landed the final blow against Lewena, it had been Casper who had taken the shots that truly ended the battle.

I frowned at the walls as we continued deeper into what I had thought was their temporary base. But the small cinderblock buildings the military had constructed in Saint Charles didn't have hallways as long.

"Where are we?"

The cinderblocks gave way to old foundations, giant quarry rocks like those that had been used to construct the foundations of some of the oldest homes in the city.

"Underground," Casper said.

"Underground where?" I asked.

Casper looked up at the ceiling. "I don't know exactly."

"It's dangerous to dig in this area," I said. "You might find things you'd rather not." I glanced behind me, frowning a little deeper at the flickering shadows and the small gray orbs that danced around the corners of the hall. "Or you might wake something up you don't want."

"It's been okay so far," Casper said. "Aeros helped us carve out a long network of tunnels. We added onto it a bit ourselves, but now we've got an easily defensible location."

"Be pretty easy for the water witches to drown you out."

Casper shook her head. She pointed to a door as we passed by, and I cursed when I saw the hatch. It looked more like something I'd expect to see on a submarine than an underground base.

"Waterproof?" I asked.

She nodded. "One hundred percent."

We turned another corner and a very familiar voice, a very familiar angry voice, echoed through the hall.

"I don't give a dead rat's fucking ass what that reporter promised you," Sam said, her voice echoing off the walls. "You can't trust Emily Beckers."

The knot of dread sank into my stomach at the mention of

the reporter. Emily had once come to Death's Door, seeking answers to the video of a fight we'd once had with a blood mage. It had gone viral, and not even the Watchers had been able to stop it. Granted, that was because Ezekiel had carved through a great many of them, but still.

The reporter had covered darker things.

Park's response was calm, even reasoned, but that didn't stop Casper and I from jogging the rest of the way down the hall. She stopped outside and knocked, as if she planned to formally introduce us. But once I heard the words that came out of Park's mouth, I didn't hesitate to barge in ahead of Casper.

"What reason would that reporter have to lie to us about a dragon? Maybe it wasn't an actual dragon. Maybe it was some kind of Fae creature that we need to be ready for. Something you and Foster haven't yet prepared us for. I can't risk standing down."

"It's a dragon," I said, pushing in to stand next to Sam.

Sam cocked her head to the side and blinked. "Demon, are you sure?" I knew what Sam was really asking. She wanted to know if we were going to tell Park exactly what was going on.

"Yes, it's Vicky. I mean Elizabeth. Elizabeth and Jasper. You're talking about the dragon by the Arch?"

Park nodded.

"That's our friend. Tell your men not to engage her."

"Her? The dragon's a her? What does that have to do with anything?"

"The girl," Sam snapped. "The girl Emily mentioned."

I squeezed Sam's shoulder. "Vicky is still supposed to be in hiding with her parents. I don't know what the hell she's doing." I turned to Park. "But do *not* attack her. She has a very murdery guardian."

"Sorry to break protocol," Casper said. "Damian sort of appeared in front of me."

Park gave a hesitant shake of his head. "This job is going to kill me."

"In all fairness," Casper said. "It probably won't be the job."

Park released a humorless laugh and rested his forehead on his palm. "Give the order. No one is to engage the dragon."

"Glad it's not the other dragon," Sam muttered.

Park's brow furrowed into a look somewhere between irritation and exasperation. "Other. Dragon?"

I gave him an awkward smile. "Drake."

"We haven't heard any reports or sightings of Drake. Not from the troops here, and not from the troops stationed around Falias. I'm not sure if I should be happy about that, or concerned."

"We'll know next time we see him," Sam said.

"This is a pretty nice underground base you have," I said, hoping to catch Park off guard with a violent change of topic.

Park raised an eyebrow at Sam. "You didn't tell him?"

"You said not to," Sam said. "It didn't exactly seem like a critical bit of information."

Park pursed his lips. "Yes, after last year's assault burned our camp to the ground, we decided to put some safety measures in place."

"Smart," I said. "I especially like the submarine-looking doors."

"They don't just look like submarine doors," Park said. "They're made of the same material, and they're deep inside the stone thanks to Aeros."

I waited to see if Park would elaborate. He didn't, so I let it drop. "Where's Foster?"

Park started to say something, but looked at Casper instead. "Did you leave him there?"

Casper frowned.

"Shit," Park and Sam said at the same time.

Park jumped to his feet. "We left him with Ms. Beckers. There's a tunnel that leads to the archives. We'll find them there." He dashed out of the room.

Sam gave me an awkward wave and then rocketed through the door, catching Park in an instant. Casper and I followed.

CHAPTER FOUR

THE WALLS AROUND us changed from the ancient stone of long-forgotten foundations to the cinderblock I was so used to seeing in the temporary military constructions. The hall faded to nothing but dirt with stone arches placed every ten to twenty feet. They were unnaturally smooth, and I had little doubt Aeros had built this section.

"How far?" I asked as we closed on Park and Sam.

"Quarter mile at most," Park said, his voice barely betraying any sign of exertion.

"You don't think Foster would do something stupid, do you?" Casper asked.

Sam released a sharp laugh. "How many months have you known him now? Do you even need to ask? We'll be lucky if that reporter's head's not on a pike."

Casper's eyes went wide.

"She's totally exaggerating," I said. "Totally."

But in the back of my mind, I wondered how far Foster would go. Emily hadn't directly sabotaged us in the past, exactly. But she was certainly part of the media machine. The media could be a serious pain in the ass when you were the underdog in a Fae war.

Park took a sharp left, and we followed. Around the corner was an old concrete staircase. Our boots echoed as we started up the flights. Two floors, four, and we finally found a door on the fifth flight. Park pulled the iron bar off the center of the door and shouldered the creaky hinges open without ceremony. The dim light of the tunnels gave way to the harsh fluorescence of what looked like a room full of floor to ceiling filing cabinets.

"Come on." Park dragged us out of the room into another hallway, refocusing my mind on our task. Park nodded to a middle-aged woman who didn't need any further prompting.

"They're in administration." Her calm façade crumbled into hand wringing. "Please calm them down."

Before anyone could respond to the woman's words, raised voices echoed down the hall. Foster's words rang clear as we closed on a room with a frosted glass window set in the top half of the door.

"I don't give a shit if it's a local newspaper," Foster shouted, his voice growing shrill. "You think they won't have people watching this?"

"You're being ridiculous," Emily snapped back.

Sam pulled the door open, and Park stalked through, followed by the rest of us. For all Foster and Emily took notice, we might as well not have been there.

"The only people in the video are Nudd and the dark-touched," Emily said, her voice rising to a savage note. "There's no way he'd know who shot it."

Foster's hand flashed to his sword where his knuckles whitened around the hilt. "Or maybe he knows *exactly* who shot that video, and you just handed them a death sentence."

"*I'm* putting your friends at risk?" Emily asked. "You're the most suicidal bunch I've ever seen. And I've covered some pretty horrible black ops shit."

"You think you can take her, Foster?" I asked. "I give you 50/50 odds."

The focus of the entire room turned to me. Park frowned before slowly raising an eyebrow.

"Hi," I said, giving Foster a sideways smile.

The fairy narrowed his eyes. "We're just talking."

"And before you even start on me," Emily said, meeting my gaze with steel in her eyes, "I didn't' steal anything from the base. An anonymous source sent that video to me."

I frowned. "What are you talking about?"

"Ha!" Foster said. "Ms. Beckers published a story on Vicky, and in the process has likely got Enda and her family killed."

"I gave Ms. Beckers permission to run a story about Casper," Park said. "It was supposed to be a propaganda piece, to complement the campaign you've seen."

Foster stomped across the newspaper on the desk he was standing on and unsheathed his sword. He used it as a pointer. At first, I thought he was indicating the headline. But his sword moved to the photo included in the article.

I cursed.

"Christ," Park said.

Sam leaned over the table. She frowned at the photo for a moment before her gaze shot up to the reporter. "That's surveillance footage that Enda shot. That *only* Enda could have shot!"

"You've put that entire family at risk," Casper said. "Send word to the Obsidian Inn. Get them *out*."

"You don't have to worry about the dragon. It was eating Fae." A knot twisted in my stomach. If any ally of Nudd's had already seen this, Liam, Lochlan, and Enda were in terrible danger. "If anyone gets Vicky or my friends in Falias hurt, you can't even comprehend the pain I'll rain down on them."

I struggled to keep myself in check. I knew the dead in the city, and I could call on most of them without having some awful flash of knowing I hadn't already experienced. It might be more dangerous around them, and sometimes I feared it made me more unstable, but I pulled my aura back together, even as it tried to reach out to the ghosts.

To Emily, it might have simply looked like I was trying to intimidate her, and she wouldn't be wrong. She'd caused me more than one headache over the years, and now she was putting my friends at risk. And that was unacceptable.

"Ms. Beckers," Park said, "you're coming to interrogation with me."

"I know my rights," Emily said. "This is beneath you."

"Nothing is beneath me in this war," Park said. He tipped his head toward Casper, and she moved into action. She placed one hand on Emily's wrist and the other on her shoulder. To the untrained, it might look like she was gently escorting her out of the room. To me, it looked like she could break the woman's arm in a split second and put her face into the dirt at the same time. Casper knew how to be prepared, and she was someone I'd never want to cross.

Park waited a beat before he turned around and closed the door. He stared down at the image in the local newspaper and cursed. "How fast can you get someone to get Enda and her family out?"

Foster flexed his wings and grimaced. "I don't know, but I'll send word now."

"It's time to go see Vicky," I said.

"Let me know if we should expect any more dragon sightings," Park said, glancing at the newspaper.

Sam stepped closer to Park. "Your soldiers are more than capable of handling a leak to the newspapers. Get them on it. Damian and Foster and I can handle the fairy stuff. Concentrate on what you know."

Park sighed. "I know more than I wanted to know. Just when I think I have a handle on it, something else crops up. Dragons, reporters, and I don't even know which is worse."

"I *have* to go see Vicky," I said. "I think it's time to talk to her family, too."

"What?" Foster and Sam said at once.

I nodded. "There's too much at risk. There's too much that puts *her* at risk. I need to be sure they understand everything going on."

"Uh huh," Sam said. "You mean about how you traveled to an alternate dimension and killed the being that was taking over their dead child's *soul* before you brought her back to *life*? I'm sure that'll go over *great!*"

I fidgeted and rubbed my hands together. "Okay, maybe they don't have to hear all of it."

"You want us to come?" Foster asked.

I shook my head. "Stay here. The training is one of the most important things we have going for us right now. More soldiers mean more allies."

"Except for the soldiers that want to kill us," Foster said. "I'm literally training some of these assholes to kill me."

I glanced at Park.

He gave a half shrug. "A few, yes. Most of the troops are

quite fond of Foster, though. At least those that aren't terrified of him. Stabbing that private probably didn't help."

Foster grunted. "I assumed that idiot knew his right from his left. Bet he won't make that mistake again."

"We'll stay," Sam said. "But if you need us, you call. Frank's doing PT with some of the privates. He'll be here too if you need him. You know he will."

I paused. "Who's running the shop? I thought Frank was there today."

"Aideen is," Foster said. "She's back from the Obsidian Inn. Business still hasn't picked up as much as we'd hoped since the battle with the water witches, so she's comfortable running things by herself."

"Good. Good." I nodded to myself as if I was silently trying to pump myself up for going to Vicky's house. I suppose that's exactly what I was doing.

"But we're clear?" I asked, turning to Park. "No shooting the dragon?"

"You see," he said, "this is exactly the kind of thing I'm talking about. I've been having a relatively normal day, but now I have to tell my men not to shoot at the dragon. A *dragon!*"

I nodded sagely. "The dragon's quite friendly. But if you have any collectible Barbies around, I'd probably hide them."

Park muttered under his breath. "No shooting the Barbie-eating dragon."

Sam and Foster chuckled as I backed out of the room and closed the door behind me.

CHAPTER FIVE

I WALKED TO the main hallway, my boots echoing around me as I left the dead acoustics of the filing cabinets behind. The light grew brighter, until the sun streaming through the windows washed away the harsh fluorescent light that had surrounded us before.

Another member of the archives nodded to us as I crossed the threshold and exited onto the steps of the old building. I wondered how much time Koda had spent there, or if the building had even been around when he was still alive. The weight of a great many spirits inside hadn't escaped me, but Saint Charles was a place where the dead were always close.

The wide steps led to the uneven brick of the sidewalk. I glanced to the south and frowned at the edge of the site where not so long ago the military had set up thousands of tents, right in the heart of Saint Charles, right in the heart of Main Street. It was still hard to reconcile some days that we'd fought that battle here, but Lewena had brought the water witches to our home and destroyed so much of the riverfront.

Aeros and the Undine's had done an amazing job rebuilding things. And I'd seen more than one green man tending to the trees that had survived. But I'd seen something else in the shadows, too. Something I'd once seen in the darkness of Greenville. It towered like a green man, but the savage gouges in the bark-like flesh that formed its face made an unsettling impression. The creature had seemed to have no ill will toward the green men, but anything I couldn't identify tended to concern me.

In the last three months, we'd seen a good influx of commoners returning to the area. Some of them thought they'd be safer staying near the supernaturals and the military they'd trained. But others had bought into the propaganda. They'd come to realize who we were. That we were the ones Gwynn Ap Nudd had called out in his infamous television appearance.

Now we were just as likely, or perhaps far more likely, to receive a death threat at the store's email as we were to receive an order. Frank had managed to set up some excellent filters, which kept the worst of it out of our sight, but there was still something disconcerting about seeing all that hate documented so thoroughly.

I turned away from the open patch of ground, now sprinkled with dead grass, and headed north toward Death's Door. Some of the usual county construction had started up again along Main Street. It was a rare day where you didn't see some amount of cobblestones torn up, or the sidewalks dug up, to either repair the sewers and pipes beneath them, or simply fix the sidewalk to help keep the pedestrians from snapping their ankles. The old cobblestone roads required quite a bit of upkeep, but I always felt like it was worth the cost to preserve that history. I hoped the city would also continue to believe it to be worth it.

The rains had stopped. Puddles still waited in the uneven cobblestones across Main Street. A few brave souls had already ventured out, unsure if the last wave of the thunderstorm had already passed, or if they'd be trapped in another deluge. A family of red-haired children stood on the corner, seemingly beyond the worry of rains or the coming storm. I suspected the family may not have been entirely human. We'd been seeing more Fae lately around Saint Charles. Some who had moved from Falias, and others who claimed to have done the same. I wasn't the only one who was concerned that there might be spies among them. Foster and Aideen were already looking into that.

A few large drops of rain crashed against the glass plates of the gas streetlamps. A flurry of umbrellas rose across the sidewalks, shielding those less tolerant of the rain. Lightning lit the brick of the restaurant beside me and thunder shook the sky a moment later. It was perhaps an omen of things to come, the gathering clouds of a storm none of us would want to be in.

I made my way past the print shop where we sometimes had flyers done for the store, dodging around another bit of street repair. Farther up the street, I paused in front of Main Street Books. It was a modern shop, and while they didn't carry the things I was generally looking for, they did stock quite a few titles on the history of Saint Charles, written by modern historians. But instead of the bookstore, I'd been sequestered away in the attic of Death's Door, nose deep in the library doing research. It had been months since I'd read a book simply for entertainment, and the thought made me groan.

When this was over, the first thing I'd be doing would be turning off my phone and locking myself in that library with a good read.

I passed a couple of bars, and eyed the crowd gathered around an old antique store. The rain started to pick up, and I frowned at the old metal awning declaring the area historic Saint Charles. That part of the street always looked dark to me in the rain. Like some ominous thing, ready to swallow anyone who wandered too close.

I picked up my pace, passing restaurants and the occasional pedestrian and only a handful of soldiers. The rain was a steady drizzle, but by the time I made it to the shop I was still soaked.

The bell jingled on the front door as I walked in, the old handle cold beneath my fingers.

"Damian," Aideen said as I stepped inside.

"Hey."

"That's 15.98 with tax," Aideen said, turning her attention back to the customer at the counter. I smiled as the fairy danced barefoot across the tablet, before shoving it toward the customer. "Just swipe your card, and you're all set."

A little girl with light brown hair stepped out from behind what I supposed was her mom. She went up on her tiptoes and smiled up at Aideen. "She's beautiful." And it was said in that matter-of-fact way only a child can speak. There was no deception to her words, no exaggeration or manipulation. She was simply stating what she felt was the truth.

"Thank you, dear," Aideen said. "That's always nice to hear as we get older."

The mother ran her hand through the child's hair. She looked back to Aideen. "You can't be that old. You look like you're in your twenties."

"We do not age quite the same as humans," Aideen said, giving the pair a broad smile. "I am much older than you might think. Although I did have a very good friend that lived to be almost 5000 years old. Now that's old."

The child giggled, and the mother just stared blankly at Aideen for a moment. She shook herself and signed the tablet.

"Thank you, dears," Aideen said. "If you'd like a bag, feel free to help yourself. I hope to see you again."

The customers thanked our Fae proprietor, gathered up their purchases, and headed for the front door. I stepped into the far aisle to give them plenty of room to pass. The mother's steps slowed when she saw me, and I braced myself for whatever words she might have to say. Her arm wrapped around her child's shoulders in a protective stance.

"Thank you," she said. "Some people in the city don't understand what you've done for us. They say you brought hell to our streets. We saw what you fought back in the river. Thank you."

It was my turn to stare blankly, as the woman took her leave and the bell jingled on her way out into the rain.

"What the hell was that?" I asked, waving at the front window as the little girl waved back.

"They stayed in town when the water witches attacked," Aideen said. "They saw you and Bubbles and Nixie take down the harbinger."

"We didn't take it down," I said.

Aideen held up her hand. "They saw what they saw Damian, nothing can change that. I for one am grateful we have goodwill among some of the commoners." She glanced at the now-empty window. "And perhaps we have more than we realized."

"Thanks for watching over the shop," I said.

"Of course," she said.

"I'm heading to Vicky's now."

"You never responded to their letter. The letter her parents sent you?"

I grimaced. "I know. What the hell was I supposed to say to that?"

"I'm sure they've grown more accustomed to her by now. They may have missed out on some years, but they have their child once more. They'll understand you don't have all the answers they're looking for."

"Let's just hope it doesn't come up. Because now I have to talk to them about their daughter's *dragon*."

Aideen gave me a huge grin. "Good luck."

I narrowed my eyes and pushed my way through the saloon-style doors, passing the Formica table and the old grandfather clock before Bubbles ripped an enormous snore from the safety of her lair. The closet door creaked when I pulled it open, pondering a change of shirts. I could don one of the vampire-skull T-shirts Vicky had given me. The vampires certainly seemed to be amused by them, but this wasn't exactly a social call. I hadn't even *talked* to Vicky in a few months. It felt best to leave her be, so she could have a normal life.

The umbrella on the shelf caught my eye, so I grabbed it and headed through the back door. I glanced back at the deadbolt, surprised it hadn't harassed me. If I hadn't known better, I would've sworn it was sleeping. It made me wonder if Aideen had found an effective way to threaten it into silence. The thought made me happy.

I pulled the door open on my thirty-two Ford, the car I'd taken to calling Vicky before the little ghost had taken on that name. Before she'd been trapped in the Burning Lands. Before she'd been resurrected.

And now I was going to talk to her parents.

I slid into the small seat and collapsed against it. The car started with a roar, and I made my way onto the streets.

CHAPTER SIX

THERE WAS ONE thing I was sure of: Vicky wouldn't have come out of hiding without reason. The question was, how good of a reason? And how dangerous? The thought of what might be out there hunting her caused my pulse to spike. Was it the vampires? Nudd himself? Something from the Burning Lands that had snuck through the cracks between realms?

I turned the wheel and the car veered around the entrance ramp to Highway 70, starting the short trip east before I merged onto 141 and headed south.

I'd almost reached Manchester Road before my nerves really kicked in. As I tried to take my mind off things, I recalled a particularly eventful trip to the old altar. We'd managed to summon a demon, and then kill it at Zola's cabin. I couldn't be sure, but I thought I might have more nerves about this trip than I'd had then.

And with that, my thoughts returned to Vicky like a rubber band. I thought about talking to Vicky's parents, telling them part of what had happened. But how would I do that? How did you tell someone about the hell their child had been through? Would Vicky even want them to know?

My knuckles whitened as I strangled the steering wheel. It was a conversation I'd tried to have in my head a dozen times, a hundred times. But I never had a good answer. So here we were. Time had passed, and some things had perhaps gotten better, but others had most assuredly gotten worse. Nudd was here, in our world. He spent more time stalking the palaces of Falias than he spent in Faerie. He put on such a benevolent show, like a magnanimous ruler returning from obscurity. I feared he'd hoodwinked half the commoners.

But benevolent wasn't a word anyone should use with Gwynn Ap Nudd.

His treaty, or partnership, or whatever hellish agreement he had with the dark-touched gave him an edge I didn't care to think about. The Morrigan told us Nudd was a fool for entering into such a bond. The dark-touched could not be controlled like that. They were too elemental, too undisciplined, but I'd seen them fight with the water witches and their harbingers, and I knew we hadn't seen the last of them.

I took a deep breath as I turned onto a street lined with old oak trees. Neatly trimmed hedges rose up sporadically, and it didn't take long for me to find the one that I'd hidden behind the night we'd taken Vicky home.

My stomach flip-flopped as the old car bounced into the driveway. I wouldn't be hiding in the shadows anymore. I supposed this was inevitable. The desire to see Vicky again warred with the dread of meeting her parents.

The car door thudded closed. A few footsteps carried me up to the porch. I watched my finger ring the doorbell, as if it was someone else's, cast upon a movie screen in a dark theater.

Footsteps and muffled voices sounded inside the house before laughter grew louder and the deadbolt clicked open. The hinges whispered, and the face of a man not much older than me appeared in the doorway. I remembered seeing him that night. He'd been broken, with nothing but routine to keep him moving from day to day. But that wasn't the man who stood before me now. This man stood straight and looked well, though his grip on the doorknob turned his knuckles white, and his smile was strained.

My brain didn't fully register what I was hearing as I stared into the dark blue eyes of Vicky's father.

"Jasper, no!" a woman's stern voice shouted.

I frowned slightly as Vicky's father stumbled out of the way and a large gray thing exploded through the screen door. I didn't so much as have time to curse before the wide ball of gray fluff smacked into me and sent me to the ground, flailing into squarely trimmed bushes that were not nearly so soft as they appeared. Jasper chittered and squeaked, his size shrinking then expanding as the round ball snuggled up against my neck and bounced on my chest before shooting back into the house.

A woman about my age appeared at the hole in her door. She looked down at her husband, who lay sprawled across the foyer. "James, I told you we needed to take that screen out."

"I was thinking about it, Lori, but I didn't think Jasper would get *that* excited about anyone who would be visiting us. You must be Damian. Please, come in."

"It's the—" I started. "It's nice to meet you." I accepted a hand when he offered, and he helped me out of the bushes.

"Vicky's in her room," her mom said. "She's been waiting for you."

I frowned at that. Elizabeth was the name I'd expected to hear. I didn't want to ask why they weren't calling her Elizabeth, but I guess my expression wasn't so subtle.

"That's her name now," her dad said with a sigh. "Just have

to get used to it."

I pulled the door shut behind me, the punched-out metal screen dragging and squeaking along the concrete until it clicked closed.

"Can I get you a drink?" Lori asked. I frowned at her for a moment before shaking my head. For years, I'd been friends with this family's daughter, with the ghost of their daughter. In all that time, I'd always thought of them as Vicky's mom and Vicky's dad. It was strange to think of them as something else, as their given names. It felt right, but it also brought their loss crashing back down onto my shoulders.

"I'm good, thanks," I said quietly.

"Vicky's room is down the hall to the right," James said. "It's right at the end. Why don't you talk to her?"

Getting a chance to speak to Vicky alone sounded a hell of a lot better than ambushing the whole family at once. I hadn't seen Vicky in person in over a year.

I nodded. Mirrors mounted on the wall to the right caught my attention before I turned the corner into the hallway. The house wasn't very big. It appeared to be three modest bedrooms, two barely large enough to comfortably fit a twin-size bed, and the other the master bedroom. I froze in the hallway for a moment. I'd done more than fail Vicky. Was I really going to risk taking her away from a real home? What the hell was I thinking?

Jasper purred on my shoulder. I reached up and scratched the furball between his giant black eyes. The deep trill woke me from my reverie, and I started down the hall again, my boots silent on the old beige carpet.

Even if James hadn't told me which bedroom was Vicky's, it

wouldn't have been hard to figure it out. The door stood open, but I still stopped and knocked on the frame. I stared across the room at a wall covered in newspaper articles and photos that had clearly been printed off the net on a cheap printer. Some of the pages were wrinkled, unable to maintain their form under the weight of the ink. Pictures of Nudd hung in one section of the wall, while red string tied between tacks trailed to an ethereal drawing of what I was quite sure was Hern. I traced those lines and found the Morrigan and Edgar and Camazotz and the dark-touched. Farther down the wall was a photo I didn't remember taking. Four of us huddled in the library above Death's Door—me and Happy and Foster, with Vicky asleep on one of the overstuffed chairs.

But the warm feeling I got from that photo, of seeing Vicky and Happy together, fled when I saw the photo next to it.

I stepped into the room, vaguely aware of Vicky sitting at the desk on the nearest wall, refusing to believe what I was seeing. But as I grew closer, there was no doubt. It was her, and a fairy, and two dragons.

Rage like I hadn't felt in months boiled in the pit of my stomach. "Drake," I snarled.

"At least he returns phone calls," Vicky said, pulling her headphones off.

The growing fire in my gut fizzled. "You have Drake's phone number? The right hand of the Mad King? Murderer, deceiver, and number one Fae who ought not be trusted?"

Vicky gave me a half smile that lit up her eyes. The only word I could think to describe it was sarcastic. "Some of the fairies say the same thing about me. So it seemed like a good fit."

"Fairies? Plural? How is this keeping a low profile?" I asked as I gestured uselessly at the photo of her and the infuriatingly charming-looking Drake. "Is he why you were flying your dragon around downtown? I didn't pull you out of the Burning Lands so you could live an extremely short life. I yanked you back so you could have a normal life!"

Vicky's mouth pulled into a flat line. She held her hand up, curled it into a fist, and lit a brilliant soulsword.

I blinked at the dense blade.

"Not one call, Damian," Vicky said, holding up the index finger of her free hand. "Is this normal?" She gestured to the soulsword before letting it snap out of existence. "You left me with a dragon and fragments of memories."

"I was hoping you wouldn't get those back. Kid, you know now I can't be around you. It's not safe."

"Bullshit. If there's a weak link in the Devil's Knot that binds us together, it's not me."

I felt a light pressure on my shoulder as Jasper compressed and launched himself across the room into Vicky's lap. She scratched the furball between the eyes, and with her legs crossed and her shoulders back, she could've been mistaken for a Bond villain. It was then that I noticed the black clothes, the antique enamel skull pin that adorned her left shoulder, the dark eyeliner.

"Are you a goth?" I asked, completely losing the grip on my anger again. The kid could disarm me in a moment. I wondered subconsciously if that was really why I had been avoiding her.

"I'm undead," she said. "It seems fitting."

"I'm sorry." The words felt inadequate. "I don't want to put you at risk, but you're exposed now."

She ran her fingers through Jasper's fur. "It's not your choice anymore. It hasn't been your choice for the last year."

I frowned, fishing for the right way to apologize to her, to tell her how happy I was she was home, to tell her how much we all talked about her, to tell her she had another family at Death's Door.

Instead, I stood there like a mute idiot while the child—young woman, if I was being honest with myself—rose to her feet, walked over to me, and put her arms around me.

"I missed you," Vicky said.

"Missed you too, kid." I failed to fight back the tremor in my voice.

"Next time, just talk to me. Don't make me ride a dragon through the Arch to get your attention."

Jasper trilled on her shoulder, and I let a tiny laugh slip.

"Let's go talk to the folks," she said. "You could've at least responded to my dad's letter. That was just rude."

"But I—" I started, remember the words of gratitude her father had written me. But how could I respond to that? What could I say? She grabbed my wrist and pulled me out of the room, dragging me down the hallway while the realization dawned on me that I hadn't gotten a single answer I was looking for.

CHAPTER SEVEN

A MINUTE LATER, I was sitting in the living room, my back against a rather uncomfortably rigid floral-patterned chair. The family on the couch across from me looked like any other. A nuclear family, two parents with their arms around an irritated teenager and a fluffy dragon pacing back and forth on the back of the couch.

Okay, so maybe they weren't like any other family.

I waited for them to say something until I couldn't take it anymore. "Was there anything you wanted to talk about? Because I have a few things to tell you."

James glanced at his watch. "Let's just give it another minute. Then we can say what needs to be said."

I frowned and looked at my own wrist before remembering I didn't have a watch on. In fact, I almost never wore a watch. It was just one of those annoying things, if you see someone else check their watch, you glance down to check yours, even if you aren't wearing one.

I doubt it was more than another minute, even though it felt like an eternity. For a split second, the room shook like a rare Missouri earthquake had struck beneath our feet. Lori patted Vicky on the shoulder and stood up, heading for the front door. Voices drifted in from outside.

Just as Lori cracked the door open, I heard the old New

Orleans drawl of an irritated Cajun.

"You crushed their *petunias*," Zola said, not even trying to hide the exasperation in her voice.

"These things can be hard to judge," Aeros's voice boomed back. "There are many rocks in this property, and I do apologize for moving the wrong ones."

"Crushed them flat," Zola muttered. "Ah'm sorry about that, Lori."

Aeros crouched down until he was peering through the front door. "Greetings, Vicky. It is good to see your family doing well. I rather miss your visits with Shiawase."

Zola interrupted the rock. "I'll ride back with Damian. You head to the base. Make sure that fairy hasn't stabbed anyone else." Zola sighed and shook her head.

"Be well," Aeros said to no one in particular as he vanished into the ground once more. There was a brief rumbling as the sod closed over the hole and the mulch churned to cover the flattened petunias.

It was about then I realized I was now standing, staring slack-jawed at Zola. "Zola! What the fuck?"

"Language," Lori said.

My eyes flashed to Lori before returning to Zola as she stepped through the front door.

"Ah asked them to call me when you showed up. Thought it might be best for everyone."

"It's good to see you again," James said.

"Likewise."

"Again?" I felt like I'd accidentally skipped several chapters of a very important book. "What do you mean again?"

"You know damn well what Ah mean by again, boy," Zola

snapped.

Vicky blew out a slow breath. "Zola was worried my parents were going to flip out when my memories returned. The whole death resurrection now I'm a teenager thing. You remember that?"

I blinked at Vicky. The friendly girl I'd come to love had turned into a miniature version of my unbelievably sarcastic sister. I was both horrified and impressed.

Zola let out an exasperated breath. "Ah would not have put it so crudely, but yes, Ah spent some time with the family a couple weeks after Vicky came home. Wanted them to understand what happened, and Ah wanted Vicky to understand why *you* might not be around that much." She stepped forward and poked a finger into my chest.

"Ouch," I said.

I made my way back to the chair and watched as Vicky hopped up and hugged Zola. The things Zola sometimes did without me knowing, or without anyone knowing, surprised the hell out of me. She didn't have to make time for these people. Zola had done enough with her life. She'd saved enough people, and the world was better for her work.

"I just wanted to thank you," James said. "The letter I sent you was never enough. Nothing could ever be enough."

"You gave us more time," Lori said. "Every day has been a gift."

"I didn't …" I started. "I couldn't …"

And I felt the dam breaking in my chest. That hopeless sense that I was going to tear this family apart again.

I tried to speak, but no words would come. Moisture gathered at the edges of my eyes a split second before Zola's palm cracked across my cheek.

"*This* is why I'm here boy." She stepped closer to me, and despite the difference in our height, she stared me down. "You may never think what you did was good enough, but it was better than that. You saved that girl, boy. And there is nothing more you could have done."

"Nothing," James said, echoing Zola's words.

"I told you he's stubborn," Vicky said.

I choked out a halfhearted laugh and smiled at the kid.

She scratched behind her ear. "I know you felt you had to stay away. And I know I have to go with you now."

"Although that does lead me to a question," Lori said. She exchanged a glance with James and wrung her hands. "If something happens to our daughter, and that means it happens to you, why exactly would you give her a dragon?"

I laughed nervously. I wasn't sure I had the best answer to that question. "Jasper's a guardian. He kept me and my sister safe when we were kids, when my powers first started … causing issues. And a couple years ago, he helped us fight off the fairies that destroyed so much on the east coast. You guys know the whole story?"

"Once my memory started coming back," Vicky said, "it wasn't like I was going to keep it from them. I don't think they were any safer not knowing."

"Certainly not with what's been going on in the world," Zola said. "They need to have an understanding of what could come calling."

I cursed under my breath and sank back into the chair. "Why didn't you tell me?" I looked up at Zola.

"You had too many close calls, Damian. Ah was a little

worried you might do something stupid and end up getting all three of you killed. But as you've been doing stupid things all your life, and haven't ended up dead yet, Ah figured the time had come."

She winked at me, which told me a lot in one gesture. There was truth to her words, lord knew I'd done some stupid shit over the years, but there was more to her reasoning. I trusted Zola, maybe more than I trusted anyone else on this earth. And that would be enough for me, for now.

"Did Vicky tell you she knows Drake?" I asked. "That was a new one on me."

Zola turned toward Vicky, who had retaken her seat on the couch. One of the old Cajun's eyebrow slowly arched, and I watched Vicky try to disappear into the couch cushions. I knew exactly how she felt.

"Who's Drake?" James asked, exchanging a look with Lori.

"Yes, Vicky," Zola said, settling into a chair across the room. "Why don't you tell us who Drake is to you?"

Vicky frowned at Zola. "Drake's just an old fairy with a dragon. Like Jasper. He's nice enough, even if you've had your differences with him." She sounded angry, like Zola had made a ridiculous accusation about a childhood friend. But Drake had fought alongside the Fae for millennia. Aideen and Foster thought he was older than they were, and that left his true age to be anyone's guess.

"He attacked Casper and Park's squad," I said.

Vicky blew out a breath.

I cocked my head.

"What has he told you?" Zola asked.

Vicky crossed her arms. "It doesn't matter. I believe him."

I blinked at the girl. She sounded wiser than she should, and confident in her convictions about Drake and his dragon. I'd been face-to-face with them before, and while I thought the dragon seemed pretty okay, I couldn't say the same for Drake. I suspected his agendas had agendas of their own. He wasn't someone I'd be quick to trust.

Zola drummed her fingers on her knobby old cane. "Drake was responsible for your aerial performance downtown."

Vicky crossed her arms. "I was helping a friend out of a tight spot. And speaking of friends, I hear Hugh has been having problems of his own."

I leaned forward. "Hugh and the River Pack have been in Kansas City, facing down some of their leftovers."

Vicky shook her head. "You don't understand. You haven't seen the worst of them yet."

Her words curdled in my stomach. I still remembered the dark-touched from the Burning Lands. I remembered how well-spoken it had been, and even though that one had been a Geryon, Graybeard said he'd seen the like in the ranks of the dark-touched. A small part of me had hoped they'd been lost or had vanished completely when the Seal was restored. Vicky's words made me think they hadn't been.

Zola frowned. "That would make a terrible kind of sense. None of the creatures we've battled would've entered into a contract with Nudd. They may have been controlled by him, or manipulated by him, but not part of a conscious agreement like so many of the Fae seem to think exists."

I nodded. "You told them about Koda?"

"The old ghost likes books," Lori said. "She's mentioned him once or twice. But mostly the panda bear."

"Panda samurai," Vicky said under her breath.

I grinned at the kid for a moment. "Koda thinks the dark-touched might be a hive mind. But not in the traditional sense of the word. He thinks it's more ordered, like a military structure, where a few in charge give orders to those below them, and so on. Until it trickles down to the ground troops, like the rabid creatures we fought."

"And is that good or bad?" James asked.

Zola shrugged. "We don't know. And Koda might be wrong. Though Ah think Ah could count on one hand the times that ghost has been wrong."

"I want to help," Vicky said.

I leaned back, unable to stop my eyebrows from rising. "I have to get you out of here for your own safety, but that doesn't mean I'm putting you in harm's way."

"Why not? I'm faster than you. And I'm better armed than half your allies. Maybe more than that, if you count Jasper." The ball of fluff on her shoulder puffed up and trilled.

"Kid." I rubbed at my forehead.

Vicky narrowed her eyes. "You can't stop me. You might as well use me."

I looked helplessly over to her parents.

James tilted his head to one side. "This is her decision. It's true you can't stop her. Trust me."

Lori patted him on the knee, and her words sounded rehearsed. "Our daughter is strong, and brave, and she's fought battles we can scarcely imagine."

I slowly turned back to Vicky. "You told them about the Burning Lands?"

She nodded.

I tried to imagine what that must've been like. Did her parents think she was insane? Or did they just accept it? They already knew their daughter had come back from the dead. They'd seen the power she could wield. They'd seen her dragon. Stories of the Burning Lands probably weren't so much of a stretch after that.

"It sounds like her friend Carter took good care of her," Lori said. "She wants to fight for his memory."

"And Maggie," Vicky said.

The words gutted me. Every logical argument I was scrambling for fled in a heartbeat. Carter and Maggie had watched over her. The whole Ghost Pack had. This girl had been through hell, died, been to a different kind of hell, and come back. It wasn't my place to stop her.

Zola nodded once. "I think the real concern here is what happens if Nudd loses control of the dark-touched. The military can't drop a nuke on every harbinger that pops up. And if Koda's suspicions are right, and there is a chain of command within the dark-touched, we don't know what's coming."

"But it's what we have to be ready for," I said. "Vicky, it's why I am worried about you getting into this. And Drake is a manipulative bastard. I'm worried about that, too." My words came out in a hurry to preempt any protest. "I won't stop you from helping, but you have got to be careful. Stay close to one of us as often as you can. If you're not at home, I'd feel better if you were with Foster and Sam, or even Frank."

"The arms dealer?" Lori said, raising an eyebrow. "*I* may take issue with that."

"He's not a …" I started before turning back to Vicky.

"What have you been telling them?"

"Only what they need to know," Vicky said.

Zola let out a slow laugh. "Oh, Ah do like this one. It's good to have you back, girl."

I groaned and sank back into my chair.

"What can we do?" James asked.

"If you'd like," I said, "I can give you my parents' phone number. They don't live far from here, and they're pretty well experienced with some weird shit, too. They do have a necromancer for a son and a vampire for a daughter."

Lori shook her head. "That would be wonderful, thank you. It would be nice to speak to some fellow ..." She glanced over at Vicky. "Some fellow 'commoners,' as our daughter calls them."

Zola smiled. "Ah think you'll like them just fine."

CHAPTER EIGHT

WE SPENT A few more minutes talking to James and Lori. They seemed to be trying to convince us they were happy with whatever decisions their daughter made, but I didn't understand how anyone could be happy knowing their daughter would be put in harm's way. Or worse, knowing she was always in harm's way, being tied to me and Sam.

James held up a finger before asking, "Are we safe here?"

I hesitated, cutting myself off before I could even begin to speak words that weren't true. "Probably not. I don't think anyone who's friends with me or my family is safe. You'll be safer if Vicky isn't here."

James nodded, though we hadn't really answered his question. "Sounds like a good time to visit the relatives in Texas."

I stood up to go, and Zola followed me to the front door. Vicky trailed behind her, scooping up her backpack from behind the chair and tossing it over her shoulder.

"She always keeps a backpack," Lori said. "Ever since she got home."

"I wonder where she learned that?" Zola said, her forehead wrinkling.

I laughed nervously and ducked out the front door, hoping to avoid an awkward conversation about how I'd turned their child into a prepper.

"Damian," Lori said.

I paused and started to turn, unable to hide the surprise as Vicky's mom wrapped her arms around me.

"Thank you."

James reached over his wife and clasped my shoulder. He didn't say more, but he didn't need to. I nodded to them both, and headed for the '32 Victoria parked in their driveway.

"Aeros really flattened those petunias," Vicky said as the door clicked closed behind us. She followed Zola around the car and hopped in the back seat.

"Aeros did good," Zola said, closing the car door behind her. "He didn't accidentally crush me, and he got the job done he needed to get done."

"Probably would've been easier to call a taxi," I said. "Why didn't you drive yourself?"

"Ah was at the cabin, boy," Zola said. "It would've taken me over an hour to drive back up here. Who knows what kind of stupid things you would've said by then."

I frowned for a moment. "So, you basically used Aeros as your own personal express subway?"

"Oh," Zola said, a smile stretching out her face. "Ah rather like that."

Vicky leaned up onto the back of the front seats. "Where to?"

I glanced at her and said, "Put your seatbelt on."

"Are you serious?" Vicky asked. "Aren't we a little beyond seatbelts at this point?"

"Hell no," I said. "No one in this car is beyond a seatbelt. I'm not scraping anyone off the inside of this windshield."

Vicky blew out an exasperated breath and flopped back into

the seat. I heard the click of a belt a moment later.

"The girl did ask you a question," Zola said. "Where are we going?"

I glanced down at the clock. "Sam and Foster will be in training for another hour. We can meet up with them for dinner after that. Let's head to the shop and keep Aideen company."

✦ ✦ ✦

WE MADE IT back to Manchester Road before a memory flickered to the top of my mind. Foster had eviscerated a vampire in the basement of a parking garage. That same vampire had killed a dozen people. One of those people had been a child, and her ghost had appeared in the back of my car, this car. That night had set off a chain of events I could scarcely imagine. I don't think anyone could have foretold that Vicky's ghost would've led us to the Burning Lands, would've put us up against the Destroyer, or would've given so much power to the Ghost Pack. The question I had now was, why did she still have so much power?

"So how long you still been able to summon a soulsword?" I asked.

Vicky shrugged. "I don't know. It may not have ever changed. I just remembered one day."

"What I wonder," Zola said, "is where is she pulling souls from? It's possible there's something else, some leftover vestige of the ties to the Burning Lands."

"But how?" I asked.

"You yourself left the gateway in the Seal," Zola said. "A gateway that perhaps only you can access, but a gateway nonetheless. So she may draw power from the Burning Lands in much the same way you drew Graybeard into our world."

I glanced up in the rearview mirror and found Vicky tapping away on her phone.

My cell rang, and I pressed a button on my car stereo to answer it. Frank's voice boomed to life in the old car.

"Damian, I'm here with Park. Safe to say Nudd found out about the article. You got about twenty minutes to get to a TV."

"What's going on?"

"Nudd called a press conference. They're gathering on the eastern side of Falias, near the gates."

Zola cursed. "That bastard has too many eyes."

"They published it in a freaking newspaper," Vicky said. "It's not all that surprising."

"Was that a kid?" Frank asked.

"Hi, Frank!" Vicky said, raising her voice. "It's Vicky."

Frank hesitated. "When did that happen?"

"Uh … about fifteen minutes ago," I said.

"Try to keep that nut job in line, kid," Frank said. "And I mean Damian, not Jasper."

A small burst of static signaled the end of Frank's call, and the stereo went dead. I caught a hint of Jasper's fur in the rearview mirror, rippling as the dragon chittered.

"We should have enough time to get to the shop," I said as I pushed on the accelerator a little harder.

"Don't drive so slow on my account," Zola said.

"This is great!" Vicky said a few minutes later as I swerved off 270 with the engine roaring and took the ramp onto Highway 70 at a nearly suicidal speed. The tires didn't so much as bark, but Zola still rolled her eyes.

It was a straight shot to 5th Street. I slowed down enough to avoid terrifying the other drivers on the exit, but if we passed a cop, we weren't going to be on time.

Zola tapped the clock on the dashboard. "Seven minutes. Slow it down."

I'd been thinking the same thing. I merged onto Booneslick and, in an instant, modern strip malls and architecture vanished. The homes grew older, and gas streetlamps lined the brick sidewalks. It wasn't until we got down to Main Street that the cobblestones started. And until that point, I kept our speed at the edge of what I thought a cop would let slide.

"It's weird," I said, turning the wheel and bouncing on the cobblestones. "I'm so used to seeing Graybeard's ship docked down by the museum, that it looks like something's missing now."

"That must've freaked out the commoners," Vicky said. "A bunch of skeletons taking orders from a dead parrot."

"From a *talking* dead parrot," Zola muttered. "That is one of your missteps Ah did not expect to stay with us for so long."

I grinned. "That's me. Fuckups that last. Maybe I should change the slogan for Death's Door?"

Zola snorted.

Vicky leaned closer to the window as we passed Oh Fudge. "Where's that ice cream shop? I thought it was around here."

"It's down the stairs," I said, steering around a particularly deep pothole.

Vicky frowned. "I didn't remember that. I feel like I should have remembered that."

"Just wait until you get older," Zola said. "You'll be lucky if you remember to put on pants."

"That why you always wear a cloak?" I asked.

Zola's voice was deadly. "Boy, if you weren't driving right now, Ah'd knock you out."

I smiled at Zola as we rumbled past the last stretch of bars and shops before we reached Death's Door.

The parking spaces were all taken on the curb in front, so I slid into a spot by Talayna's, the pizza joint across the street.

I looked at the clock. "Come on. Two minutes."

We piled out of the car, and I watched as Vicky gracefully slipped out the back of the '32 Ford. I was pretty sure I'd never been that graceful. My legs were too long for that small of a seat.

I frowned at the front doors across the street. The closed sign was turned, and I hoped Aideen hadn't had too much trouble while we'd been gone. I tried the handle, and it opened.

The bell jingled, and I held it open for Zola and Vicky as they passed through.

"We're closed," Aideen said.

"It's just us," I said.

"Get over here." Aideen hopped up on the old mechanical register we'd recently replaced with a tablet. "It's about to start."

Aideen turned the tablet toward us.

"You finally got out of the 1990s?" Vicky asked.

"Ha ha," I said. "The TV's in the back."

Aideen shook her head. "We can stream it here." She swiped at the screen and tapped an icon with the flat of her hand. The tablet went dark for a moment before returning with a cacophony of sound, and a camera pointed at a podium that stood before the gates of Falias.

CHAPTER NINE

I'D SEEN THOSE gates before, but not in person. I'd seen them in the great murals that decorated the halls of the court in Faerie. I'd seen them in mosaics in the ruins of Falias. They were a symbol of hope to some, and one of threat to others.

Ornate marble pylons stood to either side of the massive gates. I suspected each was at least as tall as the Washington Monument, only wider and carved with the great wars of Faerie. For a moment, I forgot the dread those gates pulled up from my gut. I sat in awe of the detail I could see even on such a small screen. The hand of the Mad King, a violent vein of red stone showing both a severed limb and a gateway through the Abyss. Nudd was always quick to remind his people that he'd been the one to slay the Mad King. His keen timing with propaganda had been on full display in the past, when he worked to cast his enemies in a bad light for the commoners. Beside the severed hand waited a dragon, a legion of Owl Knights, and many more that warred across the stone.

I leaned forward and frowned. "Is that a basilisk?"

Aideen nodded.

"I don't remember that being there."

"The gates are living stone," she said. "They change as Falias changes. Look at the other pillar. The pillar of the opposition."

But my eyes were still locked on the left pillar, and the crown of antlers that sat atop it. Slowly, I shifted my gaze, and my frown deepened. The top of the stone appeared to be more liquid than solid, with veins of blue struck through, so the stone looked more like a wave, and in that wave were dozens of faces.

"The water witches?" I asked.

"They are a threat."

Just below them sat the ghostly vision of the Bone Sails. I couldn't make out any individual skeletons, but I had no doubt the upturned skull and the sails represented Graybeard's ship. I searched lower, studying each strata, stepping back in time, until I came closer to the bottom. Perhaps three-quarters of the way down, I found the terrible visage of a raging gravemaker. I had little doubt what the pillars and spikes were, set against a massive wave. This was me, battling the undines in Saint Charles, only here the commoners were displayed on spikes made from the flesh of gravemakers.

"That didn't happen," I said, pointing at that section of the pillar.

"No," Aideen said. "The pillars may show history, they may show conflict, but they do not always show truth."

I grimaced. "That sounds dangerous."

"Yes," Aideen said as a cloaked form stepped up onto the stage and strode toward the podium. "Perhaps the biggest threat to Nudd at this time is the world's military might, combined with the knowledge we've given them. But do you see the soldiers on those pillars? Do you see the tanks or the bullets that can strike down a Fae?"

"No," I said.

The picture zoomed in on the podium as Gwynn Ap Nudd

took his place.

✦ ✦ ✦

"WELCOME ALL," NUDD said, flashing a disarming smile that I suspected was the same expression he'd wear as he cut an enemy's throat. "I would like to say I am glad we have found harmony between our people. The hard work of your governments and my own has allowed us to find a peace in these trying times. But I know all is not well, and I am not here to offer you hollow words. While some things are much improved, there is much yet to be done."

Zola stifled a shiver.

"I'd like to speak to you of the refugees from the calamity that happened in the town you once called Gettysburg. Your government failed them. Unable to provide basic necessities such as water and food before the people began to starve and turned to violence. But *I* did not fail them."

"What is he talking about?" Vicky asked, sidling up to the counter behind Aideen.

"I have delivered the details of this project to your media. For while we have provided refuge to some of your people, I am sad to say that some of your people have murdered ours."

Harsh whispers rose throughout the audience. The camera panned to show a mixture of Fae and commoners gathered before the gates.

"It is not all humans," Nudd said, raising his hand to ask for silence. "It is only those I have previously warned you about. You must be vigilant, for our enemy has managed to strike down the great queen of the water witches and has seated in her place a murderous imposter.

"My people and I only seek peace with humanity, and we must not let the actions of a few warmongers destroy our hard-won peace.

"I fear one of my own people has sown the seeds of untruth and discord. Under the guise of being a family, three Fae infiltrated my city and returned with footage that has been twisted by your media. For that, they must face punishment for their crimes, as they would in Faerie. For that, they must be executed."

"He's a bloody dictator," I muttered.

"A king," Aideen said, a note of sadness in her voice. A low growl sounded in the back of the shop. I glanced toward the saloon-style doors as Bubbles pushed through.

"I don't like him either, girl," I said.

Bubbles cocked her head when she saw Vicky. Her ears perked up and her long braided tail wagged, springing to life where before it had been still with anger. Bubbles sprang past me and took up a post beside Vicky, nuzzling the girl's hand while Jasper slid down to rest on the cu sith's back.

Nudd went on, spewing more rhetoric about how alike the Fae and the humans were.

"This should be easier to see through than glass," Zola said. "He's spoon-feeding those people trash."

As if on cue, polite applause rose from the audience on-screen. "Some of you fear me, as some of my people fear you. The tragedy that happened in these lands will not soon be forgotten by any of us. But we must move ever forward. We must be ever vigilant. And we must always work toward the greater good."

Nudd gestured at the front of the stage, and the point of

view of the camera switched. Below him stood three podiums, surrounded by cameras and what I suspected were members of the press.

I narrowed my eyes. "What the hell is he playing at?"

"As a token of our good intention, I wanted to allow your media to ask us questions. I admit, some we may not be able to answer. But there is no question that is off limits. Ask of me what you will, and I will answer what I can."

"Well, that seems stupid," Vicky said.

Aideen shrugged. "It's most likely staged."

A string of reporters lined up. Some I recognized from the major news networks. I had no idea who the others were. A few looked like they were teenagers, possibly there on an insane school project.

Nudd gestured to the first podium.

One of the youngest-looking of the bunch shuffled note cards before stepping forward. He leaned into the microphone. "What happens when you die? Several reports say you vanish. There are videos where it seems like only clothing is left behind."

Nudd frowned slightly at the question. If he was faking surprise, he was damned good at it.

"We are not so different from you," Nudd said. "Once our bodies expire, we return to the ley lines, the magic that connects this world to many others. Dust to dust, if you will."

It looked like the kid was going ask another question, but a Fae who would've appeared human, if not for the fact his chest was as wide as two bodybuilders standing together, ushered him away.

A middle-aged woman walked up to the second podium.

"Carla Casey, with channel 5."

"Glenn Nudd, King of Faerie, ruler of all you see."

Carla hesitated, clearly taken aback, but other than a slight stutter in her movements, she hid it well. Some of the things reporters faced in their day-to-day lives were truly horrible. Their ability to remain calm was impressive, at the least.

"You claim you stand for peace, but a great deal of evidence has surfaced showing you plan more for war than anything. How do you expect us, how do you expect humanity, to accept you at your word when there is clear evidence you do not abide by it?"

"That woman has no idea what she's doing," Aideen said. "Nudd's balls, he's going to kill her."

Nudd just wrapped his fingers around the edge of his podium as he leaned forward.

"Now?" Vicky asked.

"No," Aideen said. "But she's not long for this world."

"There is not much more important to a fairy than their word. You will have to take me at mine. Go in peace."

"That's not even an answer," Carla started, before she was not-so-gently guided away from the podium.

The man standing at the last podium watched Carla's departure with some interest. He ran a shaky hand over his close-cropped hair and steadied himself with a deep breath.

"William Macleod," the man said, his voice steady, almost stern. "I'd like to follow-up on Carla's question. It was your doing that brought Falias here. It was you who murdered the commoners and Fae alike in so doing. You consort with the dark-touched, scum of the lowest sort. We know what you did to Falias will one day befall Gorias, Finias, and Murias, all the great cities of the Fae. You aim to bring all of Faerie into the mortal realm. But this place is no longer our place." MacLeod pounded his hand on his podium and stared defiantly at Nudd.

Nudd remained silent.

A burly Fae stepped forward to escort Macleod away from the microphone, but a flash of yellow light interrupted him before he reached Macleod.

Carla returned to the second microphone. "You feign benevolence. We have no evidence of it. There is no proof of this proffered benevolence."

Silence thundered across the screen. Murmurs started in the crowd as Nudd stood silent.

"You wish *proof*?" Nudd closed his eyes, and the picture on the screen darkened. The camera shook briefly, and screams rose from the surrounding crowd before the color on the screen returned to normal before Nudd said, "There is your proof."

"What did he do?" I asked.

"Macleod …" Aideen whispered. "You idiot."

"You know him?" I asked, turning to face Aideen.

"I know of him. He's an old warrior. From the time of the Mad King. But what does it mean?" she whispered to herself as she stared at the screen. "What does it all mean? Drake has returned. Macleod, champion of Gorias, has appeared after nearly a millennium in hiding."

"What does your gut tell you?" Zola asked.

Aideen grimaced and looked up at Zola. "I fear for this world."

"What have you done?" Macleod asked on the screen as the burly Fae finally gave up trying to break through the shield of yellow light.

"The vile weapons this world loves so have been banished. Forthright and forever more, your nuclear arms are lost. Build more, and you will answer to the Lords of Faerie. You want proof of the peace I offer? You have it. Once, humanity sent bombs into our city to destroy us, but now I have taken that power from your governments and your madmen. Do as you will."

The camera focused on Macleod's face, his astonishment plain to see. "You know not what you do."

"The traitors—known to the commoners as Liam, Lochlan, and Enda—shall face execution. Their trial was set, and the courts have declared their guilt. Now all shall see the fate of those who threaten this peace. Go, son of Gorias, lest you soil the name of your ancestors."

I steepled my hands and cursed. "I've seen enough. The military won't stand idly by, and he damn well knows it."

"Maybe." Aideen turned her attention away from the screen. "Get to Park. We need to get in front of anything that's going to be done locally. Nudd came too close to naming us outright. The fact he hasn't is disconcerting."

"Games within games," Zola said, rapping her cane once on the hardwood floor.

Vicky adjusted her backpack. "I'm going with you."

I raised an eyebrow. "They don't even know who you are. And thanks to Nudd, things may have just gotten a hell of a lot more tense out there."

"I'm going with you, or I'm flying my dragon over Saint Charles. Your choice."

Zola laughed quietly.

I snapped my gaze to her. “Not helping over here, Zola.”

“Please,” Vicky said. “Who better than Jasper to infiltrate a military base?”

I shook my head violently. “We’re not *infiltrating* anything. We’re going to see our allies, our friends, and find out—” My phone buzzed. I frowned at the screen, then answered it. “Hey, Frank. Are you watching this—”

“Damian!” he shouted. “Damian, I couldn’t stop them. Oh god, I couldn’t stop them. They took Sam and Foster.”

I ground my teeth and flipped the phone to speaker. “Who took them?”

“I don’t know! Park didn’t recognize the unit, but they had Fae with them.”

“Where?”

“I don’t know. They arrested them for colluding with Nudd and providing intel. They’re saying our nukes are missing, Damian.”

“How many?” I asked, dread and rage warring in my gut.

“*All of them!* Get over here now! I don’t know what to do. Some of Casper’s squad got beaten down.”

Aideen stood slowly. “This was always a risk, trusting the commoners.” She methodically checked the sword sheathed at her waist and the daggers in her greaves. She pulled a quiver and bow from behind the register and looked up at me. “Do what you can. Find my husband.”

“We’re going with you,” I said.

“Meet me there. You’ll slow me down.” She streaked to the front door, exploded into her full-sized form, and slipped out while Bubbles hurtled after her.

“Let’s go,” Vicky said.

My eyes trailed back to the television as Nudd waved goodbye to a split crowd: half somber, half celebratory. Division was growing among the Fae.

I cursed and then said, “Come on.”

CHAPTER TEN

"WE HAVE TO get to Sam, now," I hissed as we hurried out onto Main Street. I watched Vicky as she walked beside me. If they'd put Sam down with something, Vicky was at risk. All three of us were.

Zola's cane cracked against the cobblestones. "We will, boy."

I glanced at Zola when her cane went silent. She had her head down and trailed Vicky. I slowed a bit to see what she was doing. Her old fingers blurred across the screen of her phone. To say she'd improved her texting skills was a vast understatement.

"Who's that?" I asked.

"Vik," Zola said. "Ah've found that vampire replies faster when people type at him than he does when they talk."

"It's called texting," Vicky said. "Or call it messaging."

"Girl," Zola said, flipping her phone off. "You get to be older than one hundred and fifty years, you can call it whatever the hell you like."

An old man smiled at us from a bench, giving Zola and I a look. I gave him an awkward smile, and he tipped his Fedora at us. It was good to see the locals moving back into the area. For a while, it had been hard for them to do that. There'd been so much debris around from the battle with the water witches that it had made the recovery slower than expected.

"Let's go," I said, increasing my pace again. It was only another minute before we were hurrying up the steps to the archives. I threw the door open, yanking it out of the hands of the woman who had been standing on the other side.

"Sorry, we're closed," she said.

"We're here for Sam and Foster."

She frowned.

"I was just here this morning," I said, flashing her the most plastic smile I could muster.

"I know. It's just we're not supposed to let you in."

"According to whom?" I asked.

Her eyes flashed up and to the right to a camera mounted above the door.

"Military? But not Park? Are they recording sound?"

She shrugged.

"I'm coming in," Zola said, stepping in front of me.

"What's going on?" Vicky asked, pressing up beside me. Jasper chittered on her shoulder, and at that point the woman in front of Zola didn't need to fake the surprise and fear on her face.

Zola might appear small, or even frail at first glance, but she shoved the receptionist into a stumbling sprawl with little effort.

"Come on," I said stepping between Zola and the woman on the floor. "To the basement."

I didn't look back. Zola padded along behind me, her cane cracking on the floor every few steps while Vicky hurried behind her. We passed filing cabinets and shelves, twisting through the hall until we reached the stairs. I hurried down them as shouts rose from below us. I worried what Aideen might be doing to Park's unit.

The anger on Aideen's face flashed through my mind an instant before my focus shifted back to Sam. They'd taken Sam, too. If she died, Vicky and I died with her. If she was injured, other people were going to die. Of that, I was sure.

Our pace increased to a jog and finally a sprint. Before I could so much as consider the danger, my aura reached out to the dead buried all around, until it caressed the dormant gravemakers that had arrived after the battle with the undines. We crossed through a section built of cinder blocks before the screams began.

I slowed as we came into the base proper, where we'd met Park earlier.

Shouts filled the hallways. Where it had been silent near the archives, now it was chaos. It took a moment to realize part of that chaos was due to me. Fragments of black flesh and bone oozed from the cracks between the old foundation's stone.

"Stop," Vicky said. "You're scaring them all away. We'll never find out anything."

Zola put her hand on my shoulder. "Vicky is right. You need to stop."

I breathed deeply, but didn't stop moving forward. I probably wasn't putting as much effort into controlling myself as I should have until one of the fluorescent lights burst with the influx of the gravemaker flesh. The pop of the bulb slowed my steps, and I focused my will, pulling my aura back tight against my body. The hum of the dead receded, and what flesh didn't return to the earth at least stopped crawling across it.

"I figured that was you," a somewhat irritated female voice

said from around the corner. A glint of light vanished near the floor before Casper stepped forward, rising from a knee until she faced us. She folded up a small contraption, and I suspected it was either a camera or a mirror she'd used to look down the hall.

"Where are Sam and Foster?" The words that came from my throat weren't smooth, but rather were gravelly, more the growl of a demon that'd been chain smoking for the past century.

"Bloody hell," Casper said. "We're working on it, but you have to get yourself under control."

"Would you like to meet my dragon?" Vicky asked.

Casper glanced down at the girl. "She's joking, right?"

"Oh no," I said, my voice slowly returning to its normal timbre. "Vicky, meet Casper. Casper, Vicky. Vicky is the one who decided to sail her dragon through the Arch."

Casper ran both of her hands through her hair. Her fingers massaged her scalp, and I suspected she was trying to stave off a headache of monumental proportions. "Come on, let's go find Park."

Casper turned around, and Zola flashed Vicky a grin.

"Don't encourage them," I said.

Jasper whined on her shoulder.

"Now you've hurt his feelings," Vicky said.

I gave Jasper some side eye. "Don't worry. I'm sure we can find something to feed you soon. I suspect that will make everything better."

While Jasper had been keeping a low profile on Vicky's shoulder, at my words, he flashed his rather large silvery gray teeth. When I looked up from the furball, I found Casper staring at us down the hallway.

I held my finger up to my lips, like a librarian might when shushing an unruly child or a jackass who answered his phone in the reference area.

"What is that?" Casper asked.

"Teeth," I said. "Now let's move it." I stepped toward her. She could either decide to move with me, help us, or block me. She glanced back at Jasper for a moment, shook her head, and then led the way.

We only made it through two turns in the hallway before we ran into what looked like some very paranoid soldiers. One of them started to level the rifle at us before his eyes locked on Casper, and he let the black weapon fall back onto its shoulder strap.

"Where's Park?" Zola asked.

"Interrogation," Casper said before taking a narrow hallway off to the right when we reached an intersection of three tunnels. The fluorescent lights seemed brighter here, but I wasn't sure if that was simply because the ceiling was lower, as I felt the need to duck as we passed each fixture.

"We caught one," Park said as we filtered into a small room. Behind him was a window into a room with walls blanketed in what looked like geometric acoustic foam. A soldier was cuffed to the table, with guards standing nearby. "I don't know how long she's been in the unit. The only time we can think a breach might have occurred is when some of our privates were in the infirmary for a week last month."

"What you mean by a breach?" I asked.

Park pointed. "I mean that whoever that is somehow replaced Private Reese."

"Is this room soundproofed?" Aideen asked.

Park nodded.

"Who discovered her? And how?"

Casper raised two fingers. "I did, with the seeing stone Foster gave me." She fished around in a pocket near her belt and pulled out a marbled circular stone with a hollow center.

Aideen frowned at the seeing stone. "Foster should have detected the magic. You shouldn't have needed that." She turned back to the window into the little holding cell. "How did she hide her disguise?"

The death's head grin on the captured fairy's face made her look insane. She uttered a low, guttural laugh. It was the most inhuman sound I'd ever heard a fairy make, like the laughter of a child mixed with the scrape of a blade on a whetstone. "Vesik."

That word alone, just my name, set Casper off.

She burst into the interrogation room with no announcement. One of the guards standing inside looked like he was about to say something. She silenced him with a glare. On the far wall was another mirror, much like I imagined would be on the opposite side of the room we were in, only much, much larger. But if it was reflecting us, who were the other interrogators? Or was it just another piece of psychology to throw off their subjects?

Eerily calm, the captured fairy watched us with almond-shaped eyes as Casper moved through the room. The fairy's eyes were narrow, and her face was thin. But she wore a satisfied smile, a knowing smirk. It was likely she had far more intel than we would ever know.

We followed Casper in as she leaned toward the fairy. The

prisoner's calm cracked a hair before Casper crossed back to us and into the strange L-shaped room we were all huddled in. The door clicked close behind her, and it sounded almost like a vacuum seal engaging. "Whoever she is, she'll break."

Park rubbed his hands together. "Private Reese was known for constantly wearing hats."

"Even in the showers," Casper said. "She wore some kind of shower cap thing. She'd always been particular about her hair." Casper frowned and glanced away for a moment. "Some of us gave her trouble about it. But that thing in there …"

"She's Fae," Aideen said, "just like me. Just like Foster. Which is why I assume you have falsely arrested him?"

"We know who gave our nuke locations to Nudd," Park said. "We needed to convince the chain of command that Sam and Foster weren't colluding with anyone. Foster went willingly. He was just trying to keep the response nonviolent."

I blinked. "Are we talking about the same Foster? I feel like the general outcome of that would be lots of soldiers with severed limbs on the ground."

"Nonetheless," Aideen said, refocusing on the soldier. "How did you discover her?"

Casper blew out a breath. "She looks human enough as long as she had a hat on. I only caught a flash of her ears when she was changing. It bothered me, because the movement was so fast I almost couldn't see it. So I followed her."

"That sounds subtle enough most humans would dismiss it. A flicker of light from the corner of their eye, or a shadow they can't explain."

Casper nodded. "But I know you. And I know Foster, and I've seen what the Fae can do. So I followed her. She was the last one in the showers. I waited in the locker room. It was then that I heard the voices."

"Whose voices?" Aideen said, stepping forward.

"I don't know," Casper said. "I managed to catch a glimpse from around the corner. It's easy enough, the way the room is laid out, to stay in the shadows. She'd written a pattern of what almost looked like blood on the wall, a series of runes maybe? Sigils? I don't know what they were." As she spoke, she started flipping through her phone. "Here." Casper slid the phone toward Aideen.

Aideen hopped down off the stack of books she had been standing on and frowned at the photos of the sigils. "What exactly did you hear her say?"

"Not much. Just that the stage had been successful."

Aideen looked up. "Meaning the removal of your weapons? And you're sure she said nothing else?"

Casper shook her head. "She whispered something. I can't be sure what it was. But it sounded like 'hail to the marketing King.' "

Aideen cursed in English, and then her tongue rolled over into a language I didn't understand. But the meaning was clear enough. She was infuriated. "Hail to the Wandering King," she spat.

Laughter echoed up from the other side of the mirror.

"Hell," Zola said, shouldering her way in front of Vicky. "This goes deeper than we imagined."

"You know those words?" Aideen said. "You understand what that means?"

Zola nodded. "Ah understand that was the clarion call of the man who became the Mad King, the man Nudd slayed to take his throne."

That's why the words had been eating at me. That was the stray thought chewing at the back of my brain, an old reference to the Wandering War, and the madman who had spawned it.

"Is she an acolyte?" Zola asked, leaning over to look at the phone beside Aideen.

"I don't know," Aideen said. "But Drake has reappeared. Who's to say some of the others didn't survive? I can see why they'd fall in with Nudd. The birth of Falias onto this plain? Nudd's manipulation of the humans, and their government?"

"Let's see what she knows," I said, turning to head back toward the door as my voice lowered to a growl. "Get my sister out of that cell."

I stalked to the rear of the bunker before cracking the door open and stepping through into the interrogation room.

CHAPTER ELEVEN

THE FAIRY'S LAUGHTER cut through my anger.

I stared down at the Fae chained to the table. "That was a hell of a job you did, infiltrating this squad. Shame you're on the wrong side."

The Fae's smile faded. "There are no sides. There is only the king, and those who serve him."

I gave her a half shrug. "Sure, that's one perspective, but the other side has everyone who doesn't serve the king."

The Fae stared at me blankly.

"What's your boss planning to do with the world's nuclear arsenal?"

"Is that all?" The Fae cocked her head. "That is information I will give you gladly."

I waited a beat. "Yes, I would like to know that." I spoke slowly, as if she was perhaps not fully understanding my words.

"They are destroyed," she said.

"I don't believe you," I muttered. "Don't make me peel all your skin off."

She relaxed into her chair. "I would think you a friend of the Mad King with such sweet words."

"Mad King, Wandering King, why don't you all pick one name?"

The fairy drummed her outstretched fingers on the table.

"You do not know him, so you cannot know."

I cursed under my breath and rubbed at my forehead.

"How is it you are not an ally," she asked, "when you carry his hand in your sack?"

It took a moment before I realized she was talking about the hand of glory. "That's not his hand, but I expect you already know."

"It is a hand the Wandering King owned; therefore, it is his hand."

That told me enough. She knew it wasn't his hand, but I wondered if she knew it was Gaia's. I didn't want to risk sharing that knowledge. "Are you loyal to the Mad King?"

"Of course," she said. "All those who understand the way of things are."

I snapped in an instant, her vague musings wearing through my patience. The stone floor shattered beneath our feet and vine-like tendrils of long-dead flesh and bone snaked out of the earth, spiraling up the Fae's legs and torso while she grinned. The darkness reached her wrists before she turned her palms up and caressed the dead flesh of the gravemakers.

"Your powers have grown more than we realized," she said, smiling down at the bark-like flesh solidifying around her. I could feel the same stuff crawling up my chest, reaching my neck, and slithering through my hairline.

"This will end badly for you," I said.

"Perhaps, but it will end badly for far more humans. The commoners will take their rightful place, at Nudd's feet. The common filth with whom you so foolishly ally yourself, Damian Valdis Vesik, have no weapons left to fight us. What can they hope to do now? They can only bow before their rightful king."

I narrowed my eyes, letting the tendrils of pulsating darkness tighten around the Fae's neck.

They licked at her flesh, hungry to cut into it and pull out whatever soul waited inside.

The Fae laughed through her teeth.

The door clicked open behind me, and a rush of air almost popped my ears before Park's voice said, "Don't kill her."

I hesitated, staring down at the Fae's bared teeth.

"It is not your choice to release me," she said. "I can leave whenever I wish, for this body is only a vessel." The last line was a whisper, meant just for me. I felt something bend and stretch beneath my power before the Fae laughed, and her eyes rolled back into her head. I let my power fade away as the screams began.

"What the hell?" Park shouted. "You weren't supposed to kill her!"

The guard at the far side of the room raised his rifle and pointed at me.

"I didn't!"

The screams of the dying fairy filled the room, cutting off any chance of an immediate conversation. I stared at the guard, at the weapon leveled at me. Park shouted something I couldn't hear, while the shrieks of the dying clawed at my eardrums. A darkness flickered through the shadows, and what had a moment before been a man with a gun became a man pinned to the floor with a dragon standing on his back.

Park backpedaled. Jasper roared and thrashed his head from side to side. It was the first sound that eclipsed the dying fairy. The soldier tried to curl into a ball when Jasper raised his foot from his back. The dragon stepped on the M-16 with his talons, and the gun fell into three distinct pieces. A moment later, the dragon vanished into the shadows.

Park stared slack-jawed at the uninjured soldier, the fractured gun, the remaining armor of the dead fairy, and me as the fairy's dying wail faded away. "What the fuck just happened?"

"I didn't kill her."

"Okay," he said. "How about the dragon? Why in the hell was there a dragon in here?"

"Because my friend didn't think this through?" I said, slowly turning to the doorway where Vicky was standing with her arms crossed.

"I didn't tell him to do that. It's not like Jasper would just stand here, waiting for you to get shot."

"Furball," I said. "Get out here."

The shadows in the corner shifted, and a small gray ball of fur rolled toward me until it reached my foot. I bent down to pick him up.

"While I appreciate your help, these are our friends."

Jasper trilled, before turning a deep red.

"He wasn't going to shoot. He was only doing his job. Don't eat him."

Jasper bared his teeth.

Aideen fluttered over Vicky's head, and Zola pushed in behind the girl.

"What happened?" Zola asked. "Are you sure you didn't kill her?"

I gave one quick nod. "Hell no. I didn't even draw blood, but I couldn't tell you what the hell happened."

"She was possessed," Aideen said.

Park frowned. “Are you talking about exorcist shit?”

Zola shook her head. “Not a demon. She was controlled by another Fae. The true spy could be in Falias, though Ah thought that magic was forbidden among fairies.”

Aideen grimaced. “The Unseelie Fae have a way of excusing any means, if the ends justify it. I have not seen such a clean possession in a very long time. Many parts of Faerie are warded against such magicks.”

“We aren’t in Faerie,” I said, Aideen’s words weighing on me.

“I know. The chaos this type of magic can breed is incalculable. It can be used as both a weapon, and an excuse. What concerns me more is the sheer power it must take to reach and stay with a body who was gone so deeply underground.”

“There are a great many ley lines here,” Zola said. “Would it not ease the difficulty of that magic if they were stationed beside one, or perhaps within one?”

Aideen nodded. “Zola, I thought you were just trying to get under her skin when you asked if she was an acolyte. Did you or Damian realize how much power she held?”

Zola shook her head.

“No,” I said. “But if we’re certain Drake is who he says he is, couldn’t more of the powers from that time have surfaced in this world?”

Aideen looked down at the vacant armor of the dead fairy. “I fear what that might mean.”

CHAPTER TWELVE

I TURNED BACK to Park. "Take me to Foster and Sam."

Park ran a hand through his hair. "They're in detainment. They aren't … She didn't lie about that part. I'll take you to them, but I can't release them without being court-martialed. Then we all lose." Park hesitated, and his voice quieted. "We haven't confirmed with all of our bases yet, but at least some of our nukes are missing."

"Ah believe that even if only one was missing it would be considered a crisis," Zola said. "But I suspect the entire stockpile has gone missing …"

"Nudd's been playing nice so he could get his spies in place." I looked back to the private huddled in the corner of the room. "He's in shock."

Park glanced at the private. "Casper, get him down to the infirmary, and meet us in the cells."

Casper nodded. Some of her formality had fled, and the only other time I'd really seen that was in the heat of a conflict. But maybe that's where we were. Maybe that's all they saw. Me, murdering the prisoner.

I ground my teeth together. Some lines were blurred in our alliance, and I prayed they wouldn't become a breaking point. I needed to keep my temper in check. Three deep breaths brought the throbbing pulse in my ears back down.

Park led us into a hallway before opening a well-hidden door in the stone. The rocky surface swung open silently, and we followed him down a winding metal staircase.

"Don't you have an elevator?" Vicky asked.

"We do," Park said. "But it's on the other side of the bunker, and it's a long walk to get to it."

"Girl," Zola said. "You're far too young to be complaining about stairs. Get another hundred years on those bones, and then you can come talk to me."

Park hesitated for a moment before he shook his head and continued down the stairs.

I was beginning to wonder just how deep the stairwell went when we finally came to the end. It had to have been at least three or four stories beneath the earth.

Park glanced back at me. "There's something else I haven't told you. I don't know if you already knew or not. There are some very old ruins under this land."

"There are ruins across much of the state," Zola said. "Civilizations have come and gone, and been driven out and slaughtered."

Park nodded. "That may be, but not like this."

He pulled the door open, and I glimpsed the golden stone lining the hall before us. At first, I thought Aeros might have arranged the rocks, and perhaps helped straighten them out or cleared the way of dirt and mud, but I'd never seen him build anything like this. Massive stones, ground down and polished until they almost shone. It was like marble, but there was only one place I'd seen stone like it. The Royal Courts of Faerie.

My voice came out a mix of awe and confusion. "What the hell is this?"

"I was hoping one of you could tell *me*," Park said, gesturing to the walls. "A section of it was a prison of some sort. We added some bars, and UV lights for the vampires, but the rest was already here."

Aideen's curiosity soured. She glared up at Park. "You locked Foster away in this place?"

"He's safe," Park said, but his eyes flashed between Aideen and the hall. I didn't miss the crease in his brow, and worry warred with anger in my gut again.

Aideen's lips curled into a snarl, and her hand moved toward the hilt of her sword. She stormed off down the hallway, exploding into her full-size form a second later, a glittering shower of fairy dust sparkling in the light that I now realized was emanating from the walls.

She pushed past Park, leaving a thin layer of fairy dust smeared across his uniform.

I let my vision slip, focusing on the energy around us, and the dead. I didn't stifle the gasp when I realized what was flowing right through the place.

"Aideen," I said, calling to her retreating form. "We're standing in one of the biggest ley lines I've ever seen."

"Of course we are," she said. "How else would the Mad King have sent a piece of Faerie into another world?"

My easy gait faltered. So it didn't just look like the stone I'd seen in the Royal Courts. This place was of Faerie, and I wondered, was it a piece of the courts themselves? But if the Mad King had sent that, it meant this place had been beneath the earth of Missouri for millennia.

"It is part of the prison at Gorias," Aideen growled. "Meant to house war criminals, kingslayers, and the thieves of children.

This is not a place for the Demon Sword."

Park started to say something, but Aideen took a sharp turn, before taking two more and leading us down a narrow hallway.

"How do you know your way through here?" Park asked.

"Because I was here, when it was still part of Gorias. I locked monsters away in this place. Those we couldn't kill, or those who were awaiting their date in the Court."

I blew out a breath and turned toward Park. "A long time ago, this place used to be in Faerie. Two or three millennia back, they had a war with their king, the one you heard them refer to as the Mad King. He had the ability to create portals, and he owned the hand of glory before I did. Before Philip did."

"So, Gettysburg wasn't the first time someone pulled something through from Faerie," Park said.

"Apparently not," Aideen said, coming to a stop before an iron-barred cell. It wasn't simply a cell, though. The bars ran across the floor and ceiling as well, looking like they'd been knotted into squared-off spirals. Even something as small as a fairy would have a hard time negotiating through them to escape. Unless they were ironborn, the touch of that metal could kill.

In the back of that tangled mass of metal was a tiny platform made of wood. And on that platform lay the unmoving form of my friend.

Concern and dread boiled up in my gut. "What's wrong with him?"

But a second before that dread turned to rage, Foster ripped a massive snore.

I blinked at the fairy, wondering how such a thunderous

noise could come from such a tiny body.

Aideen breathed a sigh of relief. "He needs more space than that. At least get a larger piece of wood."

Park nodded. "I'll see to it."

"A larger piece of wood?" Vicky asked. "They should be letting him out. Jasper could get him out."

"No," Aideen said. She gave Vicky a small smile before nodding to Park.

Vicky's lips twitched into a frown. "Why?"

Jasper chittered on Vicky's shoulder, and I had little doubt he was wondering the same thing.

"Because our alliance is fragile," Aideen said.

"What does that matter?" Vicky didn't hide the blatant tone of irritation in her voice. "We're less vulnerable without anyone holding us back."

"In some ways," Aideen said. "But we share this world now. It is not right for the Fae to rule the commoners."

Park nodded slowly. "And humans can get rather violent about that sort of thing. It's best to keep what alliances you have. You never know when you'll need them."

Vicky rolled her eyes. "Oh gods, he sounds like Carter."

I barked out a laugh, thinking about what kind of conversations that old wolf must've had with Vicky when they were running in the Ghost Pack.

Park typed something into his phone. "They'll have a bigger platform down here for him shortly. I'm sorry, Aideen. I didn't realize."

She nodded. I half expected her to give Park some kind of verbal forgiveness, or indicate her understanding, but all he got was the nod. I wondered if he knew her well enough at that point to understand how angry she was. And how angry she had a right to be.

The thought sobered me. "Where's Sam?"

"Down here," a familiar voice rasped. The hot glow in the old stones around us was enough to create a dim reflection on Frank's bald head. His voice was gruff, but he didn't sound stressed.

Frank's words grew more heated and his hands balled into fists. "Look at what they've done to her."

"Frank," Park said. "I told you, no one will hurt her."

I squeezed Frank's shoulder and then pushed past Park. I was done listening to excuses and concerns for our alliance once I heard the fear picking at Frank's voice. I jogged down the hall, Jasper now rolling beside me, having left Vicky behind.

Sam huddled in the back of the cell. A small travel umbrella was opened above her head, reflecting the harsh light of the ultraviolet assembly. The lamps looked more like a cannon.

"Damian's here," Frank said.

Sam cursed under her breath. "I'm fine, Demon. Don't kill anybody."

"Fine?" My voice cracking with rage, unable to keep the words from turning into a growl. "Fine! You're locked in a dungeon of a lost city, dead in the middle of a ley line. You might be many things, but you're not fine."

Sam tilted the umbrella back a hair. "I'm good enough. Don't attack them. I can do this, Demon." Jasper rolled toward the gate, but he stopped outside the bars. His black eyes roved up and down them, focusing on the lamps in the corner.

"I'm fine." She held her hand out as if asking Jasper to stop. Her flesh was blistered. She'd sustained more damage than I'd ever seen the sun inflict on her. Whatever these lights were, they were damned powerful.

I slowly turned to Park. He hesitated when he met my eyes, but instead of turning away, or trying to make excuses, he hurried to the cell. I watched him as he looked inside, as Sam lowered the umbrella a bit more, revealing her blistered cheek and a blood-red eye.

Park exploded with a string of curses. "I don't know who the fuck did this, but they're done. I will end them."

Vicky caught up with us, and her breath hitched when she saw Sam.

I ground my teeth and bit off my words. "Jasper, take out the lamps."

Before anyone could protest, a jet of blue fire exploded from the furball, and a moment later, the UV lamps fell to the floor as so much slag.

Sam let the umbrella fall and looked up at Vicky. "I'm fine, kid. For now, just … trust me." Sam waited a beat, and when no one moved, she turned her head toward me. "Okay?"

The muscles of my jaw flexed, but I nodded.

"Let me heal you," Aideen said.

Sam shook her head. "Stay away from the bars. I'm good."

Zola had been watching silently. She cracked her knobby old cane on the floor with a brutal strike. Everyone turned to look at her.

"Ah don't know what this game is, First Sergeant Park. You have earned our trust, and I hope we have earned yours. But this …" she said with a nod toward Sam. "This is cruel. If you tortured a human like this, you'd be held accountable in the highest courts. You'd be branded a traitor. And a very long time ago, in an age Ah sometimes do not care to remember, the only ones who sank this low ran slaves."

"Zola …" Park started, cringing under her gaze.

Zola held up her hand. "No. If you intend to torture supernaturals, or enslave them, you're no better than Nudd."

"It wasn't my doing," Park said through gritted teeth. "Some things are above my ability to control."

"I suppose you were only following orders," Zola said, and her voice held a weight that spoke worlds.

Vicky stepped closer to the old Cajun. "We can't leave them here."

"You don't have a choice," Sam said.

Vicky's brow creased, and she shook her head.

Aideen's wings sagged a little. If I hadn't known her so long, I might not have noticed. "Sam is right, little one. Our alliance is young, and while not everyone is on our side, Park and his people are. Give them a chance to resolve it promptly." She eyed Park, who nodded once.

"Go," Sam said. "Frank is here. We have friends here."

Frank grunted.

Vicky wrapped her right hand around one of the bars and leaned in toward Sam. "This is bullshit. You change your mind, these won't stop me."

Sam smiled up at Vicky. "It's good to see you, kid."

Aideen didn't hesitate. "Now, make for Falias. We need to speak with our allies there and take stock of the situation. I doubt it was a coincidence Nudd held the press conference before the eastern gates."

I patted Frank on the shoulder and looked into Sam's cell. "If the situation changes, you let me know."

She nodded and leaned back into the wall.

I turned away from the cell, trying to wipe the vision of Sam and Foster behind bars from my mind, an exercise in futility. “Vicky, you’re coming with us. I’d feel safer knowing you’re not taking Jasper for another joyride.”

“Next time, answer your phone,” Vicky said.

Sam let out a weak chuckle from her cell. “Go. Tell me what you find. Get me out of here, Damian.”

“I will.”

CHAPTER THIRTEEN

We returned to the entrance to the archives. Casper had rejoined Park as we exited the hallway with the cells. Seeing where they'd imprisoned Foster and Sam had fractured my confidence. I took two slow breaths to calm the rising rage.

Casper eyed me, hesitating before she asked, "What next?"

"Falias," Aideen said, back in her smaller form and perched on Zola's shoulder. "We have allies there. They may have information we desperately need."

"What do you need from us?"

"Get our people out," I said, "and make sure they aren't tortured in the meantime."

Zola drummed her fingertips on the head of her cane. "Ah think what Ah'd recommend is using that seeing stone to ferret out any more spies among your ranks. You are clearly not so secure as you thought."

Park nodded. "That's a good call. Casper, organize an inspection. You'll either find more people who are possessed, or those who don't show up will tell us as much."

"I could stay and help them," Vicky said.

I shook my head. "You'll have more fun with us, kid. Unless you think Drake's going to attack them again?" I raised an eyebrow.

"How could I know that?" Vicky asked. "I don't think he

would, but fairies are weird."

Zola let out a slow laugh. "Not all fairies, girl."

"We'll take the Warded Ways by the old church," Aideen said. "It'll take less power, and I'd like to conserve as much as I can for our arrival in Falias."

"Expecting trouble?" Casper asked.

"Always."

Park frowned. "We have our mission, and you have yours. Best of luck to you all." With that, he spun on his heel and returned to the stairs that would take him into the underground halls. He paused before vanishing down the steps. "I'm sorry." His footsteps faded as he descended the stairs.

Casper hung back for a moment. "He didn't know what they were going to do. You need to believe that. None of us did. If I had …" The muscles in her jaw flexed.

"Someone did," I said. "But I believe you. Find out who orchestrated it." I let my gaze trail back to where Park had vanished. "He may not have known ahead of time, but he knows now."

Casper nodded. She looked down at Vicky and said, "Keep them out of trouble, yeah?"

Vicky bit her lip. "I'm probably not the best person to ask for that."

Casper blinked at the girl and then followed in Park's footsteps.

"I'll go with Gaia," I said. I wanted to walk with the Titan, but I also wanted to avoid the nausea-inducing thrill ride of the Warded Ways. "Where will you exit the Ways?"

Aideen glanced down as if she was studying the weave of Zola's cloak in order to determine just where they would come out of the Warded Ways. "I believe we can reach the guard room from the old church. That shouldn't be a problem."

"Good," I said. "So, no randomly appearing in front of a wandering dullahan today, right?"

"Probably not?" Aideen said, her voice rising.

I narrowed my eyes. "You don't instill much confidence."

"Just be ready for anything. If Nudd's press conference was a lure, gods only know what we're walking into."

"Would they not have contacted you?" Zola asked.

"They should have," Aideen said. "But today has been an odd day."

"You have a gift for understatement," Zola said. She turned and started toward the main entrance of the archives. "Enough talk. We move."

"See you there," I said, fishing around in my backpack. My fingers brushed the cold dead flesh of Gaia's hand. I laced her fingers between my own and stepped into the Abyss.

✦ ✦ ✦

"IT IS NOT usual for me to see you so many times in one day," Gaia said as she materialized beside me. The motes of her golden light outshone the stars of the Abyss in the distance.

"And we're probably not done," I said. "I need to get to Falias. Just outside the Obsidian Inn. Preferably by the guard room, if you can do that."

Gaia frowned. "I know the room of which you speak, but it is warded against many magicks." Her musical voice was both soothing and a stark reminder of where we were. "While I may be able to get you into that room, I do not know if you would survive the experience."

I groaned. "What about the old courtyard? With the basilisk skeleton? That's close enough to the entrance that I probably won't die."

"Your standards for travel have decreased somewhat of late."

"Was that a joke? I'm not sure how to take that, Gaia."

"I can bring you to the courtyard of which you speak. There are many more beings gathered near the eastern edge of the city. Would you not prefer to go there?"

I shook my head. "We need to talk to the Inn. Nudd is making a move, but we're not entirely sure what it is."

Gaia pondered those words, her gaze trailing off toward the dim horizon before returning to me. "I have sensed the fear in the humans. A panic rose like I have not felt since Falias, and for nearly a century before that, the last time one of the great wars scoured their world."

"You can sense that from here?" I asked.

"Of course," Gaia said. "My body still rests upon the earth. It is only my consciousness that roams this place, and a segment of my power."

"And your hand."

Gaia gave me a flat look.

"Sorry," I said. "I thought we were making jokes."

"Indeed."

A far-off sound rose, the deathly silence of the Abyss fractured by a basso roar like that of a rising earthquake.

Gaia stared into the distance and frowned. "Some of the old ones have been stirring."

"Why? It's not like they can escape this place."

"Perhaps not," Gaia said. "But that does not mean they

cannot be released. We are here."

"Thank you. You'll probably see me again shortly. I don't think this meeting will take long."

"Ready yourself, Damian Vesik, for you are not alone."

I had a split second to wonder what in the hell Gaia was talking about before the Abyss tilted into a violent spiral and I fell.

✦ ✦ ✦

THE DISORIENTING BLUR of my trip back to earth was blissfully smooth. Sunlight nearly blinded me as the darkness of the Abyss vanished, and I was left stumbling beside the massive skull of the long-dead basilisk. It was a good thing Gaia's aim had been good, or I might have been impaled on one of its massive fangs.

"That would've sucked," I muttered, trying to orient myself.

Something crunched beside me, and I frowned as I turned toward the noise, backpedaling as I gazed at the hooded form. A helmet beneath the cloth hid flesh that would burn in the daylight. I fumbled in my backpack cursing at myself for not drawing the focus before stepping into the Abyss.

"Vesik," the gravelly voice boomed.

My fingers wrapped around the butt of the pepperbox and I drew the gun while my other hand fumbled awkwardly for the focus. It was only then that I realized what had snapped. The dark-touched held an Utukku in his claws, her neck snapping and crunching as his red right hand crushed it into a pulp.

"Vesik is here!" The dark-touched vampire screamed in his gravelly voice.

"You can talk?" I said, a split second before I started pulling the trigger on the pepperbox. Bullets whined and ricocheted as they cracked against the dark-touched's helmet. More of my light blindness faded, and I began to understand just how not alone I was. A few piles of clothes were tangled up in Faerie armor, and the corpse of more than one dark-touched lay amid the wreckage of three Utukku bodies.

"Goddammit," I snarled, holstered the pepperbox, and held my hand out as the dark-touched who had spoken charged.

"*Tyranno Eversiotto!*" I screamed the incantation. The ley lines snapped through me as the hairs on my arms stood at attention before electric blue lightning scoured the earth in front of me. The bolt cut through the stone beneath my feet and ripped its way to the vampire. What had been an uncomfortable distance of 30 feet had closed to half that in the blink of an eye. The lightning met him about ten feet out, the explosion rocking me back on my heels. I dropped the incantation when I realized I'd singed the hair on my forearms.

Movement caught my eye. Distant, but not for long. Cloaked figures flew across the rooftops and slid down the slender spires of Falias. Far more vampires than I could hope to fend off by myself. And what patrol had been here—the usual ten-member mixture of Utukku and Fae—were either dead or broken and running. They had the right idea.

I didn't hesitate as the dark-touched at my feet groaned. I ran. Slipping into the shadows of the nearest alleyway, I cringed as the visceral cries of the dark-touched followed me down out of the light. I'd only been here once before, when Ward—or was it the Old Man—had shown us the basilisk. There wasn't much doubt I was moving in the general direction of the Obsidian Inn, but I didn't know if the alley would lead me to a haven, or a trap.

I sprinted toward what looked to be a dead-end, and my heart hammered as something scrambled over the brick above me. To my left was an archway, and I dove through it. I turned as I fell and shouted, "*Modus Ignatto!*" A torrent of fire, unrefined but massive, belched from my hand and splattered out into the alley. I didn't stop to see what it had done. I scrambled back to my feet and sprinted through the rest of the arched alley. As soon as I broke into the daylight, I jaunted to the right and ran hard until the burning of my lungs threatened to send me to the ground.

"Here," a female voice hissed.

It was either a trap, or help. But in my escape, I'd managed to grasp the focus. If it was a trap, I had a much better chance of surviving it. The golden stone of a half-collapsed building revealed only a sliver of shadow, but again the voice said, "Here."

The dark-touched bellowed above me. I risked a glimpse backward, and I saw nothing above me or behind me. I slipped into the shadowed space and squinted at a distant light.

"What happened here?" I asked.

"Nudd happened," a whisper said. "Too many of us went to the gate. Fools."

"Morrigan?" I said, fairly certain I recognized the snide tone in the word "fools."

"Yes. Now, come. We must return to the Inn." She started through the hall toward the light. It only took a moment before I realized we were headed down a gradual slope.

"Where are Foster and the others?" Morrigan asked.

"Foster's in jail, along with my sister, but Aideen's on her way. She has Zola and Vicky with her."

"The Destroyer?" Morrigan asked.

"She's not the Destroyer anymore."

"Yes, yes, you humans and your semantics. Is she still bonded to the reaper?"

"Jasper?" I asked as we reached the torch that I'd seen from the start of the passageway. "Yes, I asked him to guard her. To keep her safe."

Morrigan slid the torch off the wall and led the way to a staircase that vanished into shadows as dark as the Abyss.

"Good," Morrigan said. "We may need a reaper of our own before this day is done."

"Who else is here?"

"Some of the Utukku. At least those that are left alive. Hess remained at the armory with a few of her most loyal soldiers. This is my fault. I never should've sent that family to infiltrate Nudd's ranks."

"I doubt you forced them into it," I said, remembering the fear on Liam, Lachlan, and Enda's faces when we'd met them in the catacombs. "They're fed up with Nudd."

"Aren't we all?" Morrigan said. "Aren't we all."

CHAPTER FOURTEEN

WE CONTINUED FARTHER down the darkened halls, Morrigan in her crone form. I could have mistaken her silhouette for Zola in the shadows and the wavering torchlight. It felt like we had been walking for an hour, but I knew that couldn't be right. Time hadn't truly slowed. Quiet scratches and distant thumps echoed around us in the musty air. My gaze shot toward every shadow that moved or shifted in the distance.

It was impossible to lock down my senses in their entirety when I was this stressed. Impossible to ignore the floating gray orbs of long-forgotten guardians in this place. Morrigan glanced back at me and hesitated.

"You sense more than I expected."

"What do you mean?" I asked.

She gestured at a cluster of the gray orbs that seem to flit through her hand and out of my field of vision. "The old ones. Those who once lived, but do no more, whose purpose is not forgotten." Morrigan studied me for a moment before glancing at the ceiling as something thundered overhead.

"Are we close?" I asked.

"Yes," Morrigan focused on corridor ahead of us. A rumble built in volume, and I didn't think it was outside the tunnel this time. Morrigan exhaled. "I'd hoped to avoid this."

She hurried forward, and I followed.

I lowered my voice. “Avoid what?”

“Nudd has sent all manner of Unseelie Fae into the tunnels, hunting for the Obsidian Inn.”

“Why doesn’t he just send the dark-touched down here? This is practically their natural habitat.”

“He tried. They perished. The dullahan has called more than one name in these corridors, and the dangers that lurk here are powerful protections for the Inn. I have known Nudd ten times longer than Zola has been alive. He will not stop so easily. It is only a matter of time before he sends less … stable things down here.”

We turned the corner, and I frowned at the hallway. I thought I recognized it, the place where I’d once appeared below Falias. A place of cells and violence, and the charred brick on the walls told me I was right. But Morrigan had been right, too. We weren’t alone.

In the distance, two blue orbs floated together as if they were weightless fire.

“Dullahan,” I said, my hand reaching for the focus at my belt.

“It’s not the dullahan you should be worried about, boy,” Morrigan snapped. “We make for the stairs. Don’t hesitate to kill anything between us and our goal. Go now!”

Morrigan broke into a sprint. My focus was still on the distant floating eyes of the dullahan, as I remembered what a monster that creature could be on the battlefield.

I finally saw it about the time the intersection appeared, the crossroads with the stairs to the Obsidian Inn. At first, the mass appeared to be a wall of snakes, surging out from one of the cells and splattering against the far wall. But instead of a wet thump, the shadowy forms cracked into the very stone. Among the undulating mass of slithering things, I heard the fall of rock and metal clattering across the floor.

I tried to concentrate on my footing, careful not to twist an ankle, as we attempted to outrun the massive shadows. A moment later, the dullahan's eyes disappeared in the distance, and those snakelike forms broke into a halo of light. As they crossed through, I could see they were caked in mud, blood, and other viscera I couldn't identify. One thing I was sure of: they weren't snakes.

"What the fuck is that?" I shouted.

Morrigan glowed. Between one step and the next, the crone became the raven, and she rocketed forward on oily black wings. "Burn them!" the bird squawked.

Throwing an incantation while running was a sure way to miss your target. But one thing Zola had taught me was if you threw a large-enough ball of fire in an enclosed space, you didn't really need to aim. "*Magnus Ignatto!*"

I stumbled as the power ripped through me. I felt what was left of the hairs on my arms burn to a crisp. Morrigan, almost distant now, made the turn through the intersection and flew up the stairs. She'd be safe from the heat, though I wasn't sure if she was susceptible to fire incantations. The chaotic wall of flame shot forward at irregular intervals until it crashed into the writhing mass of what now looked very much like lampreys or dying gray vines draped in gore and dripping blood I suspected was from our allies.

Whatever they were, they were sentient. The instant the flames hit and widened to the point that I couldn't see down the hallway through the fire and pain in my arms, something else screamed. It wasn't immediately recognizable as pain, as the sound was so deep and basso it took me a moment to understand the earth wasn't shaking around me. I let the fires die away and gasped for breath as I stumbled forward, making my way for the staircase as the soles of my boots sizzled on the superheated stone beneath them.

The fire faded, but it took time. I closed on the staircase that would let me climb to salvation. But even as the fires died, revealing the charred tentacles of roots and flesh and whatever else that thing had dragged down here, the snakelike vines moved again. Perhaps it was an illusion that they stuttered and stopped and restarted, but I liked to think they were injured.

But that didn't mean they couldn't kill me in a heartbeat.

A roar sounded in earnest, but this time it was a roar I knew. A wall of gray exploded in front of me. The long tail of a lizard that shouldn't exist stretched out from the mass as four enormous legs materialized beneath it with a whumph. Ash and debris flew up from beneath Jasper's massive wings. He reared back, unhinged his jaw, and a hellish blue flame exploded from his mouth. I dove behind the dragon, taking shelter by one of his hind legs. I sagged against him as the air thinned, and I felt like my lungs would catch fire at any moment. But they didn't, and the flames receded, and the gray flesh moved no more. For a time. Then Jasper shrank, staying large enough for me to lean against, but losing the sheer level of intimidation he had as a full-sized dragon.

I was making the turn into the intersection when the smoke cleared to little more than wisps of gray, allowing me to see the eyes of the dullahan, still watching in the distance. As I looked back, I caught movement. The charred flesh flicked away, and the creature raced toward a cell before a voice boomed through the halls.

"Dragon fire?" the thing said. "Who walks these halls? Who dares interrupt my hunt for the Abyss creature?"

Exhaustion settled into my bones, but I stood my ground. I patted Jasper on the head and kept one foot on the first step that would lead to safety. Unless this thing was faster than I'd seen so far, I could still escape. Curiosity had its claws in me.

A hunched form swept through one of the cells as a tangle of vines and wood retreated toward a shadowed form. It stepped forward into the edge of the torchlight that had been ignited by Jasper, or me.

My breath hitched as I stared at the bark-covered face and the jagged openings of the glowing green eyes. Its mouth was little more than a serrated break in the bark it wore like armor.

"You?" I said. "I saw you in Greenville. What are you doing here?"

The being froze. Its face shifted, and the bark almost seemed to frown.

"Speak carefully," Morrigan said from the top of the stairs. "The forest gods are powerful."

I frowned. "Forest gods?"

"You have met others of my kind," the creature said extending a hand, palm open before curling into a fist. It was formed of tightly knit vines, and some of them appeared to be charred. "There are not so many of us as there once were. Where is this Greenville of which you speak?"

"Missouri."

"The war-torn lands," the creature said, her words trailing

off as if lost in thought. "I have family in that place. Though some are not so benevolent."

"Like the green men?" I asked.

The treelike face swayed toward one wall and then the other between releasing what I can only think of as a scratchy laugh. "The green men are followers, for we are their gods."

"Like Gaia?" I'd spent many hours, days even, looking for any information on the thing I'd met on the battlefield of Greenville. I'd mistaken it for a green man, but of that it most surely wasn't. But now Morrigan seemed to know what this thing was, and if I was judging by appearance alone, I suspected it was the same kind of creature.

"The goddess left us long ago," the forest god said. "Some believe she will return one day. But I fear all of our lands will be ash by that time."

"The forests?"

"Yes," the forest god said, her form shrinking as she appeared to settle into the corner of the intersection. "Even if our goddess returns, it will be too late for my child. It is the way of things, though, for all of us beings who march against time. Even the oldest of us cannot remember the beginning of this world."

I hesitated, then spoke the question in my mind. "What happened to your child?"

The glow around those green eyes narrowed, and it gave the forest god's face a hardened look, nearly as full of rage as the creature I'd encountered in Greenville. "Humanity. And what humanity couldn't finish on their own has been lost to the Fae. Fae who should know better than to let the children of Gaia die."

Morrigan crept down the stairs. She was no longer the crone or the raven, and for a moment I didn't realize it was her. But I caught a glimpse of her black eyes, darker than the shadows around us. "You are Gund. Shepherd of the old mountains. What the humans call Appalachia."

The forest god shifted to the other side of the hall. "I have been called that name before. But I am not the only one of my kind. My husband rules to the north, while my child waits for death in the war-torn lands. A forest grown in the blood of men, risen through the metal and death they left in the earth."

"But you think Gaia could save him?" I asked.

"The forest gods who once ruled here are already lost."

A hoarse whisper sounded behind the forest god.

The mass of vines and bark and ash turned toward it, opening enough of the view down the hallway for me to see the dullahan.

"That thing sure is persistent," I muttered. "Is it a danger to you? Because it sure as hell is a danger to us."

"No," the forest god boomed. "I have no quarrel with the dullahan. And it has no quarrel with me. If you wish to have a formidable ally, it is the dullahan you should seek a pact with. A slayer of mortal and immortal alike."

Something thundered deeper and distant in the catacombs.

"Leave this place in peace," the forest god said as she turned to leave.

"I know Gaia," I said, unable to stop the words, wanting to reach out to this creature and learn more.

"Many beings know Gaia," she said, "but many more have allowed her to die."

"I've walked the Abyss with her. I call her friend. She still lives. There's still hope for your woods."

The forest god turned back and met my gaze. It felt as though those glowing eyes, carved of crystal and light, looked deep inside my thoughts. "Then tell her she is needed. And the time for slumber is long past."

With that, the vines and wood that formed the forest god's body slipped out of the light, moved through the shadows, and vanished back into the cell they had come from.

"Follow me," Morrigan said, "before something else finds us."

For a moment, I stared at the empty space where the forest god had been. In the end, I trailed after the Morrigan.

CHAPTER FIFTEEN

WE REACHED THE top of the stairs, and Jasper trundled forward, his miniature dragon form shrinking further and losing shape until he was once again an oversized dust bunny with enormous black eyes. Vicky stood beside Zola, and a pair of Utukku each held a spear in their right hand, the butt resting on the floor and the tip pointed toward the heavens. I nodded to each of them, and they briefly touched their spear hands to their chests in acknowledgment.

Vicky crouched and scooped up Jasper. He took up his usual perch on her shoulder while Zola eyed the mass of fluff.

Zola turned to Aideen and Morrigan in turn. "What in the hell is a forest god?"

Aideen took a deep breath then snapped back into her smaller form. She glided down to a white pedestal against the wall. A series of fairy-sized seats adorned the top of the stone. The backs of the chairs were odd, narrowing greatly toward the base, but when Aideen sat in one, I understood why. Her wings fit perfectly without having to be bent or folded. It gave her a grand appearance, with wings spread and her posture rigid. I wondered what purpose those chairs had been built for, but it didn't distract from the question at the front of my mind.

"So, what are they?" I asked, bringing the focus back to the forest gods.

"They are old spirits," Aideen said. "Predecessors to the green men. Commoners might refer to them as ancestors, but it is different than that. It would be like saying that a creature more powerful, and more fit for survival, evolved into a weaker form of itself. That is how I think commoners would best understand it, and perhaps even you. A reverse evolution, if you will. Those gods did not need so much power anymore, they did not need such levels of violence to survive, so those abilities fled. The elements of their being that tap into the ley lines are not the same as those of the green men."

"I've seen them before," I said.

Aideen nodded. "I know. You told us many times of the strange green man you met on the battlefield at Greenville. But that is not what I expected. I never would've thought it was a forest god. It's been a long time since they've shown themselves."

"Forest god or not," Morrigan said, "they are not the threat we face this day. We should rally the Inn and make ready for Nudd's assault."

"Our soldiers are prepared," one of the Utukku said. "We have made the sacrifices required of us, and we will fight at your side. We will die at your side, if needed."

"And you will have your honor," Morrigan said. "Though I hope the cost is not too high."

"Do you wish to review our ranks?" the Utukku asked.

Morrigan nodded. "I would. Our guests have not seen the expanded grounds. Show them what's been done here."

"Of course." The Utukku inclined her head to Morrigan before leading the way to an arched hallway at the other end of the room. Our group followed, but Zola made a low sound, something like a hum.

I turned to glance back at her.

Zola frowned as she brushed a series of braids behind her ear. "There is something more valuable we must discuss."

"Such as?" Morrigan asked.

Aideen fluttered above us for a moment before settling on Zola's shoulder.

"A simple question," Zola said. "What Fae would have the power to possess another and cast a glamour so thoroughly that only a seeing stone could pierce it?"

"That's an answer I'd like, too," Aideen said. "Do you have anyone here that powerful? Or have you heard of anyone?"

"There are always rumors," Morrigan said as we crossed into the hallway. "As to which of those rumors are true, and which are misdirection, I cannot say."

"There aren't many Fae that have the abilities to match what you've described," Aideen said. "Many of them are thought to be lost to time, were thought to have died in the Wandering War, but our new knowledge of the forest gods makes me wonder what else has survived the ages."

"Perhaps we should ask those who saw those darker days," Morrigan said. "Perhaps even a man who has worn the cursed dead as his armor."

"The Old Man," Zola said. "He is certainly knowledgeable when it comes to killing."

"Nixie said he's in Faerie with Ward," I said.

Morrigan nodded. "They journey to Gorias, to seek allies and those who are willing to fight alongside the commoners."

"The *Old Man* is on a recruiting mission?" I asked, slowly raising an eyebrow.

"There is no one better," Morrigan said. "He has the respect of much of Faerie, and a history of walking between two worlds. His time in warfare is no small measure, even by the standards of the immortals."

My eyebrow settled down. "When you put it like that … I guess." But I just remembered him kicking my ass during training and being an obstinate mentor to Dell, for the most part. Useful, yes, but a good first impression? I wasn't so sure.

"There is another who may help," Morrigan said. "Come, I will show you to the training grounds, so you may witness the growing strength of the White Hand."

"White Hand?" Zola asked as we stepped into a sloppy formation behind Morrigan.

"The White Hand of Nudd was a mark once used to identify his followers," Aideen said. "Only those who wished to declare their allegiance to him bore it."

"Yes," Morrigan said. "The irony is not lost on us. It shall be his own hand that strikes him down."

I frowned as we passed another hall and saw what I could have sworn was one of the Utukku's instant-death rooms. A place where, if someone used the Warded Ways uninvited, they'd be skewered immediately. For some reason, I'd thought it had been closer to the stairs we'd used to come out of the catacombs. It was odd how the brain played tricks sometimes. How you could remember something so clearly, but when you saw it again, it was almost as if it had changed.

We followed Morrigan deeper into the hall, walking shoulder to shoulder until the expanse narrowed. I fell back behind Vicky so we had more room to walk, until the width lessened yet again and we were nearly walking single file. Morrigan vanished as she took a shadowed doorway I could scarcely see in the torchlight.

"This is a little creepy," Vicky said.

Jasper chittered in agreement.

"Some Fae used to say it was the mad tunnels of the Mad King," Aideen said. "This was a stronghold in Faerie. The narrowing hallways and twisted corridors gave the defenders ample chance to fight back and eliminate their invaders."

We came close to a torch mounted higher on the wall before I realized it was a Fae light. There was no warmth, only illumination from the small flickering orb. Aideen pointed up to a slit near the light.

"You can still see the arrow slits. Archers could hide behind the wall, and only the most accurate of their enemy could hope to strike back."

"Or a powerful-enough incantation," Zola said as she pulled back her hood. Her braids swung free and her face wrinkled as she squinted at the tiny slits in the wall. "Not much range of motion. Most of the arrow slits in the old forts would give you a wide berth."

"Some of those slits were not manned by fairies in their larger states," Aideen said. "Some of us would wield bows from tiny platforms set just inside the wall. And as for incantations, the stone was enchanted. Only the strongest of mages could have broken through it."

Morrigan harrumphed. "There were other ways in those times. When basilisks were more common, and a few twisted Fae would use the magic of life with deadly intent."

Vicky perked up at that. "What do you mean?"

Morrigan glanced back at the girl as we continued forward.

"It is something your necromancer can speak to you of. Twisting a magic meant to bring life, forcing a plant to kill, a root to rise and impale your foe, a vine to strangle them, a tower to collapse on top of them."

"Like that spiky forest you used to kill the demons in the Burning Lands?" Vicky asked.

I gave an uneasy laugh and glanced at Morrigan. "Yeah, kid, exactly like that. You can't claim plants don't kill, too. Look at the pitcher plant or the Venus fly trap."

"Did you hurt your back?" Zola asked. "Trying to twist your logic around that much, boy? Ah have the name of a good chiropractor if you need one."

Aideen stifled a laugh, and I glared at the fairy before cracking a smile of my own.

The narrow hall took one last bend and then expanded like the stage of an amphitheater. We spread out within the room of gray stone. The change from the golden ambient light was harsh, and it hardly felt like fairy work until I saw the doors. Massive battle scenes rose from those towering bronze monoliths. And it reminded me of the pillars outside the gates of Falias. Some I recognized: legends of the Morrigan, the crow perched upon a broken branch, Hern leading an intricately carved mass I had little doubt was the Wild Hunt, and even Nudd throwing down the Mad King, and raising the hand of glory. Gaia's hand. The flesh that rested in my backpack at that very moment.

"There is no fighting in these halls," Morrigan said. "Once you pass through these doors, this is a place of peace, unless you are one of those standing within the ring."

I exchanged a look with Zola, and was glad to see I wasn't

the only one somewhat confused by Morrigan's words. But before we could so much as ask her to clarify what in the ever-loving hell she was talking about, Morrigan threw open the doors. Whatever the intent of her comments had been fled my mind.

CHAPTER SIXTEEN

THE DOOR OPENED to reveal a massive cavern, its gently sloping walls polished to a mirror shine, that stretched to a strip of rough stone some 30 feet above our heads. But that wasn't the truly awe-inspiring sight.

As far and wide as I could see, an army of Fae trained. They moved as one, one section of the floor wielding swords, rising with the grace of a crane before striking forward like a viper. The mere sight of their lunges was enough to make me wonder how I'd survived more than one battle with any fairy.

Another group used halberds. A third line of fairies sat on the backs of their owls, still in their small forms, the movement of the birds so perfectly synchronized with the riders it was an unnerving sight to behold. Even the owls cocked their heads at the same time, flashed a wing, and struck out in unison with talons as sharp as any dagger.

But beyond that ocean of Fae was the noise. The grunts, shouts, and war cries of an army.

Vicky stared out at them, her gaze taking in the crowd from one side of the cavern to the other as she entered the room beside Zola. "Wow." She stretched the word out, and I understood the awe in her voice. Jasper hopped off her shoulder, and rolled to the right until I lost sight of him in the throng of fairies.

Looking at that intimidating force left one question in my mind. “Why didn’t they gut the dark-touched?”

“Their mission was to keep this army a secret,” a voice said, a bit too much emphasis on the s syllables. “Until the right time.” I turned, expecting to find one of the Utukku, but not *the* Utukku. She bared her fangs in what I’d come to think of as a friendly smile. Her lizard-like eyes blinked sideways, and I returned the smile.

“Utukku! What are you doing here? I thought you’d be with Hess, or somewhere else, even back in Faerie, no?”

She reached out and patted my forearm. “No, Damian Vesik. There is no more important place than here. I was saddened to learn of my people who died on the street. But their sacrifice will keep us hidden for a time. Nudd does not know his doom grows beneath his feet.”

Morrigan glanced between me and Utukku. “Our time is running short. Some of the elite dark-touched have been seen here.”

“The ones that can talk,” I said.

Morrigan inclined her head. “Yes.”

Utukku stroked the hilt of the dagger sheathed at her hip. “They are formidable, but a formidable enemy can still die.”

A break in the rigid routine, playing out deeper in the cavern, caught my eye. “What’s going on back there?”

“The ring?” Utukku asked. “You must come and watch our allies spar.”

“A foolish way to get our allies to kill themselves,” Morrigan said. “I still do not approve of this.”

“There are more healers,” Utukku said. “And more importantly, Ward finished laying his runes before he left for

Faerie with Leviticus. The incantations inside that circle are far weaker than those cast outside of it."

Morrigan crossed her arms.

Vicky frowned and looked around the group. "Where'd Jasper go?"

"Don't worry," I said. "That furball can take care of himself."

"As long as there aren't any dolls around," Vicky said.

"He still eating their heads?" I asked, remembering how many of Sam's Barbies I'd fed to him when we were kids.

"It's not the toys I'm worried about," Vicky said. "You know what could happen if he got a hold of a voodoo doll?" She shivered.

And I tried to envision it, those gleaming, razor-sharp teeth slicing into the flesh of a voodoo doll, rending all the stuffing from it. "Thankfully, voodoo isn't real, right?" I raised an eyebrow as I looked to Zola.

"Whatever helps you sleep at night, boy," Zola said.

I laughed nervously.

"Come," Morrigan said.

I expected her to lead us around the drilling soldiers but, instead, we strode up the middle, only a few inches separating us from the thrusts of the swords and the overhead strikes of a hundred halberds. Zola frowned, looking unimpressed, though I suspected that wasn't the actual emotion she was fighting with. Vicky, on the other hand, looked downright excited. And I could understand some of that excitement, knowing all these Fae were our allies.

I flinched as a halberd thrust came uncomfortably close to my right arm. The Fae at the end of the pike gave me a small smile and a nod before shifting his weight and swinging his halberd back in the other direction. I wondered how many of the Fae considered us their allies. Or were we something their leaders simply told them they had to deal with? Or, more perhaps more disturbingly, how many of them were actually spies for Nudd?

The thought sent a chill to my bones. But if I was honest with myself, I had little doubt that some of the Fae before us did not have our best interests at heart. If we'd been smart enough to send spies into the ranks of Nudd's army, you could be damn well sure he'd done the same.

We started past the Owl Knights, and I would have thought they were adorable, if I hadn't seen them fight. The damage the talons on those owls could do to a Fae that was still in its small form was immeasurable. Two of the larger barn owls at the back raised their right wings, concealing the flash of their riders' swords. It was graceful, deadly, and terribly effective.

Beyond that, the skirmish in the ring had picked up in earnest. Three Fae squared off, and it appeared to me they were all on their own side. None of the fairies in the circle were armed with the narrow Fae blades I was so used to seeing. We were just close enough I could hear the words of the fairy in the circle with his back to us.

"Nudd be with you," he said.

His two adversaries stiffened and raised their fists, as if they were about to engage in fisticuffs that would've looked more at home in a silent movie. But it wasn't their fists that struck out. The Fae on the right made a half turn, and when the fairy closest to us moved to block, the attacking Fae changed direction so fast my head spun. Instead of a forward kick, a blindingly fast roundhouse caught the defender on the shoulder. The fact that he managed to get his shoulder in the way to block spoke greatly of his speed. He grunted as the third Fae closed on him. The defender whispered an incantation, too quiet for me to make out, but his laugh was clear. He grabbed the wing of the first attacker and dragged the fairy into the path of the wave of force from the second. Even though I didn't hear the incantation, I was fairly certain it was a *pulsatto*. It hammered into the fairy's chest, and he collapsed to the floor, only to rise in a rage and attack the third fairy.

"Too easy," the defending Fae said. And something tickled my memories. It was a voice I knew. A voice I'd heard before.

Before I could say anything, a thunderous roar echoed from the back of the cavern. A small tower of blue sparks fired into the air, drawing my attention completely away from the fight.

"Shit," I said. "Jasper. Nothing to worry about indeed."

"That's not Jasper," Vicky said. Another barking roar sounded, and a second tower of blue flame went up beside the first. A gray neck rose, towering over the distant edge of the training grounds. "That's Jasper."

"Then what ..." But I didn't get a chance to finish my sentence before another massive gray neck stood tall above the crowd, and a dragon equal to Jasper's size made its way toward him. I took a step in their direction before Vicky cursed and grabbed my backpack. She had it unzipped and was rooting through it before I understood what was happening. I heard the bag of jerky crunch in her hand a moment before she sprinted off toward the dragons.

"Another dragon?" Zola turned to Morrigan. "Who is that?"

I knew the answer. And so did Aideen.

"You let him in here?" Aideen said. "We can't trust him."

"Trust who?" Zola asked, but the tone of her voice told me she already knew.

I stared at the back of the fairy in the ring. Watched the lithe, graceful form that I'd faced before on the battlefield and I called out his name, "Drake!"

He turned his attention to me for a split second and flashed me a smile. But his opponents, now fighting more as a team than individually, didn't miss their chance. Drake's face was smashed up against the dome of power a moment later. His wry smile turned into a grimace of pain. He tried to escape, but unarmed against skilled opponents, he was done.

"I yield," Drake said.

The barrier around the fairies fell, and Drake's opponents released him. He turned the fairies and nodded. "Your training is going well. I'm happy to see the improvements."

"One day it won't be my bare hands, betrayer," the larger of the two Fae said.

"I did not murder your brother for joy," Drake said. "It was on the battlefield, a long time ago. Some things are best forgotten."

I raised my voice. "You should come talk to the military with me. I'm sure they'll buy that line."

Drake flashed his teeth, somewhere between a grin and a sneer. "Vesik. Care to join me in the ring? Loser has to do whatever the winner says for a day?"

"I'm a bit more concerned about what your dragon might do," I said.

"You ruined my dragon, Vesik," Drake said. "I owe you for

that."

He cocked his head toward the back of the cavern. I frowned at him, and then followed the motion to the dragons. Vicky was sitting on Drake's dragon's head while the dragon stuck out his tongue so Vicky could pile Frank's face-melting jerky onto it.

"I …" But I couldn't find the words.

Drake turned and watched the dragons and the young teenager. "I doubt I'll ever get him to eat humans again. Dried out cow, on the other hand …"

I blinked at the fairy. The right hand of the Mad King, a Demon Sword, who somehow retained his powers through the loss of his monarch—powers to rival Foster's own, powers that he'd used to burn down Park's base in Saint Charles. I glared at him.

For a moment, I wondered just how much the circle dampened powers, and if I could fire a spell through it with enough force to strike him down. I'd been willing to give him leeway after the minimal help he offered, but the fact he was now in contact with Vicky put my tolerance on the back burner.

A small smile lifted the edges of Drake's mouth, giving his sharp cheeks and chin a deadly appearance. "I didn't realize we would have guests so soon." He glanced at the Morrigan.

"This was easier than trying to explain it to either one of you." The Morrigan brushed at her sleeve, and a crease formed on her brow. Just a small expression of irritation I'd seen on Zola's face more times than I could count. "I don't care what differences you had in the past. We will have peace in this place."

"The skirmish by the river?" Drake asked. "Hardly what I

would call a difference."

I choked back a growl. "People died."

He scoffed. "I doubt it was anyone important. The commoners and their military." He frowned, like he didn't like the taste of the words. Much like I didn't like the fact the military was occupying civilian streets.

"Vicky doesn't need to be involved in your schemes," I said, unable to think past what the fairy's manipulations might be.

"*My* schemes?" Drake spread his arms wide. "It surely was not me who brought her to these grounds, who gave her the burden of a reaper, who gave life to that which should not live." His words grew quieter as he spoke, until the last sentence had been little more than a whisper.

"Enough, boy," Zola said. "What's done is done. He only spins yarns to rile you up."

"Is it true?" Aideen said, standing up on Zola's shoulder. "You're a mercenary now? A sword for hire? One who would work for the Unseelie Court as quickly as they would defend their own brethren?"

Drake crossed his arms. "Typical. I saved your friend's life," he said, nodding in my direction. "The fool would've walked right into Nudd's trap. I could have let him die on the battlefield. I didn't."

"And why didn't you?" Aideen asked. "So you may beg a favor of him one day? Win a favor of mine? Or that of the rightful Demon Sword?"

Drake let out a hollow laugh. "You don't have the whole story."

"Then tell it to us," Aideen said.

Drake glanced at the dragons before returning his attention

to me. "I mean her no harm. And I know of the bond you share. To kill you would be to kill her, and I won't do that."

I eyed the fairy.

"Come, necromancer. Spar with me here, while my powers are muted, and so are yours."

"Not without reason," Aideen said, stopping me in my tracks. I'd scarcely realized I was already stepping toward the circle. "If Damian is victorious, you tell what you know of Nudd's spies."

I clenched my fists.

Drake smirked. "I accept your offer. I don't want either of us to die here, so why don't we say first takedown wins. Put me on the floor, and I'll tell you what you ask. But if I put you on the floor, then you leave me alone about my time spent with your apprentice."

"My apprentice?" I spluttered.

"Yes. I do not care to consider the grief my dragon would give me if she did not see her new best friend." Drake looked back to the massive forms of the gray beasts. They were now flinging a giggling Vicky back and forth, catching her gently on each other's noses like a rag doll. "It is … trying."

I tried to imagine then what the time Drake had spent with Vicky had actually been like. If she'd been bonding with his dragon, his reaper who had been his compatriot since the age of the Wandering War, just how much had that gotten under the fairy's skin? A slow smile spread across my face. "Agreed."

"Sweep the leg," Aideen said.

I hesitated, glanced back at her, and found the fairy grinning broadly.

"Oh, and don't lose. Apparently, Morrigan doesn't know

whatever Drake's about to tell us. She's been trying to get it out of him for the past week."

The Morrigan shrugged.

I cursed under my breath and stepped into the circle.

CHAPTER SEVENTEEN

DRAKE BACKED TOWARD the opposite side of the circle. "You humans haven't changed in a thousand years. Faerie could've ruled you then, and if you're not careful, Nudd will rule you now."

"A thousand years?" I asked, shrugging off my backpack and throwing it outside the circle to Zola. "I think you give humanity too much credit. We've been killing each other far longer than that."

Zola caught the heavy bag like it weighed nothing. It was one of those rare moments where she revealed the strength beneath what most would think was an ancient and frail body. Though she aged, and time had taken its toll on her skin, I doubted many could match her pound for pound when it came to strength.

"What of the rules of the circle?" Zola asked.

Morrigan gestured to the wards on the ground. "There are none. When the circle is engaged, their powers will be limited."

"It will be hard to draw on line arts," Aideen said.

"Is that all?" Zola asked.

When no one else spoke, I glanced behind me. Morrigan wore no expression. "It's supposed to be."

One of the Owl Knights stepped closer, a decorative halberd grasped in his left hand. He raised it high and spoke. "Die with honor." He brought the haft down on a ward inlaid on a dark gray tile. A second before the glassy dome snapped closed over our heads, I realized most of the hall had gone silent. A great many eyes were on us. When the incantation completed, the silence was almost deafening. I could see those around us speaking, but few words penetrated the spell.

"Finally," Drake said. "Whisper and they won't hear what we say in this place. But you must fight as if you mean to kill me."

"That shouldn't be a problem," I said, shrugging my shoulders and pumping my fists as if it would somehow intimidate the Fae warrior, who had likely seen more battles than I'd seen days above the earth.

"Nudd has to die," Drake said, hopping forward in an odd feint before lashing out with his right leg. I barely had time to say *Impadda* before I remembered spells wouldn't work right in the circle.

A shield spluttered on my arm, and perhaps it slowed Drake's leg a fraction, but it still hurt like a bitch when he caught my upper thigh. I sagged to one side, and Drake danced backward, as if he were taunting me. It was jarring to hear the words coming from his mouth, but see a different expression on his face. I wouldn't be surprised if the man could lie to himself without batting an eye.

"No shit," I said. "But I don't think that's your priority."

"He's lost his mind, and he's going to get *everyone* killed. Vanity is his weakness. Nudd believes himself too powerful, too intelligent, to be dethroned. So he plays both sides as if they were marionettes."

Drake's eyes lit up, and he danced forward again. Instead of waiting for a response, or an attack, I lunged, reaching back as if I intended to throw a wide hook.

The fairy followed the motion, but I feinted the attack with my right hand, drawing up short and grabbing the collar of his mail shirt before drawing his chest down to my knee in one vicious strike.

Surprise widened Drake's eyes, and I suspected he would've been in a bit more pain if he hadn't been wearing armor. It was about then I realized I was wearing a T-shirt, and he was wearing armor.

"Shit."

"You fight like the old legions," Drake said. "But you're sloppy. You take risks you don't need to."

"Not killing you is a risk," I said.

Drake landed two quick jabs. Trying to block them was like trying to block a hummingbird. "You could at least try to make this a good fight," the fairy said.

"*Pulsatto!*" I shouted, straining my will to put as much energy into the incantation as I could.

Drake danced away, but I hadn't been aiming for his chest. Weakened though the magic might have been, his sprightly steps made his legs vulnerable. When the wave of force hit, it was enough to take one of them out from under him. He went down on one knee, but popped right back up.

"That was close," Drake said. "I'm impressed."

"What do you want with Vicky?" I asked. "Why did you seek her out?"

"I didn't seek her," Drake said after an awkward pause.

"You're lying," I said.

"She's pure, untwisted by years spent in the service of a

madman. I was like her once, long ago, and that child deserves the choices I never had."

I narrowed my eyes, but I didn't have a counter to Drake's words.

"And the two of you have ruined my dragon. The beast won't touch a piece of human, or broccoli, instead subsisting on chocolate and dried meats. But you're avoiding the topic at hand, Vesik. You're walking blind into a fight with Nudd, a Fae who is truly mad."

"What do you mean?"

"The simplest answer is most often the truth," Drake said, a half-psychotic laugh on his lips.

It was a ridiculous statement, practically quoting Occam's razor, but his words gave me pause. I shook my head.

"What are you hiding from us?" I asked. "Because whatever you're hiding, you're hiding from the Obsidian Inn. You're hiding from the resistance."

"You're an idiot," Drake said. "The enemy is already in your head. You're just too distracted to see it. Nudd isn't your true enemy. He never was."

This time he attacked in earnest, a quick jab to my left kidney before his heel struck my shin. I wasn't even sure how he'd gotten around me so fast. But before I knew it, I had an elbow in my sternum and was gasping for air.

Drake's eyes narrowed, and his lips pulled into a tight line. "Never question my friendship with that girl again."

He came forward, and I knew the fight was over. But he was so sure of it that he didn't see my aura change, didn't see my power reach through the shell of that circle and grasp the mass of dead beneath us. The circle had done its job. I couldn't pull a million dead things up from the earth at once and wrap Drake up in them like an enchanted burrito, but it was enough to catch him off guard. He crashed through the flimsy wall, sending a shower of black ash across the circle. His arms raised in front of his face, perhaps to defend from an attack he couldn't see coming, but I'd already stepped around him before his eyes cleared. My elbow caught the back of his neck, and my knee was already in his inner thigh. All I had to do was reach out with my foot and put his face on the floor. Drake went down with a grunt and a curse.

"How the hell did you pull that through the shield?" he asked.

"I don't think that matters," I said. "I seem to recall there aren't any rules."

Drake conceded, bowed his head for a moment, and rolled over.

I extended a hand. The Fae eyed it warily, and then let me pull him up to his feet.

The shield went down, and the glassy dome that included the circle vanished. Drake grimaced when the Morrigan smiled at him. The shouts in the hall were deafening.

Drake took a deep breath. "I suppose I owe you a conversation."

"Let's get Vicky before we go." I tried uselessly flailing my arms, but it was unlikely she'd see me amid the mass of movement in the cavern. Morrigan was planning on taking us somewhere quiet, where we wouldn't be overheard, and I didn't want to leave Vicky behind.

Zola stuck two fingers into the edges of her mouth and whistled loud enough to shatter glass. A hush fell over the immediate vicinity while everyone turned to look at us. I kept waving my arms like an idiot, and Vicky finally saw me.

"I'm sure she'd be fine here," Drake said. "She has two reapers looking after her."

Jasper lowered his head and set Vicky on the ground before both of the dragons melted away until we couldn't see the small furry forms I knew would be following Vicky through the crowd.

"I'd feel better, knowing she was with us," I said. "And whatever you have to say, she'll probably find out anyway."

"Come." Morrigan gestured for us and we followed her to the edge of the cavern. I occasionally glanced back to see Vicky weaving through the fairies until she got to an aisle, and then she sprinted after us, two oversized gray dust bunnies flowing along the floor behind her. While I wouldn't admit it, Drake was probably right. She was likely safer with the dragons than with any of us.

Morrigan placed her right hand on the stone wall, and a small mote of light started tracing a complex knot in the stone. Small at first, but as it reached each intersection of the line, it broke into more dots until, in the end, it looked like a dozen people were etching out a pattern with laser pointers.

Vicky caught up to us as the pattern of the door fully revealed itself.

"Not good for a quick escape," Drake said.

Morrigan looked over her shoulder at him. "That is not what it was designed for." We followed Morrigan through the doorway, into a well-lit hall carved from the yellowish stone so commonly seen in Faerie.

"That was a great fight," Vicky said, weaving past Zola to

stand beside me.

"You saw that, huh?"

"Everyone saw that," Vicky said. "They seemed pretty surprised Drake lost twice."

The fairy stiffened slightly. "The first time was on purpose."

"So you didn't lose to me on purpose?" I asked.

Drake gave me a sly look. "I suppose we'll never know."

"That's a no," Vicky said. "Now we all know."

I grinned at the kid, and Drake rolled his eyes.

"Here," Morrigan said. She pushed on a section of the wall, and it swung open as smoothly as if it was a hinged door. But I didn't see a handle, or a way in, and as I stepped inside, I didn't see a way out either.

A round table sat in the center of the room. What looked to be wheeled leather office chairs in varying states of decay circled the table. It looked so out of place after passing through so much stone and using a warded doorway to enter that for a moment I just stared at it. The table was ornately carved from stone. An intricate mosaic of colorful tiles decorated the top, but the old, beat-up chairs kept drawing my eye.

"That's an … odd choice of decoration," I said.

Morrigan dismissed my comment with a wave. "Take a seat. The only ears here are our own." Aideen glided off Zola's shoulder and walked to a trio of small chairs in the middle of the table. Drake frowned at the office chairs before snapping into his smaller form and following Aideen to the miniature chairs. He dragged his a little farther away from her before sitting down on the opulently carved wood.

I pulled out one of the crappy office chairs and flopped down into it. The stone floor was slightly uneven, and it made the wheels incredibly annoying. They spun back and forth before finally settling into divots.

Vicky hopped into the chair beside me, while Zola took a seat beside Morrigan across from us. The reapers nestled underneath Vicky's feet like a pair of very bitey ottomans.

"You gave your word," Morrigan said. "Tell us what you know."

CHAPTER EIGHTEEN

DRAKE SANK BACK in the chair, his black and white wings arcing back over the finials. "You already know Nudd has spies in your ranks." He leaned forward. "But his spies are everywhere. They are among the water witches, and the commoners. I would not be surprised if at some point we learn there are more spies in the remnants of the Watchers."

"We already figured most of that," I said.

"Damian is correct," Morrigan said. "You offer us nothing."

Drake crossed his arms and sank back in his chair again.

I glanced at Vicky. If Drake was already going to try to clam up, maybe a switch in conversation topics could trip him up. Or at least change his mind.

"What are you doing with Vicky?" I asked.

Drake's easy smile hardened, and a crease formed along his brow. "I already told you I did not seek her out."

"He didn't," Vicky said.

"Then how in the hell did you two meet?" I asked.

Vicky looked down at her hands, and something between a purr and a growl echoed out from under the table.

"It is not my place to tell you," Drake said. "If Vicky wishes to tell you where she found me, how we met, that is her prerogative. I will not break my word to her, no matter what you threaten me with."

I frowned at Drake's words. He was either being sincere, or he was once again proving himself a liar of exquisite skill.

Zola steepled her fingers together and eyed Drake. "She knows something of you. This child …"

"I'm not a child," Vicky muttered.

Zola nodded to Vicky, but she didn't change the term. "This child knows something of you. Something you don't wish us to know. Why? Why put a scar in your armor for her?"

Drake's normally calm, irritating façade turned to stone. A liar he might have been, but his poker face seemed off today.

"Our reapers were drawn together. I will speak no more of it."

"Leave him alone," Vicky said. "He's not your enemy."

An almost pained look crossed Drake's face at her words, and Zola, gifted with the knowledge of more years than any mortal had a right to live, didn't miss her chance.

"But he clearly is, child," Zola said. "He withholds the knowledge of the Fae strong enough to possess another. He withholds the knowledge of who Nudd's spies are, and every secret he holds onto puts you in more danger. Puts *us* in more danger. And your friends, child … your friends will die for it." Zola pounded the flat of her hand on the table and Drake, the ancient stoic knight of the Court of Faerie, flinched.

"There are few who have the power," Drake said. "The immortal, Geb, is one. I don't know if Nudd has somehow brought her to his side, but she would have the strength. There are old ghosts in the Society of Flame who might have the skill."

I exchanged a glance with Zola. The Society of Flame was supposedly a well-kept secret. The fact Drake knew about it likely meant Nudd knew, too. Maybe Koda hadn't been too paranoid after all.

"I don't know who Nudd has recruited," Drake said. "But he is much like you, Vesik."

I slowly raised an eyebrow. "What do you mean?"

"I mean he's assembled a network, an army of his own, of spies and allies that stretches across this country, that's concentrated here in Falias. But the larger you grow a network like that, the more vulnerabilities become exposed. There's always a weak link, a pliable mind."

Drake leaned forward and rested his elbows on his knees, letting his hands dangle down between his legs. He glanced at Vicky and held her gaze before closing his eyes for a moment.

"So be it. Nudd has erred. He's given trust to the forest gods and the green men. He believes they are all spies working for him, but the forest gods hold loyalty to no one."

"Except Gaia," I said.

"Yes," Drake said. "But who holds Gaia's hand? Who keeps their queen, their goddess, from being resurrected to this plane? It's not Nudd. Not any longer."

I sat back in my chair. "Shit."

Drake nodded. "He earnestly believes they are loyal, but you have created chaos among the green men. Stump speaks on your behalf, he takes a mortal name, and while some of the forest gods frown upon this, and even plot the destruction of Rivercene itself, others whisper things to your allies. And more of them could."

"You believe the forest gods could tell us who is controlling the Fae inside the military?" Morrigan asked.

"Yes," Drake said. "Understand that if this succeeds, it will not be hard for Nudd to realize where the leak came from."

"You can stay with me," Vicky said.

Drake laughed, a sad smile etched across his face, and he shook his head. "I do this only for you, little one."

"You do this for more than me. You do this for everyone who suffered. Your siblings, and the lost children who may never know different."

I frowned at Vicky, and wondered just how much she knew about Drake.

"You honor the mantle of the Demon Sword," Aideen said. "If what you say is true, we may yet free Foster."

"You can free Foster at any moment," Drake said.

"Yes," Aideen said, "but I would prefer not to kill our allies in the process."

"And that is why you will lose this war," Drake said.

"Some believe it better to lose a fight than to lose everything they are," Morrigan said.

Drake turned his head to look at Morrigan, now the old crone once more. "Not this fight. Not this war. If you lose, humanity will become little more than servants, enslaved to the King of Faerie, and victim to his every whim."

Zola unlaced her fingers and spread her palms out on the mosaic tiles of the stone table. "That Ah cannot abide."

"You've seen the worst of humanity," Drake said. "But Nudd has had far longer to perfect his insanity. He's ruthless, and a manipulator with skills beyond any I've seen before."

"We know," Aideen said with a sigh. "He fooled Cara for years. His own wife, and in the end, he let her die."

"To a degree," Drake said. "The Sanatio missed many clues over the years, or chose to ignore them outright."

"I owe her my life," I said. "As do my family and countless others."

"And yet ..." Drake said, hesitating as he eyed Aideen. "And yet, if she had seen the signs, acknowledged them, acted on them, how many would have been spared? Would we even be sitting in the ruins of Falias right now? Upon the corpses of the commoners' cities?"

"Not even the greatest seer could tell you that," Morrigan said.

Drake nodded. "But it's that uncertainty you have to live with, and for some of us, we have had to live with it for a very long time. Wondering if we could have done something different, if we could have *been* something different." His gaze trailed to Vicky, and then dropped. "Go, find Appalachia's child in your woods. He may be less dangerous if he is dying. Learn the truth for yourself."

The old Demon Sword stood, inclined his head to Aideen, and walked toward the edge of the table. "If you need me, you know where you can find me." He glanced at Vicky and back to me. "Keep my friend safe."

Drake glided toward the wall opposite where we'd come in. His reaper rolled after him, trailing the shadow of the fairy. When the furball caught up, Drake touched a tiny stone. The hole in the wall opened no more than six inches by twelve. He slipped inside. The rather large ball of fur broke down into what looked like a trail of dust bunnies before filtering up into the darkness after Drake. The wall glowed, and then it appeared to be only stone once more.

Aideen turned to the Morrigan. "Was he telling the truth?"

Morrigan frowned. "If he wasn't, I do not yet see the ploy.

What would he or Nudd gain from our speaking to the forest gods?"

"He's not lying," Vicky said. "He doesn't like what Nudd's doing. Can't you see that? He doesn't want this. He doesn't want to gamble all of existence on a shitty alliance, to lose everything to dark magic."

"Why wouldn't he say that here?" Aideen asked.

"Maybe he doesn't trust all of you. Did you ever think about that?"

I frowned at her question. "What have you been doing with him and his reaper?"

Vicky's mouth turned into a flat line. "It's none of your business."

"Vicky, please," Aideen said. "It might give us some insight into Drake. We need to know."

"No," she said.

"Let her be," Zola said. "Vicky can tell us when she's ready." Zola stood up and walked around the table until she was behind Vicky. She laid a reassuring hand on the girl's shoulder. I remembered what that was like, having those old bones with that strong grip reassure me when I was in some of the darkest places of my youth.

And I realized that here, prying at Vicky, we were only making things worse for her. The kid had been through hell in the last few years. I just didn't want to see her hurt again.

"I don't see the harm in revisiting this at a later time," Morrigan said. "That does not mean there will not be harm, but for now I do not see it. Go, consult with the forest gods, and perhaps they can tell us more of Nudd's spies."

"And if they are truly so knowing," Zola said, "there are a

few other things I'd like to ask them about."

✦ ✦ ✦

MORRIGAN OPENED THE door, but it wasn't an empty hall leading back to the cavern. A hooded form waited, a spear in one hand and a fist in the other.

"Do not blindly trust the word of that fairy." Utukku pulled her hood back and looked me in the eye. "His loyalties are not yours."

"Most people's aren't," I said.

Utukku inclined her head. "But, for most, a difference in priorities will not kill you."

"Who are you to judge?" Vicky snapped. "You don't know him."

I looked back into the meeting room. Anger lived on Vicky's face, carving ridges I'd not seen before into her brow.

"It's okay," I said. "Utukku just doesn't want us to shoot our own feet off. It's a warning. Take it for what it is."

Vicky didn't respond, but a flush of color lingered on her face.

I turned back to Utukku. "Thank you. I'll remember your warning, and we'll protect ourselves the best we can. But for now, Drake's lead is the best we have."

"Pray it does not get you killed." Utukku pulled her hood up over her head and exited the hall in silence.

"Utukku is upset," Morrigan said. "More upset than I've seen her in ages." The old crone became a young maiden between one blink and the next. "I only hope her words are unfounded."

A flash of light sparked from Vicky's hand as Jasper released a whine. "You're wrong about him. You don't have any idea."

"I'll meet you in Greenville," I said. "Gaia can get me there without feeling like I've been riding the tilt-a-whirl for two days straight."

"Damian," Aideen said. "We left Greenville in ruins. They still haven't finished rebuilding that park, to say nothing of the forest that was trampled by the harbinger. I don't know that the forest god will be willing to talk to you."

"If you speak the right words," Morrigan said, "anyone will talk to you."

Aideen laughed. "You *have* met Damian, haven't you?"

Vicky's face relaxed a fraction, and something closer to a smile etched its way into the stony anger on her face.

"So, you'll meet me there?" I asked.

"No," Aideen said. "The forest god spoke to you and you alone. And that is how you should return to him."

The thought of facing that creature alone didn't give me a warm and fuzzy feeling. I believe Graybeard would've called it a walking the plank feeling. "What about you?" I asked, turning to Zola.

"Ah'll go with Aideen to see the innkeeper. She knows more about the green men and their ilk than anyone else Ah know."

Morrigan started down the hall, and the rest of us followed.

"It wouldn't hurt to consult with Stump, too," Aideen said. "He's one of the few green men who travel long distances. Many of them stay close to their indigenous forests, and the very nostalgia of his visits means he has more information than most."

"If you can ever get him to just tell you," I said.

"Yes," Zola said, "Ah imagine that you trying to get information out of Stump is much like me having a student who could not keep his mouth shut."

"Ouch," Vicky said.

Jasper chittered as I followed Morrigan down the hall.

Utukku was waiting to escort us back through the cavern, which was still filled with training and sparring Fae.

"You fought well, Damian Vesik," Utukku said. "Not nearly so clumsy as I expected. You've learned much in the time since we first met."

"Yeah, I also generally try not to attack people I've just met anymore."

Utukku bared her dagger-like teeth and displayed a wicked grin. "At least no one was hurt. And I have quite the story to tell about the witch queen's necromancer."

"Any laugh at Damian's expense is a good laugh," Zola said.

I grimaced at my master. We returned to the winding halls, leaving the chaos of the drilling Fae behind us. We stood at the top of the stairs that led back into the catacombs, where the dullahan dwelled in the shadows.

I rooted through my backpack and pulled out the hand of Gaia, studying the dead gray flesh for a time before making ready to walk into the Abyss. "I'll meet you at Rivercene. You good with the Warded Ways, kid?"

Vicky nodded. "I can ride Jasper. He makes it a little … better."

"Be safe, Damian," Zola said. "There are things in motion that we've not faced before. Remember, Gaia is their goddess, and you have traveled with her many times."

I wasn't exactly sure what Zola meant, until Morrigan piped

up.

"Any story you have to share of Gaia will be a welcome one to the forest gods. Do not hold back. Do not fight them unless you must. It is better to run, for they are more powerful than you know."

"Are you coming with us?" Aideen asked.

The Morrigan shook her head. "There is much to be done here. The time for the Obsidian Inn to make itself known in force may be near. We must be ready. Now go, rescue Foster and Samantha, and then tell me what you learn."

I exchanged a nod with Aideen before wrapping my fingers into Gaia's and stepping into the Abyss.

CHAPTER NINETEEN

I DIDN'T THINK using Gaia's hand would ever be normal exactly, but the odd sensation had become routine. My nerves weren't on edge as the world turned to black and slowly returned to life with the twinkling of the distant stars in the darkness. Gaia's golden motes floated in a moment later, and for a time I walked hand in hand with a goddess.

"Welcome, Damian," Gaia said. "It is good to see you again so soon."

"You, too. I met one of your … disciples? Followers?"

"What do you mean?" Gaia asked.

I looked down at my feet, trying to remember what the term was for the Children of Gaia. Beneath each footstep, the dark path glowed with a faint yellow light. "Appalachia. I met Appalachia."

"That is a name I know," Gaia said. "But it is a name one of the spirits took shortly before I was bound to serve the king."

"They haven't forgotten you," I said. "The world has changed for them since you left. Humanity has overtaken much of the lands and forests they watched over while you still lived on the earth. I think you're more of a ghost to them now, a symbol."

Gaia walked in silence for a time. I saw a small frown cross her face for only a moment. "It has been a very long time,

Damian. Even for the immortals, two millennia is a great deal of time indeed."

"I'm sorry," I said, the words feeling hollow.

"Where do you wish to go?" Gaia asked.

I blinked, realizing that I hadn't told Gaia where I needed to go. We'd just launched into the conversation about Appalachia. "Greenville. The old ruins south of the cabin."

Gaia glanced down at me, her lilting voice a source of comfort as we passed tentacled creatures of pure madness. "You seek the spirit of the drowned city."

I didn't think it had been a question. My talk of Appalachia likely gave away exactly who I was looking for. "The forest god who dwells there. Appalachia's child? I met him last year. What's his name?"

Gaia didn't answer for a time. "Sometimes I can hear them. The whispers of the spirits, they still reach me. Some of them are in pain, and some of them are no more, spirits lost to the unrelenting force of humanity's progress."

The goddess winced as the words left her lips. She didn't have to tell me what was happening for me to know that the compulsion the Mad King placed upon her so long ago was causing great pain.

"That's what I wanted to hear," I said. "You've done well."

Gaia shook her head. "It's not that, little one. It is the emotions, the anger. If I feel it too much, I am reminded not to."

The thought angered *me*. A being not allowed to feel her own emotions without being punished for them? It was monstrous.

"But I hear their whispers," Gaia said, drawing my attention back to her. "The one you seek has taken a mortal name,

Dirge."

My brain scrambled, trying to think if I'd heard of a forest, or a landmark, or mountain range, or anything that would bear the name Dirge.

"You seem lost," Gaia said. "It is not a name taken lightly, like that of Appalachia, named for the forested mountains she protected. Dirge was named for the songs played upon the hills where the dead were buried. The old cliffs above the river, before the city drowned."

"The cemetery?" I asked. "Dirge took his name after the music?"

Gaia nodded. "And the friend he lost who played that music."

"Friend? The forest god had a friend?" I stared into the distance at a towering mass of what I imagined would be writhing serpents if not for the odd slow of time in the Abyss. "A human friend?"

"Yes. Is that so hard for you to grasp? For are we ourselves not friends?"

"Of course we are," I said.

"Dirge's friend played songs at the humans' memorials. But he did more than that. He planted trees. For every one he cut down to build the burying boxes of your people, he would plant three more. Always three."

"To revive the forest?" I asked.

Gaia nodded. "Even then, that was not a common custom among your people. I do not know the entire story, but I know that Dirge had affection for the human. When that human died, and the city drowned, and those seedlings grew no more, Dirge despaired. And a spirit in distress can be a dangerous being indeed."

"We kind of ... broke some of their forest in the battle last year. You think they'll want to talk to me? Do you think they'll even realize I'm there?"

"They know when all people are there. If you did their forest harm, I am certain they will greet you."

"Awesome," I said, wondering just how much more worried I should be.

"We are here," Gaia said. "Go in peace, and the spirits will guide you."

I thanked Gaia, released her hand, and fell through the darkness until the stars fled and the green grass of an old cemetery spun beneath my feet.

✦ ✦ ✦

I TOOK A moment to steady myself. The transition from the shadows of the Abyss to the early evening of the quiet hilltop was jarring at best. I turned to look behind me and check my surroundings, when I realized how close to the edge Gaia had put me.

A hurried step took me backward. I doubted the fall to the Black River below would kill me, or at least not kill me quickly, but it wasn't something I wanted to experiment with. "Cutting it a little close, aren't we?"

I brushed my thighs off, as if trying to remove dirt that wasn't there. I slowed when I felt them. Old ghosts, and a few angry ghosts, whose homes had been destroyed in the floods, destroyed in the wars, and now even some whose resting places had been torn apart by the battle that had come here.

"I know you can hear me, boy," a voice said, and though the

sound was barely above a whisper, the anger was plain to hear.

I let my eyes unfocus and let the gray shroud of the dead fall across my vision. It wasn't a single ghost that waited for me, but a cluster of them.

The man who spoke wore a scraggly beard and a torn-up uniform, indicating he'd once served the Union Army. Other ghosts were newer, one wearing a spectacular leisure suit that led me to believe he only died a few decades before. Others were older, buried there long before Greenville had been built up into a city. I recognized the rough straw hats, the corncob pipes that were such a common sight around Coldwater, especially near the old sawmill that had been long lost to time.

"What are you all doing here?" I asked.

"He can see us!" the man in the leisure suit said.

"Of course he can," the soldier said. "Were you not paying attention when those vampires came through here?"

"I hardly think they were vampires," leisure suit said. "Everyone knows those are just stories."

The soldier pinched the bridge of his nose and let out a slow breath. "Of course. Now that you're dead, and a ghost, and stuck in a leisure suit forever, it's the vampires you don't believe in. Of course it is."

"Uh, guys?" I asked. "Did you need something? I don't think I've ever seen a cemetery with such a lively … congregation."

"Rest has been hard to come by," the soldier said.

A couple of ghosts standing around him nodded in agreement, including a young boy holding what I suspected was his mother's hand. I couldn't place the clothing, but even as ghosts, it looked like rough wool. I had little doubt their short lives had been damn hard.

"Why?" I asked, leaning up against a nearby tree. "Being dead seems like the perfect time to rest."

"You'd think so," the soldier said. "But instead there's been fighting, and dying, like we was trying to babysit toddlers with long rifles. It's been chaos."

"The old town rose right out of the earth," leisure suit said.

I turned back toward the younger ghost. "Not exactly. That may have partially been my fault. Or a lot my fault. Probably all my fault."

"So, you are the necromancer," the soldier said.

I nodded, somewhat surprised that he would know the term in anything other than the biblical sense. "And you've seen the vampires that came through here? The ones me and my allies fought?"

"Yes," the soldier said. "We saw them, some of us fought them. And some of us … died."

"Uh …"

"I know," he said. "We all know we're dead. We ain't idiots. Those things, the ones that could talk but stayed in the shadows. They tore more than one ghost apart. Claws like an eagle, and I …" The ghost shivered. "I'd never seen anything like it."

I looked around the gathering of ghosts. A few nodded along with the soldier's story. I didn't have any reason not to trust his word, but the thought of dark-touched rending ghosts left a sour taste in my mouth. I frowned and looked past the dead, at the damage the forest service still hadn't fully repaired. Most of the old ruins were intact, but where great swathes of earth have been carved up, either by the harbinger or my own incantations, chaos remained.

"We're still fighting them," I said, studying the edge of the forest. "I'll try to make sure they never come back here again."

"I would appreciate that," the soldier said. "There's only so much I can do as a dead man. Scare a few kids off here and there. A couple vandals." He balled his hands into fists. "But there's not much else I can do."

I gave the soldier a small smile. "You can be with your friends. And that, perhaps, is worth more than you know."

"It will be nicer when the forest is fixed. Maybe then things can get back to normal around here."

I perked up as the soldier studied the tree line behind us.

"Something happen?" I asked.

"Some government folks been out here," he said with a nod toward a pile of dead trees. "They burned some of the dead wood, mulched some others. But I don't think the forest will be happy until it's begun to recover in earnest."

"Do you know the forest god?" I asked.

"The forest god?" The soldier frowned briefly, and then his eyes lit up. A small smile broke through his melancholy expression. "You mean Dirge. I've known him a very long time."

I tamped down the excitement rising in my chest. "How I can find him? We need his help. It might help us stop those vampires."

"What might?" the soldier asked.

"Information, if he has it. Some of our allies, the people and fairies fighting the vampires, they've been compromised by spies."

"Like those damn Pinkertons?"

I blinked at the old ghost, but I was quite sure he was referring to the more legitimate Pinkertons, and not Philip. But the thought still sent me reeling, wondering how many of these people had been touched by that man.

"Yes," I said.

"I used to see him when I played the dirge for a funeral," the old soldier said.

The man's words hit me like a brick. Who he was had been so obvious, I hadn't even thought that Dirge's friend could be this soldier.

"Thought I was hallucinating the first few times I saw him. But he was different then. He doesn't take too kindly to ghosts now, and I'm afraid that might mean he won't take too kindly to you."

"That and the fact we tore up his forest," I muttered.

The soldier shrugged. "Even he, unreasonable as he can be, saw that giant tear up those trees. I think he could hardly blame you and yours for fighting that thing."

"Guess we'll see." I pulled out my phone and opened the music app.

"What do you intend to do?" the old soldier asked.

"Play some music. See if he'll come out and talk."

"On one of those flat boxes?" the soldier said. "You need a real instrument, son."

I smiled at the old ghost. "Let's just hope this will do." I cued up a funeral dirge and cranked the volume on my phone as high as it would go. Out in the open, even in the calm air, the music wasn't very loud. But in the silence that surrounded us, it sounded more like a sad thunder. One mournful note followed its brothers and sisters through the darkness of loss.

The ghosts fell silent, and we waited.

It wasn't long before the trees swayed as if a strong breeze had moved them. But the air was still, and the movement of the trees was isolated. I focused on that patch of woods, until I saw the flash of glowing eyes and the bark that shifted inside the shadows.

"You picked a good one," the old soldier said. "Played that one myself once or twice. Back when I still could."

Another minute and the song wound down. The trees stilled, but the glowing eyes stayed focused on me. A slow blink was the only movement I saw. I waited, wondering if I should call out to the forest god, or if that would have me running screaming from an angry tree. It wouldn't hurt if I waited a little longer. I let out a breath I didn't realize I'd been holding when the tree line separated, and the mass of the forest god known as Dirge stepped into the clearing.

"That song," the forest god boomed. "I have not heard that song in a great many years. A lifetime, by your mortal standards. Why have you returned here, necromancer?"

"I thought you might be able to help us. My allies were fighting the vampires you saw in your woods, who hurt the ghosts here—the spirits of the people, and even your friend."

"The dead are dead," Dirge said. "They are friends to none."

I frowned at the forest god. I'd met many beings over the years, and some could perceive the dead better than others. Something as powerful as the green men, and the forest gods, I'd assumed would see them clearly.

"He's right here," I said. "He still wears his uniform. A little tattered, but you can still tell it's him."

The forest god's voice rose. "You injure my lands, my trees, and now you seek to pierce my heart. I left you in peace once, necromancer. Join the dead in oblivion."

The hands of the forest god erupted into spikes. Thorns grew down the length of the vines that formed his arms and legs.

I cursed and turned to the ghost beside me. "Hold on, this is going to get a little weird."

My aura flashed out before I could give him more warning than that. And a knowing filled with more loss and sadness than I'd ever seen sent me to my knees.

CHAPTER TWENTY

TERRENCE HOLTZMAN. HIS father had been the first man he knew that died in the war. A family torn asunder when his sister became an abolitionist. It was a dangerous time for women to have an opinion, much less an opinion on what had cut the nation in half. She left Missouri to work with the abolitionists.

It was the last time he saw his little sister. But he heard the stories of what they'd done to her. He swore that so long as he lived, he would fight in her memory.

He served in Missouri most of his years, fighting for the right to raise the first colored regiment near Kansas. And they finally won, and those proud men marched for the Union.

Terrence saw a dozen skirmishes with various units. Some were filled with his friends, some people he would've one time considered enemies, but most died. It was Price's disorganized campaign that tore through the heart of the state. They cut down his friends, and while many bodies were lost to the woods, some remained. But no matter what, Terrence played his guitar in their honor at their memorials.

The last song he played was interrupted by fire, and a ball of lead. His last vision was the boy in gray, marching over the fresh graves, screaming that Terrence's daddy had killed his, but now he'd return the favor in kind. He recognized the boy.

He couldn't be more than fourteen, couldn't understand what he was doing, taking up arms for the Confederacy, and murdering his one-time neighbor.

The boy never saw what got him. Never saw the shadow rise from the woods, the angry flare in the forest god's eyes. One moment he was alive, and the next vines had risen from the forest floor and shot through him like spears.

The lumbering shadow kneeled beside Terrence. It spoke. "Your music was beautiful."

In his last words, Terrence whispered, "I knew you were real."

✦ ✦ ✦

I BROKE AWAY from the vision with a cry. Tears stung my cheeks, and I defiantly stared up at the forest god. His charge had slowed until he came to a stop not ten feet from us. But his eyes weren't on me. They were on the glowing spirit beside me, the tattered and stained uniform of a friend gunned down.

"But you died," the forest god said quietly, the spikes on his body slowly receding.

Terrence barked out a short laugh. "Yeah. It sucked. But I'm glad you were there."

"And the shadows around you?" Dirge asked. "They are ghosts, too?"

Terrence nodded. "But I don't know why you can see me and not them. We're the same."

"I think I know," Dirge said. And he turned his gaze to me. "You spoke the truth."

"I did." I bit my tongue, not wanting any sarcasm to slip out and possibly anger the very, very large forest god. "We were only here for the vampires and those who would do harm to the ghosts and commoners of this place."

Dirge gave a slow nod of his colossal head before turning his gaze back to Terrence. The vines in his chest moved, slowly revealing what lay beneath. Dirge reverently removed an ancient guitar from where he must have held it for over a century. I didn't understand how it could be so well-preserved, but the magic of the Fae and the gods could be a strange thing indeed.

Dirge gently held the guitar out to Terrence, and the ghost glanced between me and the forest god.

"I can't, though, can I?"

I nodded. "For a time. Oh, and you'll probably be visible to the commoners, so you might want to stay out of sight for a little bit."

Terrence's solemn expression broke into a small smile and he reached out for the guitar. He hesitated at first, as if worried his fingers would pass right through the strings and the fretboard, but they didn't. Whatever magic had preserved the guitar hadn't kept the strings in tune, but they were still pliable enough for Terrence to fix that.

Dirge sank into the earth, until he was not much taller than us, though his face and shoulders were still quite a bit broader. "We lost friends here in the battle. But I could not play your song for them."

Terrence gave the forest god a sad smile as his fingers danced. The strings resonated, and the music that vibrated out of that old wood pulled me right back into the visions of loss that Terrence had tried to soothe with his music. We listened in silence: the ghosts of the cemetery, the forest god, and the necromancer.

✦ ✦ ✦

THE SKIES GREW dark, and Terrence must have been playing for an hour. The lilting notes at once soothing the loss and building a beautiful memorial to those Dirge couldn't play for.

When the last note died, the forest god didn't wear the expression of rage that I'd seen on him like a fixture in the battle, and even when I arrived here.

"Thank you," Dirge said.

"I can teach you," Terrence said. "If I have enough time." He glanced back at me.

"You'll be able to hold the guitar for at least a few days, and you'll need to watch out for the commoners longer than that. And since Dirge here seems to have better perception than them, you'll probably have a while to tutor him."

"Done and done," Terrence said. "If that don't beat the Dutch."

Dirge frowned and turned to me. "Why would you do this?"

"I need help," I said. "The things we fought here, the vampires?"

Dirge nodded.

"They're allied with Gwynn Ap Nudd, the Fae King. He's managed to infiltrate some of our allies' forces. They have spies who can control other Fae. Possess them."

"That is a magic I thought lost long ago," Dirge said. "There were not many who could use it, even in the days of the old wars."

"Can you tell us who? It could save many lives."

Dirge inclined his head. "There were five among the immortals, and a handful among the Fae, but each had disciples. It will be a matter of tracking them and their lineage."

I nodded.

Dirge began giving me the names. Some of them sounded like they were longer than the freaking alphabet. But others I recognized. On the last one, I froze.

"Koda? Are you sure?"

"Of course," Dirge said. "Why would I mention them if I wasn't sure?"

I gave a small laugh. "Fair enough." I typed Koda's name into my phone and sighed. "There's one other thing."

"Ask," Dirge said, looking at Terrence. "If I can help, I will tell you what I can."

"The commoners have weapons, extremely powerful weapons. Somehow Nudd stole them, made them vanish. It's creating more tension among the commoners than is normal."

"And they are like animals," Dirge said. "When they are frightened, they attack."

I grimaced and nodded. "Can you help?"

"What is it you wish to know?"

"Where they are," I said. "Or if Nudd plans to use them somehow." And as stupid as it sounded, I asked it anyway. "I mean, he doesn't have some kind of magic for uranium, does he?"

"The Fae have magic for nearly limitless applications. But of that, I doubt." Dirge closed his eyes and tilted his head to the side. The earth around us rumbled, and the trees shook as if a shockwave had gone out and Dirge was the epicenter. He sat like that for a time, listening. Eventually, the forest god nodded.

His eyes opened, and he turned his gaze back to me.

"I have found what you seek."

"Seriously?"

"The spirits are quiet, young one. And there is ill will toward you and your allies."

"Ill will," I said. "That's a really nice way of putting it."

"You slew the green men when the queen of the water witches fell." Dirge looked into the distance for a moment then returned his gaze to me.

"They didn't exactly give me a choice," I said. "If I wouldn't have killed them, they would've killed us."

"That is an odd thing for a green man," Dirge said. "They are not warlike. I fear that in the absence of the goddess, they are losing their way."

"Gaia," I said, remembering Morrigan's words. "I know Gaia." I placed my hand over my chest. "I walked with her in the Abyss."

"With a ghost, perhaps," Dirge said. He hesitated after those words, his eyes focusing on Terrence for a time.

I might have held back, but Morrigan's words came back to me. Anything I could share would be like a gift to the green men and the forest gods. "She was imprisoned by the Mad King. Her hand cut off below the elbow."

"How could one sever the limb of the goddess?" Dirge asked. "For she is the size of the worn mountains of this state. I know of few Fae who could defeat her."

"Gaia has more than one form," I said. "The Mad King enthralled her when she was not much bigger than a human." I hesitated, and then nodded to myself. I opened my backpack and dug out the hand of glory. Gaia's hand.

"Your goddess yet lives," I said, holding Gaia's hand reverently. "She is beneath the earth in this state."

Dirge remained silent, his eyes locked on the hand.

"She offered me her powers," I said. "But we can't trust the compulsions placed upon her by the Mad King."

"That is no mortal arm you hold there."

"No, it isn't."

He reached out slowly, tentatively. As if he was watching a dream, and any movement might wake him from it. But the vines that made the tips of his fingers stretched out just a little and rested on Gaia's palm.

"There is still much power in this arm," Dirge said. "I don't understand. She's been dead, lost to us, for millennia."

"Not dead. Just sleeping, trapped, and waiting for a new dawn."

Dirge drew his hand back. "She could not offer her gifts to a mortal. You reek of lies necromancer, but you show me truths. It is … unsettling." He frowned, the bark around his lips curling down. "A deathspeaker? A necromancer? She would keep her powers in the realm of life."

I looked at the edge of the broken forest around us and walked toward the woods. "Not all my powers are death. Promise me something."

"You seek my word? Why would I give it?"

"If I prove to you that I have the powers over life as well as death, I need you to speak to the green men, or the forest gods, or whatever spirits it was you tried to speak to. Tell them I am Gaia's ally. Tell them she still lives, and she was betrayed by the Fae who serve under Gwynn Ap Nudd."

Dirge studied me for a moment as I got closer to the tree

line. I turned and faced him squarely, a strange visage standing among the tombstones surrounded by a group of ghosts.

He once again glanced to Terrence and then said, "Prove your word to me, and you will have mine."

"*Vadonon arbustum sero,*" I said, and the power in the ley lines lanced out to meet me. I felt the roots of the grass first, before I found the dying remnants of the trees. Root balls and shattered stumps barely clinging to life, and some too far gone for me to do anything about. But there were saplings here, even seedlings, and if that's what it took to get Dirge's word, to find out what Gwynn Ap Nudd had done with the world's nuclear arsenal, then so be it.

I kneeled. The blue flashes of the ley line energy grew green, and I spread my hands out upon the earth. Power rose, crashing into my knees and toes as it railed against the earth. I never thought of this magic as my domain, but Cara had long ago proven me wrong. I didn't think she could have known I would one day have to prove myself to a forest god, but the thought was reassuring; that she was still with me, and in some ways, I supposed she always would be.

The grass curled around my fingers and grew around my wrists as I felt the specter of death creeping through lands, stalking Dirge, but I didn't let up. The ley line energy surged out, pulling life from the very earth, from the decay that ate the dead things, the life that came from death. And those magics twisted together until they found the broken trees, the shattered trunks, and new life surged through them. I leaned into the grass, and it held me up as I opened my aura to a degree I hadn't in years. Slowly, the magic started to recede, but the saplings hadn't grown more than a few inches. I forced the gaps in my aura wider, and cried out, "*Vadonon arbustum magnus sero!*"

My sight grew hazy as pain screamed through my limbs. It felt as though I might burst into flame as the power seemed to superheat the entire world. But it wasn't like the fire incantations. It didn't blister my skin or singe the hair from my body. This was different. This was peaceful, even in the pain. I screamed as my vision returned and green light burst forth from the forest around us. Bark creaked, and the green flesh of new saplings rocketed into the air.

"Stop, necromancer!" Dirge shouted, his voice booming with renewed life. "Your point is made! I will do as you ask! Let go, and I will finish this."

Dirge took a step forward, reaching out as if he could touch the power. And perhaps to some degree he could, as the burden and pain of the spell lifted away.

I let the power fade as I slowly locked down the channels I'd carved into my aura. The ley line energy drained back into its normal ebb and flow, only to be snapped up by the intricate movements of Dirge's hands. I looked around and smiled before my vision swam, and the world went black. But in that moment, I saw the new trees, the saplings born from destruction, and the seedlings that were now as tall as I.

CHAPTER TWENTY-ONE

I AWOKE TO a sad guitar. But despite the melancholy notes, the guitarist wore a smile. The ghosts gathered around a small fire in the dark of Greenville.

I tried to make sense of what had happened. It was no longer twilight—darkness reigned around me. If I'd been asleep that long, I wondered where my friends were. Why hadn't they come to find me?

I pulled my phone out and frowned at the screen. No missed calls. No texts.

"Your friends know you're safe," Dirge said. "I sent word to Stump at Rivercene."

"Did I tell you they were there?"

Dirge shook his head. "No, but I felt your connection to the goddess. I felt the line of power that stretched outside this realm and wove back into Rivercene. I understand now why Stump has made that place his home, and I see why he gathers more of the green men to him."

"Thanks," I said, a bit woozy as I sat up. I'd unleashed too much power in that spell. Exhaustion had settled into my bones.

"I believe you could have used a less dramatic means of proving your word," Dirge said. "But I am grateful for the forest reborn." He paused and looked down at his bark-covered hands. "And for my life restored. You have healed me, necromancer."

I groaned and turned slightly so I could see the woods behind me. I blinked at the restored trees. The new growth, and the long-fallen woods that had been sown back into the earth.

"Huh," I said.

"That was a hell of a thing," Terrance said. "I don't think I've ever seen Dirge impressed before."

Dirge sat down beside me, crossing his legs as part of his body sank into the grass until the top of his head was no higher than a shrub. "You have proven your word, and I have honored mine."

"Yeah?" I asked, rubbing my neck.

"The weapons you seek were taken through the Warded Ways, delivered not to oblivion."

I cursed. "If Nudd can take them through the Warded Ways, does he intend to use them on Faerie? Can he even detonate them in Faerie?" But even as I asked the question, I had little doubt Nudd could do terrible things without needing to circumvent the conventional human fail-safes.

"They are in the vaults deep beneath Falias," Dirge said. "They are still here, in your world, and a danger to all."

"Can't get much worse than that."

"The weapons cache is guarded by Hern and his army."

"I stand corrected," I muttered.

"Go to Rivercene," Dirge said. "Your allies await you, and the evidence of your sister's innocence should arrive there shortly. You need to rest, necromancer. Your fight is not yet done."

I said my goodbyes to Dirge and Terrence and the ghosts of

the cemetery, listening to the sad notes of that old guitar as I left. Dirge watched, a small smile on his face as his eyes locked on the hand of glory. I laced my fingers into Gaia's and stepped into the Abyss.

✦ ✦ ✦

"RIVERCENE, PLEASE," I said before the stars of the Abyss resolved around me.

"I could hear them," Gaia said, a crease in her brow that showed a level of pain I'd rarely seen on the goddess's face. "The forest gods call out to me in a way they have not in a great many years."

"I don't think they realized you were still alive, but they do now. I hope that's okay."

"I am glad." A frown flashed across her face. "There is no harm in them knowing I am here in some form. If I could but walk the earth once more, Damian, I could help you."

I met the Titan's golden gaze for a moment, waiting to see if that declaration would cause her some kind of pain, if it would go against the Mad King's compulsions, or if the awakening of a Titan could truly benefit us. It was a seductive thought, especially knowing what was out there in the world. Knowing that the stockpiles of world-killing weapons the commoners were so fond of were now in Gwynn Ap Nudd's possession.

"I'd sure miss having you as a guide in the Abyss," I said.

"That is not a power unique to me. What is perhaps unique to me is my ability to gift it to another. I promise to grant you some of my powers if I should awaken, and that is not a promise I will break."

Walking through the Abyss with Gaia didn't seem to tear

open the fabric of reality as the portals the Mad King once conjured had, resulting in the tangled, insane network known as the Warded Ways. But if she gave that power to me, granted me that gift, I wouldn't trust myself with it. Would I cause damage like the Mad King had? But I couldn't be sure if Gaia spoke of her own volition, or if some of the things she said were the remnants of a long-dead madman.

"We are here," Gaia said. "There are a great many of my children here. Bid them greetings, if it is agreeable."

"I will."

Gaia nodded and released my hand. Exiting the Abyss was never exactly the same. The last time Gaia had brought me to Rivercene, she had dumped me and Nixie into the river. But today I blinked and took a half step back as the front door of the old mansion materialized in front of me. So close, in fact, that I could reach out and turn the doorbell even though I already heard footsteps in the hallway.

"I'm coming," the innkeeper grumped from the other side of the door. "I'm coming!"

I smiled down at the old doorbell that worked by twisting it—the only one like it I'd ever seen—and the door frame that looked like carved rope. Multiple deadbolts clicked before the door swung open.

"We aren't buying bullshit today," the innkeeper said. "So keep it to yourself." She stepped aside to let me in. The innkeeper was always grumpy. Hell, she made Zola look downright peppy some days.

"It's good to see you, too."

The innkeeper grumbled something under her breath and gestured to the hall that led back to the large kitchen. My boots thunked on the ancient hardwood floors. I glanced up at the portraits lining the wall as I made my way past the grand staircase on my right. Beneath it waited a small upright piano, the only one in the building that had been tuned and working the last time I'd been there. The display case nestled in the corner of the opposite wall caught my eye, and I pursed my lips at the old, worn photo album within. I remembered what lay inside it. The thought of the faceless skinwalker still made my flesh crawl.

I'd heard voices when we first entered the hall, but now I could make them out: Zola, Drake, Aideen, and another with a light accent whom I hadn't expected to be here. I rounded the doorway, and my eyes roved across the old fireplace before settling on the group at the kitchen table.

"Casper?" I asked.

"I won't be here for long." Casper held up a tiny square box.

I frowned at it for a moment. "What is that?"

"A camera."

I gave her a half smile. "I mean, what's on the camera?"

"Enough evidence to get Sam and Foster out of lockup," Casper said.

Relief flooded through me, releasing a bit of tension I hadn't realized I was holding in.

"Word came through after you met with Dirge," the innkeeper said.

"What's on it?" I asked.

"It shows Sam and Foster in training at the moment the bombs went missing."

"Is that enough? Couldn't they still get them on conspiracy for it or something?"

Casper shook her head. "This on the other hand," she said, pulling a small flash drive from her pocket. "This is footage from a few of the silos. But I tell you, you're not going to like what you see.

Gwynn Ap Nudd had a man, or Fae, rather, at each facility to move almost every bomb."

I shook my head. "That's impossible. There's no way he could get someone inside all of those installations. I mean, how many are we talking?"

Casper shrugged. "No one really knows. Let's just say it's a shit-ton."

"Some of them used wards," Aideen said. "You can see the way the portals opened, but there were Fae in others."

"Inside some of the most secured areas of the military?" Zola asked. "Nudd has been planning this for a long time."

"They weren't all Fae," Vicky said, shoveling another forkful of breakfast soufflé into her face.

"What do you mean?" I asked, frowning.

"Dark-touched were there."

I glanced at Casper, and she nodded.

I pulled out a chair and sagged into it. "How can the dark-touched steal nukes? That's insane."

"It's the smart ones," Vicky said.

I rubbed my chin. "That's just what we freaking need."

"Be glad the green men noticed those bombs going missing," the innkeeper said. "If not for them, who knows how long your sister and Foster might have been locked up."

"I know, but why *are* the green men aware of what happened to the nukes?"

"It may not be my place to answer," the innkeeper said.

A moment later, something tapped on the large rear window. The innkeeper frowned and then gave a kind of half shrug as she made her way over to it. She opened the blinds, and the tangle of bark and vines that formed Stump's face appeared just across the deck. She slid the windowpane open and nodded to the green man.

"You want to explain this?" the innkeeper asked.

"You could hear us out there?" I asked.

"It was muffled, but yes." Stump rubbed at the bark that formed his beard and it sounded like a belt sander. "With some effort, if I am able to touch certain boards of this home, I can hear what those inside are speaking."

"Stalker much?" Vicky said.

I flashed a grin at the kid before turning back to Stump. "It's good to see you again."

Stump inclined his head, the vines of his neck flexing with the movement. "It is always good to see you, my friends. To clarify what the innkeeper said, we do not so much track the weapons of the commoners, but we are aware of them as a body may be aware of a cancer. And when the disease has left, one tends to take notice of it."

"The metals?" Zola asked. "The uranium?"

"Call it what you may," Stump said, "but it is poison. No different than what the commoners use to kill the growth around their homes, or murder their fellow humans."

"It's a little bit stronger than weedkiller," Zola muttered.

"Regardless," Stump said, "the meaning behind my words stands. No matter what the commoners may choose to kill with it, poison it is, without doubt."

"That still doesn't explain how we have surveillance video,"

I said. "I'm pretty sure you didn't pull that off their network."

"Of course not." Stump gave a small shake of his head. "The ways of the electric machines are far beyond what my people know, what with their lights and nonsense and all."

"He means computers," the innkeeper said.

Vicky smiled at the green man. "I could listen to him talk all day."

"Don't let him hear you say that," the innkeeper said. "Or you will."

Stump returned Vicky's smile, and the expression gave a softness to his bark- and moss-covered face. "In some ways, the young ones are wiser than all of us." He turned his gaze back to me. "You are not the only ones with spies among your ranks. The commoners have not yet developed reliable ways for identifying the Fae. Because of this, more than one spy has made their way into the ranks of the commoners' military forces. Some of them are Nudd's, but there are others more closely allied to the Morrigan, and those of the new water witch queen."

I frowned at that. "Nixie has spies in the military?"

Stump nodded.

"Of course she does," the innkeeper said. "She'd be a fool not to. Those morons now have weapons that can hurt a great many Fae. I suspect she'll keep eyes on them for a good long time."

I pinched the bridge of my nose. Put like that, it made sense. I wasn't sure why Nixie hadn't told me outright. Maybe she thought it hadn't been something I'd needed to know. It still gnawed at the back of my mind.

"Take your evidence and free your allies. I fear we will need all that we can gather." Stump turned to go, his words somewhat pointed and far less rambling than I was used to hearing from the old green man.

"Wait," I said. "Stump, wait."

The green man paused mid-stride beside one of the towering old trees and turned back to face me.

"Gaia says hi," I said. "And so does Dirge."

Stump smiled, but it didn't seem broad. It felt sad. "The goddess is always with us. One just needs to know how to listen. Whether she is awake upon the earth, or slumbering beneath us, it matters little, for she will always be with us. And that is something I wish my brethren could understand in full. We have the forest gods, and the wisdom that the goddess left behind. And that is enough. Go in peace, young one, though I fear that peace may not last long."

Stump walked away in earnest, his lumbering steps barely a whisper in the grass.

The innkeeper slid the windows closed and lowered the blinds once more. "I guess I need to learn how to lock the sound down a little better in this place. All the times I've threatened to turn him into firewood behind his back, and the bastard's probably heard half of them."

"Will they join us?" I asked.

"Join you?" the innkeeper asked, one eyebrow rising. "They never left you. Stump and those closest to him will be your allies until the end of time. You walk with Gaia, which means you walk with them. Some of the green men may have chosen to forget the power of the goddess, but now they know she lives, and I suspect the rest will fall in line. They likely wouldn't want to deal with the consequences if they chose the wrong side."

I gave the innkeeper a half smile.

"Don't flash your teeth at me," the innkeeper said. "You need to figure out how in the hell you're going to get beneath Falias to retrieve those bombs, or destroy them."

"That was damn smart of Nudd," I said. "There's no way we can approach that place without them seeing us coming. Nudd's army will be ready. We need a better way in."

"Sound familiar?" the innkeeper asked. "Hiding your best weapons so close to home. Right beneath your own feet?"

I didn't like what she was insinuating. "I'm not like him." But despite my protests, the innkeeper's words spoke to me. In some ways, she was right.

"Every time you've needed an artifact of dark magic, it's been at your hand. It is clear you keep the things you value nearby, and if you look at Nudd, he also keeps the things that may be useful nearby."

"Lots of people do that."

The innkeeper shook her head. "Lots of people do not manage to wield a Key of the Dead or the *splendorum mortem* with little more notice than a tornado siren."

I frowned at the innkeeper. "We aren't that alike."

"But more alike than you may think," the innkeeper said. "Gwynn Ap Nudd is simply willing to cross more lines than you are."

"Are you sure about that?" Vicky asked. "Damian did pull a fully crewed ghost pirate ship out of the Burning Lands." She wiggled her hand across the table. "Now it just sails around the rivers here. Think it's a perfectly normal thing? It's not a perfectly normal thing."

"There isn't much that's perfectly normal around here, girl," Zola said. "Ah understand what the innkeeper is saying, but there is much that sets them apart."

Zola and Vicky tried to argue about just how different we were while I pondered the innkeeper's words. Vicky eventually gave up, opting to dive into another serving of soufflé rather than argue the finer points of dark-touched vampires versus raising an undead pirate ship.

"Stump didn't tell us exactly where the bombs are," I said.

The innkeeper sat back in her chair, a small smile lifting the corners of her lips. "And?"

"But if you're right," I said, "wherever he has them stored will be easily accessible. Practically beneath his feet. Why wouldn't Stump be able to tell us a more precise location?"

"Because they're hidden," Zola said, leaning forward. "They aren't simply stored underground. They're masked by something."

The innkeeper nodded.

"He's done that before," Drake said, breaking his long silence as he stood up on the table. "Nudd used to hide his forces underground in a four-walled room. Always four walls with four corners, exactly at ninety degrees. We can ward them against any portal."

"Could Gaia break through it?" I asked. "Use the Abyss to circumvent it?"

"If you didn't want to survive the experience," Drake said. "It would be like opening a portal and having no idea where it came out. You could end up lodged in a brick wall, or be integrated with one of the bombs." Drake frowned. "Now, that would be something to see."

"I think I'd rather not see that." Vicky gave a frustrated sigh. "But how are we supposed to find it? Or better yet, how are we supposed to get into it?"

But my mind was already working, and I had an idea that would either be really good, or really bad. But when it came to fighting Nudd, there wasn't much in between. "First, we're going to spring Sam and Foster from their cells, if Park hasn't done it already. We need to tell him how to hunt down the Fae who infiltrated his ranks. We can assist him with that, but our priority is the nukes. And I think I know someone who can help us sniff them out."

Zola narrowed her eyes. "If that was a pun about the werewolves, so help me …"

I grinned at Zola.

CHAPTER TWENTY-TWO

PARK FROWNED AND squinted at the screen, studying the evidence. "I've seen these recordings before. You're telling me the ones in our system are faked? No one has access to do that."

"It's stored on the network, isn't it?" I asked.

Park nodded. "You're talking about military-grade hardware. You'd need someone with world-class skills just to get into that, much less swap it out without any trace of what they did." He paused and drummed his fingers on the edge of the keyboard. "Which begs another question. How did you get this?"

"Old friends," I said. "As to your other question, how much do you know about the Watchers? Or at least the group that used to be the Watchers?"

"Probably less than you're about to tell me," Park muttered.

A ripple opened nearby. I eyed it, waiting to see who came through. "Who are you letting open portals into the base? I thought that was restricted."

"It is," Park said, still looking down at the screen. "You and that creepy hand are the only ones that …"

But Park trailed off when he saw where my attention was. His eyes locked on the slash of red expanding before us, and on the armored fairy who stepped through it.

Park already had his gun leveled at the Fae. “This is full of lead and iron. Don’t make me use it.”

Drake raised his hands into the air. “I salute your defenses, First Sergeant Park, but they’re not impenetrable.”

Another fairy came through behind Drake. It was Aideen, in her smaller form, followed by Zola and finally by Vicky with Jasper.

“I think I’m gonna hurl,” Vicky said. “What the hell happened?”

Park’s gun slowly lowered. He blinked at the newcomers as he holstered his weapon. “That’s supposed to be impossible.”

“It certainly wasn’t easy,” Drake said, a small crease of frustration on his forehead. “Whoever built this structure knew what they were doing. The building itself forms a ward, which makes this place … difficult to notice.”

“Aeros built the tunnels,” I said, “or at least reinforced them on top of some old ruins.”

Drake nodded. “Did you tell him about the mage machina?”

“The hackers?” Park said, frowning.

“No one calls them hackers anymore,” Vicky said.

“They aren’t hackers,” Zola said. “They are mages with a technological inclination. Most were assassinated when the video of the conflict with the blood mages was released a few years ago. But Ah suspect Edgar has a few remaining resources.”

“You think Edgar got us the evidence?” I asked.

Zola nodded, looking over my shoulder toward the door.

A loud crack sounded on the floor behind us, and it was only then I realized I’d been hearing it for a while. Down the hall, through one of the corridors, came a sound not unlike Zola made when she wanted to call attention with her cane. And then he was there.

"I got the evidence," Edgar said, drawing every eye in the room to him. He stood in the doorway in a neatly cut three-piece suit, and a bowler seated on his head.

But Edgar only had eyes for one person. He locked gazes with Drake, and neither of them flinched. "Not all of the mage machina worked for the Watchers. The best of them, yes, but there are some who can breach whatever they set their minds to."

Park frowned. "Good to know. I guess there are still a few advantages to keeping things off the network."

Edgar shrugged and finally broke eye contact with Drake. "You have the evidence. It hasn't been tampered with, but someone did tamper with what remains on your network. I have two mages trying to track them down, but whoever they were, they were very good. From what I understand, there isn't much of a trace left on anything."

Park pressed a button on one of the consoles, and a small green light brightened. "Release the fairy and the vampire." He gave a long order, that sounded more like alphabet soup than something anyone would make sense of. But a short time later, a voice crackled to life over Park's radio.

"On our way."

Park picked up his radio and held down the button before he spoke. "Bring them to me. I'm in the control booth nearest the archives."

"Understood."

"I do have one question, though," Edgar said, eyeing Drake

again. "I would call him an imposter, but I understand his powers rival those of Foster."

"My mantle is older than his. Different," Drake said. "There are no laws to say only one Fae can be blessed with fire, just as there are no laws that say only one immortal can lead the Watchers. Or what's left of them."

Edgar stiffened, the first reaction he'd shown since joining us in the room. "I wouldn't …"

"Enough," Zola said. "There isn't time for bickering amongst ourselves. We have the location of the bombs. We just have to figure out how to get to them. Focus on the task at hand. If Drake betrays us, we'll deal with him then." She eyed Edgar. "Not before."

Vicky moved closer to the old Fae. "I'll stay with Drake. If he gets out of line, Jasper can eat him."

"So be it," Edgar said. "I'm afraid I may know the answer to who was helping Nudd's spies. Some of our networks are still alive, and some of our own spies are still in Falias."

"Out with it, then," Zola said, biting off the words. "It's not polite to make an old woman wait."

Vicky snickered, but Edgar's expression didn't change.

"It is not my place to tell you everything," Edgar said, "but I can tell you enough. Ward once had an apprentice in Gorias. A young woman with the skills to manipulate runes almost as well as the Warded Man himself."

Zola's frown deepened, the lines on her forehead folding into canyons. "Ah was not aware of this."

Edgar turned to her. "Not many are. Leviticus, myself, and perhaps a few water witches."

I flexed my hands into fists and glanced at Zola before turning my attention back to Edgar. "Are you telling us Ward's apprentice is working for Nudd? Ward, who can create ghost circles, and warded knots, *Devil's Knots*, and bend the very fabric of this reality? He has an apprentice who's not on our side?"

"A bit dramatic," Edgar said, "but yes. Her name is Heather. And she has long worked alongside the Unseelie Court. When they first started rebuilding Falias, Ward feared it might have been her help that allowed them to rebuild so much of it so fast. She can amplify some of the Fae's energies. It's a dangerous skill, and one Ward himself has not mastered."

"I didn't realize she is still alive," Aideen said, hopping down onto the console beside Drake. "I thought she died in the basilisk attack? When Falias was in Faerie?"

"Seems like a lot of us aren't as dead as you thought," Drake said, smirking at Aideen.

"You cannot be who you say you are," Aideen said, tilting her head. "Your powers would have fled long ago."

Drake rested his hand on a dagger in his belt. "Make of it what you will."

"Can we stop arguing about that now?" Vicky asked.

"The girl's right," Edgar said. "If it's Heather who warded the bunkers beneath Falias, then we have a great many challenges ahead."

The door creaked open behind us. Sam stood there, an exhausted-looking Foster on her shoulder, and an exasperated Casper standing behind her.

"Happy now?" Casper said. "I told you, they're all fine."

Sam nodded. She walked over to me and gave me a brief hug before turning to the rest of the room.

"You have a ride home?" I asked.

"Vik's on his way," Sam said. "But thanks."

I nodded. "Just get some rest. We might need you before this is all over."

"You always need me."

I exchanged a grin with Sam, but her smile didn't hide the circles under her eyes, or the rippled flesh, still healing where she'd been burned by the lights.

"There's an old story," Foster said, his voice cracking with exhaustion as he tried to raise it. "An old legend. They say it was a mage gifted in the art of wards who crafted the Mad King's hand of glory. It's just a story, maybe, but you need to understand the kind of power that Ward can wield. The power his apprentice probably can, too."

"And?" I asked.

Foster's gaze trailed to Drake, and he stopped speaking for a time.

"And those are lost arts," Aideen said, answering for him. "Koda knows of some of them. In fact, I wouldn't be surprised if it was him who planted the idea of the ghost circles in Zola's brain, or Ward's."

"There are too many things we thought dead and buried," Foster said. "Relics from wars long forgotten. And Fae thought to be dead for a thousand years."

"You're getting paranoid in your old age," Drake said. "I'd heard the new Demon Sword was a fierce fighter, nigh unkillable."

"Everything is killable," Foster said, baring his teeth. "You just have to try hard enough. But tell me, Demon Sword, what will you do if they come for the girl?" Foster turned his gaze to

Vicky, and I caught some reaction in Drake.

I wouldn't call it anger, or fear, but whatever it was left in a flash.

"My only oath was to a king who was lost long ago." Drake slowly unsheathed his sword and turned the blade over on his palm. "Pray that is the worst you endure."

"The worst?" Foster snarled. Whatever exhaustion had practically pinned him to Sam's shoulder evaporated as he surged to his feet. "I lost my king, a fairy I looked to as a father, and he murdered my mother. What do you know of loss, imposter?"

Drake pinched the tip of his sword, gave a small smile directed no one, then lashed out, leaving a red wound in the air before him. He looked down at Vicky. "We will meet again. Stay with your friends, little one. For they are fools, and fools protect their own."

Vicky crossed her arms as Drake stepped into the portal. The light dimmed, and the room held one less fairy.

"Stand down," Park said.

I wasn't sure who he was talking to, until I caught a glimpse of the gun barrels just outside the door. A small squad of soldiers had flanked Casper, and even the sniper had a hand on her sidearm.

"Perhaps it would be best if we took our leave," Edgar said.

Park nodded. "If your mages turn up anything else that's been tampered with, I'd appreciate a copy."

"Of course," Edgar said. "An old alliance must be cared for, but a tentative one, even more so."

"Walk with us, Edgar," Zola said. "I'd like to hear more of Ward and his apprentice."

"Foster," Casper said.

The fairy looked back over his shoulder, flexing his wings so he could see the sniper.

"Your sword," she said.

He nodded, and took the small weapon from between her pinched fingers. "Thank you."

"Debrief in ten," Park said. "Gather your squad."

"Yes, sir," Casper said.

CHAPTER TWENTY-THREE

I WATCHED THE black SUV bump its way down the cobblestone street, ferrying Sam back to the Pit. She'd be safe there, and I was glad of it. Now I just had to worry about Vicky, our little dragon rider.

"We could go after Nudd directly," Aideen said as we walked down Main Street, drawing my attention to her perch on Zola's shoulder. "Take him down before he has a chance to use the bombs."

Edgar stepped around a missing cobblestone on the sidewalk, tipping his hat when he bumped into me. I almost laughed at the mundane gesture.

"That's an aggressive plan." Foster rubbed his chin. "We could do it."

"No," Zola said. "We *must* retrieve the bombs, or destroy them. Even if Nudd was incapacitated, who's to say the next in line to the throne wouldn't use them?"

"And they can set them off?" I asked. "Without a secret decoder ring?"

Zola snorted.

"Yes," Foster said. "They've gone after reactors before. Meddled with tests in the deserts. They know what they're doing."

"Chernobyl," Aideen said. "It was only one of many thefts.

Perhaps the one that went most wrong. But rest assured, Nudd and his ilk can trigger those bombs with magic."

"And they may have Heather," Edgar said. "She has Ward's power, but is somewhat unhinged. The thought gives me little comfort."

I kicked a loose stone into the street. "To say the least."

We walked in silence for a brief time until the sign for Death's Door loomed large overhead.

"The Obsidian Inn is our best bet," I said as the bell rattled on the front door. "They can keep Nudd distracted, and they're going to know the catacombs beneath Falias as well as any opposition."

"Perhaps better," Aideen said, gliding into the storefront. The rest of us followed.

"Thank God you're back," Frank said, scooping a canvas backpack up off the counter. "I'm heading to the Pit to meet Sam. You mind locking up?"

He'd already sprinted through the saloon-style doors before I could respond. I heard Bubbles chuff once at the bald man running through the store, and then he was gone.

Aideen settled on the glass counter beside the register. "I guess Frank knows Sam's out."

I nodded. "And we have to get to Falias. Everything is there. I doubt Liam, Lochlan, and Enda have much more time."

"I can distract the military," Edgar said. "With the mage machina from the Society of Flame, we can, at the very least, keep the focus of those spies trained elsewhere."

"Ah don't know if that will be enough, Edgar." Zola rubbed her wrist. "But, regardless, the boy is right. It is to Falias we must go."

Vicky rolled her neck and eyed the clock on the wall. "Can we go now?" Jasper trilled on her shoulder, and I was pretty sure the furball was thinking the same thing I was thinking.

"Hell no. We need to plan. Foster needs a nap. And I need to make a phone call."

✦ ✦ ✦

A FEW HOURS later I was still awake, sitting in the reading nook on the second floor of Death's Door. Manuscripts were piled around the ghost circle, some of which I hadn't read in years, and I had little doubt that Koda had been here. The old ghost couldn't affect things outside the circle, so Frank usually helped him pull down the volume he needed to study. But the book I'd been studying had a tendency to bleed.

I yawned and pinched the bridge of my nose. Zola was snoring like someone was trying to turn over a cold engine on a semi. I grinned at my master, sprawled out on the inflatable bed that her back could tolerate far better than mine. Vicky slept on one of the oversized stuffed leather chairs, a small ball of fur purring beside her. Jasper's unblinking black eyes stayed ever-watchful for any threats. I glanced down at my phone. It was nearly one in the morning, and that's when Caroline had told me to return her call. The first time I'd tried, she'd said she was too busy to talk. Despite my protests that I had some really important shit to say, she'd still hung up on me.

So Edgar left, and the fairies retreated to their clock for Foster to rest. Peanut flopped down in front of the clock, like a very lumpy rug, while Bubbles waited across the room, camped out beside the coffee table. I doubted they'd move much before Foster had recovered. That cell had made him sick, and I hoped

Aideen could work her magic on getting him back to normal.

Whatever that meant.

I flipped through my contacts, and my thumb paused over the photo of Caroline. It was an old one she'd emailed me after we'd lost Carter. After we'd lost Carter again. He was in an old torn-up wool shirt, and she wore the uniform of the Irish Brigade. The photo had been taken during the Civil War, and the bloody clash at Antietam would be bearing down on them in a matter of weeks. Caroline knew war like most of us know breathing. Some days I felt sorry for the wolves. Their penchant for violence and pack rivalries were some of the worst in all of the supernatural communities. But I'd seen Caroline with her friends and family. They knew more than killing.

Caroline picked up on the second ring. "Sorry about that, Damian. We had a small emergency with the Obsidian Inn. Morrigan called us to help deal with a new company of dark-touched."

My mind raced, delaying my immediate determination to spew out everything that was happening with the military, and the location of the bombs. Instead, I said, "More dark-touched?"

"A lot more," she said, a small tremor in her voice. "And these are different, Damian. They're smarter." She hesitated, even after she took a deep breath as if she meant to speak.

"Why did Morrigan call you? Have you seen their training grounds?"

"I have, Damian, but they took a hit. Morrigan is still holding back the bulk of their forces, keeping them in reserve for the main campaign against Nudd. And she is right to do it."

"For what?" I hissed, my voice low, trying not to wake up

Zola or Vicky. "You don't think the wolves would've made for a better surprise?"

"In a brigade of highly trained Fae?" Caroline asked. She didn't say anything more after the rhetorical question. She didn't need to. I knew damn well she was right. The wolves may have some serious muscle and durability, but there were Fae, especially the older Fae who were reserved and polite and proper, who hid titanic magicks behind their facades.

Caroline took a deep breath. "We almost lost Dell."

"Is he okay?" I asked, my heart rate spiking.

"One of the dark-touched got its claws in him, and he didn't exactly have a measured response. I'd be proud of the idiot if I wasn't scared for him. He pulled one of those *things* out of the ground. One of the gravemakers. But I didn't think it was going to let him go."

"It attacked him?" I asked, my mind scrambling to remember when Dell had learned how to summon a gravemaker. I mean I supposed we had both always known, without realizing what we were doing. The things were naturally attracted to us, and if we were near one, it wasn't likely to be far. It wasn't too uncommon for it to make its presence known.

"No," Caroline said. "He almost lost himself to it. His arms, they're cut up pretty bad. I'm not certain what happened."

But I was damn sure what had happened. Dell had lost control. He'd put everything he had into pulling that gravemaker out of the earth and turning it against the dark-touched that were attacking his friends. I'd done the same thing myself, but part of me always thought it was the mantle of Anubis that allowed me to do it. For Dell to do it without the mantle made me feel like he was lucky to be alive.

"Morrigan is more than capable of dealing with some dark-touched, though. She could have spared a few troops. It's not like Nudd doesn't know the Obsidian Inn exists. If we're being honest, he probably has spies inside the Inn anyway."

"You haven't heard," Caroline said.

It wasn't a question, but it prompted one anyway.

"Heard what?"

"Nudd is going to execute Liam, Lachlan, and Enda," Caroline said.

"I know."

"Let me finish," Caroline snapped. "They'll be executed two days from now at dusk. It'll be broadcast, Damian. A spectacle for the humans and the Fae alike."

"We have to get them out."

"I wish *I* would've thought of that," Caroline said, "but the humans are already in a frenzy over their missing nuclear weapons. Do you know how many weapons the humans have that aren't nuclear, Damian? You understand how much damage they can still do? To the Fae, and each other?"

I'd seen what men could do. The supernaturals were capable of horrible things, but there was a side of the commoners that was anything but human. I'd seen their dead. I'd heard stories of their murders, and I'd killed more than one for what they'd done. But with governments unhinged, and the military's might decreased, the thought of what one might do to another was unsettling indeed.

"We know where the bombs are now. The green men and the forest gods told us. What if we could return them?"

Caroline cursed. "Of course you did. Since when would a forest god, supposedly allied with Nudd, help a necromancer?

That's insane, Damian."

Beyond. "I helped them regrow part of their forest in Greenville. I think it saved one of their lives."

The phone went silent. I pulled it away from my ear and looked down at the screen to make sure I hadn't accidentally disconnected Caroline. "You there?"

"Damian, that's not possible."

"It *is*," I said, drawing the word out. "Cara taught me, a long time ago."

Caroline muttered a curse in a language I didn't know. "It doesn't matter right now. Where are the bombs?"

"They're beneath Falias itself. From what I understand, it's beneath Nudd's palace."

"Palace," Caroline said, disgust plain in her voice. "More like a temple where that idiot can worship himself."

"It's in a bunker beneath the ground, and there are enough arms there to wipe most of humanity from the earth."

"And if Nudd detonates those?" Caroline asked. "We're just going to march in there and die. I don't care how fast you can heal; there isn't much that can survive a nuclear blast."

"I doubt he'll detonate them while he's standing on top of them. But I don't suppose you know any were-lichen?"

Caroline snorted a laugh. "Not the time." She paused. "Hold on, I'm conferencing Morrigan in."

"Morrigan has a phone?" I asked, but I was already on hold. "I can't believe Morrigan has a phone."

The line came back before I finished talking to myself.

"It's not my phone," Morrigan said. "We have a few, and our spies have several. We found that the commoners' technology can be moderately more difficult to intercept than that of the old magicks. You'd be wise to use one with your queen."

"You do understand people can still intercept those calls?" I asked.

"Of course," Morrigan said. "But it is more likely to be the commoners than the Fae."

"Caroline tells me you learned the location of Nudd's arsenal."

"Beneath his palace in a large bunker. I don't know exactly where, but that's what the forest gods told me."

Morrigan fell silent for a moment. "Very well. What do you intend to do with this knowledge?"

"I intend to get the bombs, or destroy the bombs, or *hide* the bombs, all while rescuing Liam, Lachlan, and Enda."

"And this is the extent of your plan?" Morrigan asked.

"No, I asked Caroline to help. You were next on my list."

Morrigan let out a humorless laugh. "I am mystified as to how you are not dead yet, Damian Vesik. While your intentions here are honorable, I do not know if the return of the commoners' weapons will calm their military. But I do know that the bombs cannot stay in the hands of Gwynn Ap Nudd."

Her voice had taken on a slow cadence and a dark timbre. The sound of her words sent a chill down my spine. Morrigan knew the kind of death magic I'd seen, she knew the kind of death magic I controlled, but she was talking about some kind of nuclear Fae magic. The very idea was insane. And terrifying.

"Are you seeing more of the elites yet?" Caroline asked.

"No," Morrigan said. "But we have seen more of the dark-touched pawns."

Morrigan's words reminded me that they'd been using the term "elites" to refer to the dark-touched who were capable of speech. I rubbed at the stubble on my chin. “You think they’ll be guarding the bombs alongside Hern?”

“It’s possible,” Morrigan said. “My more immediate concern is the commoners. The military must be calm, or we will have a war in earnest on two fronts.”

“Edgar is working on it. He has the mage machina trying to root out Nudd’s spies in the military. In the meantime, he may be able to block some of the communication between countries that may be escalating things.”

“Whatever can be done, do it.”

“Drake has returned to the Obsidian Inn,” Morrigan said. “I’m curious as to why he did not relay all of this information to me. As I understand, he has spent time with you this past day.”

“Maybe because we shouldn’t trust him?” Caroline said, practically pulling the thought right out of my head.

“It is a risk I am willing to take,” Morrigan said. “The power of the Demon Sword is not to be trifled with. The power of two could turn the tide of this conflict, and the presence of a reaper is never frowned upon.”

“So you’ll help?” I asked. “We need to get to the bombs.”

“You will have the help of the Obsidian Inn,” Morrigan said. “Caroline, if you can, move the Irish Brigade into Falias. We may have need of you.”

“What of the armories?”

“Leave that to the Utukku. If you can spare a wolf, assign them a post in Antietam, as a warning system, if nothing else.”

Caroline pondered that for a time before finally saying, “I will. I’ll meet the Obsidian Inn by the bones of the basilisk. We can keep whatever comes our way out of the catacombs and away from Damian's group. There's a network they can follow that will take them all the way to Nudd's palace."

"And whatever bunker lies beneath it," Morrigan said. "Prepare yourselves, for death walks among us this day."

Morrigan disconnected without another word.

"Tomorrow, Damian," Caroline said. "Call the vampires. You're going to need them in the dark."

"Wouldn't miss it for the world," I said, as if we'd just completed plans to meet for chimichangas, and not plans that were likely to get a great many of us killed.

CHAPTER TWENTY-FOUR

WE GATHERED AROUND the old Formica table in the back room of Death's Door in the morning. I'd slept surprisingly well after my conversation with Morrigan and Caroline. Foster stepped out of the grandfather clock and glided toward the table, much to my horror.

"Oh my god, put on some pants!" While I could appreciate the finely cut muscles the fairy seemed to maintain with practically no effort, I really preferred him with pants.

Zola froze, a breakfast burrito halfway to her mouth as the fairy glanced down, frowned, and then waggled his eyebrows at her.

Aideen smacked him and pointed at Vicky.

Foster quickly covered himself with his hands, still looking worse for wear as he sailed back to the clock. He had dark circles under his eyes, and the normal black and white coloration of his wings hadn't returned to its usual crispness. It was almost as if the iron from the cell he'd been in had leeched into them, graying the white areas, and adding to his terrible pallor.

"Didn't need to see that," Vicky said around a mouthful of eggs.

I slid a plate full of freshly microwaved breakfast burritos to the center of the table. Zola snatched up another one and juggled it a bit, waiting for it to cool down. "You and me both, girl. You and me both."

"Sorry, we're out of forks," I said. "Things have been a little crazy lately."

Bubbles chuffed in agreement from the entrance to her underground lair.

"Still tastes good," Vicky said, shoveling half the burrito into her mouth at once. Her cheeks puffed up as she chewed, and Zola gave her some serious side eye.

"Just because your parents aren't here doesn't mean you can eat like an animal," Zola said a moment before she took just as big of a bite, and her cheeks puffed out, too.

I grinned at the pair and glanced down at Aideen and a now-clothed Foster, who were seated at the edge of the table. "Feeling any better?"

"Don't feel like I'm about to die," Foster said. "That's always a plus."

I nodded. "Especially when we're about to go to Falias and probably die."

Aideen slowly raised an eyebrow. "So … you spoke to the Morrigan and the Irish Brigade. We have a plan?"

"We have to get Liam and his family out of there. They've lost enough, and they're going to be executed in one day." I glanced at the clock face. "Less than one day."

Aideen nodded.

And they damn well *had* lost enough. Their home had been torn out of Faerie and erected on the corpses of commoners. They were some of the few who had come to realize that Nudd had, in fact, meant them to die in the transition. If it hadn't been for Vicky, channeling her powers as the Destroyer, most of Falias would have died in the transition.

But Nudd had still managed to spin the manifestation of Falias, and its survivors, to his advantage. He was as bad as any human politician, making himself out to be their salvation, instead of their doom. I wondered how many more of the Fae realized it now, or how many of them simply stayed silent because it didn't affect them and their friends and their families. But there was little doubt it affected someone they knew, and perhaps that's why the ranks of the Obsidian Inn had swollen the way they had.

"Once we get to Falias, I'll have someone look at Foster." Aideen patted his knee. "I can heal him a bit more, but if we're going to be engaging the dark-touched and Hern's army, I'd prefer not to be exhausted."

"You can always stay at the Inn," Zola said.

"I'm not dead yet," Foster muttered. "These hands can still make a whole bunch of other people dead before I'm dead, so I'm not staying at the bloody Inn."

I laughed and took another bite of breakfast burrito. Apparently, Aideen and Foster had already had this conversation, too. He was clearly not happy about Zola mimicking his wife's suggestion.

My phone rang, and I frowned at Sam's caller ID. I answered and put it on speaker. "What's up?"

"Vik's already got people on their way to Kansas City," Sam said. "I don't think we have many vampires to spare."

"I'm not surprised. That may not be a bad thing, though. If Hugh and Ashley are both in KC right now, and we know they've had problems with the dark-touched there."

"You're still getting two of the best," Sam said. "Dominic and Jonathan will both be meeting you."

That gave me some measure of relief. They were two of the greatest fighters Vik had, and the fact the old vampire was sending them out with us surprised me a bit, considering the current climate. I had no doubt Sam had more than a little to do with it.

"That's great," I said.

"I had to promise Vik not to go." The irritation was plain in her voice. "He still tries to baby me worse than you sometimes, Demon. Really annoying. But I'd rather you have Dominic and Jonathan than me for this fight."

"You'll stay here with Frank and keep everybody out of trouble?"

"You mean keep the cu siths from eating people?" Sam asked.

Peanut's ears flicked up, and he finally rose from his resting spot in front of the grandfather clock.

"I think Peanut heard you," I said.

"They don't *eat* people," Aideen muttered. "They might chew on them a little bit, but they always spit them out."

Sam barked out a laugh. "Be careful out there. All of you."

"We will," Vicky said. She scarfed down her last bite of breakfast burrito and fed some scraps to Jasper.

"Take care of that old vampire," Zola said. "Lord knows, he could use the help."

"Will do," Sam said, and then she hung up.

"Is Nixie coming?" Foster asked.

I shook my head. "I talked to her earlier. She's headed to an emergency convention to meet with local politicians. They're threatening to mobilize the UK's military against the Fae after Nudd's actions."

"I hope she can influence them," Aideen said. "Drowning all the delegates would likely not help much."

I grinned at the fairy. "That's a fair point."

"We should get packed," Zola said. "It is time." She glanced at Vicky. "Ah don't feel good about dragging you along with us."

"I have a dragon," Vicky said. "I'll be fine."

Zola frowned at the round ball of fur with the big black eyes. "Be safe. Move if you're told to move, and stay hidden if we tell you to."

"You sound like Carter," Vicky muttered. "I miss him."

And perhaps that changed Zola's mind, the subtle reminder of the life Vicky had led in the Burning Lands. How she'd run with the Ghost Pack, slain dark-touched, and survived until she was once more pulled back into this world. Because my master said no more.

✦ ✦ ✦

I STOOD BEFORE the shimmering red gateway. Somehow Aideen had talked me into walking through the Warded Ways instead of taking the much-smoother path that I'd grown used to with Gaia. Something about everyone arriving at once making less of a ripple, being less likely to get noticed.

It made a certain kind of sense, but now that I was standing at the gateway, with the two fairies laughing at me, I felt like this was going to be a very bad trip.

"I really don't want to hold this open any longer," Aideen said. "Just step through. We'll be right behind you."

I grimaced at the fairy, took a deep breath, and then stepped into the Warded Ways. Some of the portals weren't that bad, like those that took you to the edge of Faerie, or those that were simply a gateway between dimensions, to step from one world to another. But the portals to travel halfway across the country, or the world, were not so nice. For a split second, it felt as if something had grabbed my ankles and my wrists and then pulled until my body twisted and elongated so it could be tied into a pretzel a moment later. A dim red light became bloody brilliant yellow, and for a moment it wasn't so bad, almost like going over the first large hill on a roller coaster, but then the fun began. It felt like being slammed into one wall and then another, jerked to the right until my head cracked against something hard, only to be flung forward into a whirlpool-like spiral of power. As I finally found my voice in that chaos, I let out a yelp a second before the light went out around me. I blinked, breathing hard against the cold, damp stone floor.

"You're alive," Zola said. I squinted at her, a dim ball of illumination floating above her right shoulder. "A little bit faster than Gaia, too, Ah'd say."

Two winged forms blipped into existence above me, and the portal snapped closed. I rolled over and groaned, only to find myself face-to-face with Jasper and his rather intimidating silver-gray teeth. The furball grinned at me, and I threw an arm over my eyes.

"Not you, too."

"Get up, boy," Zola said. "You've been practicing your control over *Illuminadda* spells? We'll be needing light in these catacombs, but not too much light."

"What are you trying to say? That I ..." Whatever witty thought I'd been about to throw out was lost to a wave of my churning stomach. I lay flat on the floor until the nausea passed. “Why did I agree to that?”

Footsteps sounded nearby. I thought I should probably get off my ass and stand up to greet whatever friend or foe was about to come into the room. On the other hand, they could kill me now, and I’d probably feel a lot better.

“Lying down on the job?” a familiar voice said.

I turned my head to the side and groaned in earnest when I saw Drake standing there, a snide smirk on his face.

“What are you doing here? I thought the Morrigan was coming?”

“She sent me instead. It’s your lucky day.”

“Oh, that’s right,” Vicky said. “Drake used to live in the palace. I bet he knows all the secrets.”

“He probably does,” Foster said, a good amount of steel in his voice.

“A little respect, Demon Sword,” Drake said. “Now come here and let me finish healing you.”

Foster took a half step back. “Morrigan is supposed to send a healer.”

“She did. I thought it might foster some trust between us.”

I narrowed my eyes. “That was a terrible pun. Please don’t ever try to make a joke again.”

“What are you talking about?” Drake asked.

“I don’t think that was a joke,” Foster said.

“Let him heal you,” Aideen said. “If he tries anything, he’s not getting out of here alive.”

“My reaper will …”

It was about that time Drake noticed that his reaper, now also in its small furball form, had perched on Vicky’s shoulder.

“My reaper will … affectionately love you to death.” The

sheer level of irritation in Drake's voice made me extraordinarily happy.

"Fine," Foster said. "Let's get this done."

Foster snapped into his Proelium-sized form.

Drake touched his shoulder and said, "Turn around."

Foster hesitated, but then did as he was asked.

Drake laid his hands near the base of Foster's wings, where I could still make out some of the discoloration that had been so prevalent the day before. "*Socius Sanation.*"

A glow, one I swore was dimmer than Aideen or Foster's healings, filled the small round antechamber we were standing in. Or at least, the antechamber that everyone else was standing in, until I finally managed to climb back up to my feet. The room only gave a little half spin, and the world seemed to settle back to normal.

Drake let his hands fall to his side as Foster straightened his back and flexed his wings. "And you wonder why I'm not so fond of the commoners. The level of iron in that cell could have killed you."

"Well, none of them have tried to stab me recently," Foster said. "That's a bit more than I can say for you."

The corner of Drake's mouth lifted in a small smile. "How are the wings?"

Foster glanced at Aideen. "They're good."

Drake nodded. "Caroline and Morrigan are ready."

Foster eyed the other fairy, but he didn't thank him. The tension between them was still there, an old Demon Sword and his successor. As much mistrust as I had for Drake, he seemed genuinely concerned for Vicky's well-being. Considering how many of the Fae I'd seen look upon her with something more akin to fear, his concern gave me some hope Drake might be an ally. But I'd been wrong before.

Drake's head snapped to the side, and he held his hand out, calling for silence. I listened, but I couldn't hear anything.

"Not far," Drake said. "Vampires."

CHAPTER TWENTY-FIVE

I THOUGHT I heard something as we crept through a corridor off the antechamber. A scratch, or an awkward footstep. I knew I wasn't the only one who heard it, because the fairies' swords almost sang out of their sheaths. The pepperbox was a comfortable weight under my arm, but without being able to see what was in front of me, it would be a stupid place to fire the gun. I reached for the focus tucked into my belt and waited.

A dull orange light appeared in the darkness around us, slowly brightening, chasing away some shadows and deepening others. One moment nothing was there, and the next a tall, bulky silhouette stood before what I could now see was a smaller form carrying a partially unsheathed flaming sword.

Drake still stood his ground. "Do you bear loyalty to the king?"

The air rippled around us, and it took me a moment to realize that Drake had imbued those words with some level of magic.

The taller form stiffened. "What the hell does that mean?"

Apparently, the bizarre response was enough for Drake. He sheathed his sword.

The flaming sword grew longer, as more of the blade was unsheathed, and I smiled when I saw the deep outlines of Jonathan's face. That told me with no uncertainty that the irritated vampire beside him was Dominic, one of the vampires' strongest enforcers.

"Zola?" Dominic said, stepping forward when Zola increased the brightness of her incantation.

"It's good to see you, Dominic," Zola said. "And you, Jonathan."

The smaller, leaner vampire let the flaming sword drop back into its sheath. "I'd prefer to be in KC. Rumor is that the River Pack has a lead on Vassili, and I owe that vampire much."

Years before, Vassili had betrayed his own Pit, and slain the vampire known as Alexi. Alexi had been Jonathan's lover for over a century, struck down by the vampire who was supposed to protect them. Jonathan's wounds had been physical, mental, and deep.

"I'm glad you're here," I said.

The vampire's eyes flicked to me. "I owe your sister. And Vik has shown himself more loyal to our Pit than any Lord I have known before. That makes us the closest thing to family we can be without you being a vampire. So, yes, I will help."

The vampire smiled, and let his fangs show just a little. The reflection in the dark corridor was eerie and homicidal in the best sort of way.

"You guys know Vicky, but I don't think you know Drake. At least not more than him trying to kill us all last year."

"I've heard many tales," Dominic said. "I suppose it yet remains to be seen whether he is an ally, or lunch."

Drake tilted his head slightly. He didn't respond, but I wondered what the fairy was thinking. I knew Drake was powerful, but Dominic was old. And you didn't live to be an old vampire without being a threat to almost anything that crossed your path.

"Let us leave," Aideen said. "We need to find Liam, Lochlan, and Enda."

"If Nudd believes that bunker to be the most secure place in his palace," Drake said, "it's quite likely his more valuable prisoners will be there, too. Or at least very close to it."

"In my experience," Zola said, "we aren't that lucky."

"Let's go," Aideen said, and led the way into the darkness.

✦ ✦ ✦

THE CATACOMBS WERE quiet. Deathly quiet. It was unnerving, and it didn't take long for me to realize that not all of the stone and structure we were walking through was made of the pale rock of Falias. Some of it was ancient, appearing to have been carved by crude tools. Whether those tools had been wielded by men, or something else, I couldn't say.

The tunnels closer to the Obsidian Inn were occasionally lit by torchlight, and while we'd seen one or two lanterns, and old burns on the stone from the soot of ancient torches, there were no lights as we delved deeper into the belly of Falias. There was only stone and shadow and a kind of impending dread that I had not felt in quite some time.

But the cold damp of the underground grew more familiar the longer we spent in it. Zola and I alternated leading the way, and trailing the pack, while Aideen gave us directions. The dull glow of our *Illuminadda* incantations provided light, but hopefully not so much light as to give away our position.

I suspected we'd been walking for almost half an hour the first time we heard it.

A creak, like an old house settling, but the groan that followed couldn't be passed off as old timbers, or any kind of natural sound. Something dragged along the floor in a nearby corridor while our group exchanged looks.

"Something else is here," Drake said.

And even though his whisper had scarcely been louder than the sound of a breath, the dragging in the stone hallways stopped. Silence reigned, and I could hear the blood rushing in my ears as I strained to make out anything in the darkness.

When nothing else sounded in the shadows for the next minute, we continued on, more cautious, perhaps, and certainly more alert. We moved into a larger antechamber, not so unlike the one that had been below the basilisk, but this one was ornate, the walls and ceiling covered in a mad mosaic. Eldritch things wove through blood-red portals while one crowned figure stood in the middle of them all, as if fearless, controlling, or absolutely insane.

"The fall of the Mad King," Aideen said. "An old piece of art, thought to be lost not long after it was made, in the time of peace after the Wandering War."

"Wasn't it supposed to be fake?" Foster asked, squinting up at one of the tentacled creatures on the ceiling. "Just a rumor it was ever made?"

"It was real," Drake said. "Put together by a Fae who had walked through the portals with the Mad King. He didn't survive walking the Ways fully intact."

"Those things?" I said, gesturing up at the tentacled forms in the mosaic. "Those are the creatures in the Abyss. The leviathans and … the others."

Drake frowned, but nodded.

I pulled my phone out and let my incantation brighten a

little more as I started taking a video of the mosaic. I'd almost finished the whole thing, capturing every detail of the leviathans and the Mad King in their center before I saw the shadow.

"Something's here!" I shouted. I spread my left palm out, letting more power flow to the *Illuminadda* incantation until it burst to life like a sun. It might have been blinding to the rest of us, but whatever was in the shadow squealed. An emaciated Fae was bathed in the pale-colored light of our incantations. Armor that may have once fit the frail-looking creature hung from a body that was little more than skin and bones and fear.

"By the gods," Drake said, hurrying forward and taking a knee before the creature. "You're supposed to be dead."

"Dead? Am I not dead? Dead many years, now. But I have fallen, into the hell the commoners spoke of. Dark things chase me Demon Sword, and these rooms are not my own."

Drake blew out a breath and looked back to the rest of us. "This is the fairy that made these mosaics. I don't know how he's still alive, trapped in a lost room like this."

"There was still magic," the emaciated form said. "Until soon, recent I mean, then there was none."

"The city is no longer in Faerie," Drake said. "You're in the land of the commoners now. Lucky to be alive."

"Then I still live." The Fae gave an awkward smile and tilted his head down. "Not luck. She brought me through." The fairy raised his hand toward Vicky before letting it fall back to his side. "Saved many, I suspect. With great power, and great sadness. But you, Demon Sword, I thought you no longer served the Mad King."

Drake remained silent for a moment. "He's been dead a

long time now."

"Dead. Dead? As I should be. But I am not. You should not be here. Go, leave this place. There are vampires far worse than these." His frail hand rose toward Dominic and Jonathan. "Older, primal. Be careful. Live by the sword."

A small crease formed along Drake's brow. "If you can follow our path back, we have allies. They call themselves the Obsidian Inn."

The old Fae nodded. "I have heard them talking. I feared them to be loyal to the king."

"No," Drake said. "Find them. The Morrigan is with them. They'll shelter you until this is over."

"Can we trust him?" Foster asked.

Drake shook his head. "But I don't think he's a threat."

✦ ✦ ✦

WE CONTINUED ON, leaving the ancient and broken Fae behind. Drake seemed to think he'd be able to find his way to the Obsidian Inn. I had my doubts.

"Who was that?" Zola asked.

"A servant of the courts from before the Wandering War. He saw the rise of the Mad King, and his fall. I believe he was originally from Gorias, but I can't imagine how he's still alive."

"I know," Aideen said. "To live in solitude, hidden away for so many centuries. And I believe it had to have been him who hid this place, or else there would have been some rumors of its existence. Someone would've known."

"Unless he killed whoever helped him," Drake said. "Those were ruthless times."

"Doesn't sound so different than now," Vicky said.

"It *is* different, little one," Drake said. "You have friends you can trust, allies who won't betray you for an extra coin in their purse. Violent times perhaps, but quite different."

We moved deeper into the catacombs, until it was Drake regularly leading us. We'd gone deep enough that Aideen and Foster no longer knew the way. The farther in we went, the more unsettled I felt. I didn't trust Drake, no matter what bond he had with Vicky. He could just as easily be using her to set us up, regardless of the respect he showed. But Vicky trusted him, and I was willing to give him some leeway for that. But we still didn't know much about the fairy, and it ate at me.

Drake stopped in the center of the next hall. It reminded me of the area where we'd seen the dullahan. Halls and doorways crisscrossed the entire area. What I'd first thought was a simple rectangular hallway, I realized was far more complex than that. Halls and doors curved in at awkward angles, leading off into a dozen different paths with no indication of where any of them led. It was confusing to look at, much less try to navigate.

"When was the last time you were down here?" I asked.

Drake looked from one side of the hall to the other, frowning at what appeared to be a steel door with a half-moon carved into it. "A few centuries. Maybe more. Not that long."

I blinked at the fairy in the dim light. Not that long, but not what most people would consider a short time.

"It's a good idea to stay away from the metal doors," Drake said.

"Why?" Vicky asked, leaning back from the door she'd been inspecting.

"Because some will harbor traps to kill an unsuspecting Fae.

Others can lead you into a never-ending hall, where the same ends of the Warded Ways are twisted together into an infinite loop. The Mad King banished more than one of his enemies into that infinity."

I shivered at the thought. An eternity spent slamming around inside the Warded Ways until one day you finally died.

We moved farther into the hall, some hundred feet, before I noticed how the pattern of the stones on the floor flowed to each doorway. Some made their way into the open halls, and others stopped dead before the metal doors, almost as if they were marking unique pathways, but if what Drake had said was true, I didn't think whoever had built this place intended for the average person, or Fae, to find their way through it.

Drake said something to Zola and the light beside her brightened, revealing a stone-lined arch with a pair of horns carved into the top. They weren't simple things, not in representation or design. They were intricately carved, covered with more detail than seemed possible on such a narrow strip of stone. As if a giant painting been made miniature.

"This is it," Drake said. "If anything is going to lead to one of the bunkers, it's going to be this."

"How do you know?" I asked.

Drake indicated the horns. "Nudd's favorite errand boy, Hern."

"Just because it's marked with his sign doesn't mean he'll actually be guarding this place."

Drake harrumphed.

"It could be like an alarm system," Vicky said. "We walked into the wrong place, and it notifies them."

Drake nodded, and I felt a little stupid for not thinking of it first. But if that was true, anywhere we went in the catacombs could be a signal to Nudd, or any of his lackeys. We might have already been in more danger than we thought, and depending on the nature of the defenses, I started to suspect why Morrigan didn't simply march the army of the Obsidian Inn into the catacombs.

For all we knew, that army could set foot in this hall, and be smashed flat by a cave-in. Or by whatever was hidden behind those doors.

"Follow me," Drake said. "We won't learn anything waiting here. They'll either be waiting for us, or they won't. Either way, by the time we make it to the bunker, you can be sure we're going to run into defenders."

And on that happy thought, we plunged into the darkness of the hallway below Hern's antlers.

CHAPTER TWENTY-SIX

"IT'S BEEN A while," Dominic said, falling back to join me at the rear of the group.

I nodded to the vampire. "It's good to see you. I haven't seen you much since Greenville."

Dominic smiled in the dim light of the incantation. "As Sam might say, things have been a bit crazy. I spent time with Hugh in Kansas City. Have you spoken with him?"

"A few times. But they've been holed up there for a while now. Ashley and Elizabeth were heading out that way, too."

A grim edge crept into Dominic's voice. "So, you haven't spoken to him in the last day."

I shook my head. "No, why?"

"A new wave of dark-touched struck the old city there. A great many casualties among the commoners, but I believe Hugh and the River Pack mitigated the worst of it. Thankfully, they weren't alone."

I frowned. As far as I knew, the River Pack was very much alone. Most of the Kansas City Pack had been slaughtered, and Hugh had gone out there to find out why, and by what. "Who's helping them?"

"Camazotz and the death bats took care of many of them. The Old God seems to have taken refuge in some caves beneath the old trading city."

"So they came for Camazotz?" I asked.

"I don't believe so. From what Alan told me when I spoke to him this morning, the dark-touched were quite surprised by the sudden arrival of Camazotz and his death bats. But the tourists who encountered them first were not so lucky."

I cursed under my breath. We'd been worried about a war on two fronts. What concerned me even more was that the dark-touched had migrated to the northwest, reaching Kansas City as a formidable force without being detected. I wondered if Hern or Nudd was uncovering lost pathways for them through the Warded Ways. That was something we might never know.

Zola's light dimmed at the front of our group, and we all came to a halt behind her. I let the power flowing to the *Illuminadda* incantation over my shoulder weaken to a trickle. I could only see Dominic beside me, and the back of Vicky's head. The furball nestled against her neck shifted, and white light glinted in Jasper's eyes.

Zola whispered, "Well, what is it?" She held up the dim ball of light, and I could just make out Jonathan's features. He frowned.

"I'm not sure if it's friend or foe," he said with a shake of his head. "But we aren't alone."

"I—" Dominic started. "What the hell …"

The vampires could hear better than us, but it was only a moment before the rumble grew loud enough for my ears to detect. "Kill the lights," I hissed.

Zola dropped her incantation before I even finished speaking. Whatever was coming for us might need the light to find us. But if it didn't, it might be tracking us through our body heat or the sound of our footsteps. Neither option was comforting.

The rumble grew louder, closer, until the soles of my boots vibrated. I put a hand out and touched the wall, where I could feel the stone shaking beneath it.

"Whatever it is," Dominic said, "it's here."

The rapid unsheathing of swords sang through the air. Something like tentacles flashed into the light cast by Jonathan's flaming sword. For a time, I feared it was some kind of leviathan down in the corridors with us, but that would be impossible. They were massive forms, and I doubted even a Fae with Nudd's resources could pull that off.

A moment later two huge, jagged eyes appeared in the hall, glowing gold and staring down at Zola. Its voice boomed through the halls.

"You walk into your doom, mortals."

One of the forest gods, I realized to great relief.

"Who are you?" I asked.

"Do you not already know, deathspeaker that brings life?" the forest god asked, sweeping her eyes down to meet mine.

Her name came to my lips. "Appalachia."

The forest god inclined her head, and her eyes flashed to the corridor behind her. "You'll find no easy path out of these catacombs. There are dark-touched and viler things left over from the forgotten times of Faerie. No matter how many I destroy, another replaces them. More evils dwell in this place than you know."

Appalachia cast her eyes down to Vicky and said, "Light your blades, little one. For there are many, and we are few."

With those words, Foster and Aideen exploded into their

Proelium forms, sending a rainbow of fairy dust into the air to flicker amid the magical lights now flooding the passage.

"Follow if you will. It is only a few hundred feet to a more defensible position, an antechamber that will give you some room to maneuver. Should you survive, the prisons of the Fae King lie close."

Appalachia surged down the hall. Masses like roots and vines stretched out and propelled the forest god through the corridor. The vibrations beneath our feet returned, but I knew it had not stopped entirely when Appalachia fell still. Even as she spoke to us, the stones still rumbled all around. We ran after her in silence, only the thud of our boots on stone followed.

We sprinted into another rounded hall not so unlike the one that had housed the mosaic. But this one was plain save for a series of shackles on the walls.

"What the hell is this?" Vicky asked.

"Commoners would call it interrogation room," Foster said. "It's not a place you want to be."

"Or a place you ever escape from," Aideen said. "Light the fires."

Foster hurried over to a trough near one of the doors. Apparently, they'd both seen rooms like this, as Aideen turned to face another trough. She held her hand over it and snapped her fingers. Something sparked from her hand, and a fire burned high. It leaped across the doorway, creating an impossible pattern in the air before settling into the trough on the other side. Foster did the same, his fire forming a similar pattern and blocking the opposite door.

Appalachia pulled away from the walls and centered herself

in the room. "They have only one way in now."

"And we appear to have no way out," Zola said.

"You never did," Appalachia said.

"I don't suppose you care to enlighten us as to what's coming," Drake said. He glanced around the fire dancing across the shackles on all the stone walls and frowned.

"It has come." Appalachia's words were the last any of us spoke before the *thing* made itself known.

A snake was my first thought. A slithering form that slipped through the corner of the doorway. Another followed, and then they were on us. The things looked almost reptilian, until their featureless faces split open, revealing spirals of teeth like lampreys. Something black dripped from those awful maws, and the rumbling as they crashed through the hallway and into the antechamber grew ever worse.

There was no pause, no moment where the enemy stopped to assess us, to determine how much of a threat we posed. They simply attacked. The things coiled up like cobras and exploded forward.

Jonathan made first contact. His sword swept forward in a lightning-fast arc, slicing sideways through one of the lampreys, sending black gore to splatter across its brethren. Before he could so much as line up another sword strike, three of the things slammed into him. As it got closer, I realized what at first seemed like a large snake was closer to the size of a small anaconda. They were fast, and considering the yelp of pain that Jonathan released, most of us weren't going to survive a hit from one.

I lit the soulsword, power flooding through the old claymore's hilt, until the brilliant golden light bathed us all. I'd gotten better at using the souls locked away inside me, to the point where I could balance tying them together with my own aura and not cause myself to practically black out every time I drew the blade, which, at the moment, would've been a very bad thing.

Sealing the doors with fire felt like a worse and worse idea as more and more of the lampreys poured into the room. With nowhere to run, I couldn't see a way out of this. They were choking the entire hall, and we'd blocked off our only other exits.

The fairies dove into the chaos as Vicky and Zola danced away from a wild strike from the creature. Jonathan may have had the speed and fury of a vampire, but Foster and Aideen had centuries more experience. They made short work of the lampreys that tried to strike from above, slithering along the ceiling as if defying gravity. Before the pair of fairies could get behind us, I cut down most of the lampreys that succeeded in passing them.

Drake slammed into the opposite wall and shouted, "Get them in the fires!"

"Duck," Appalachia said.

Me, Zola, and Vicky dropped to the floor. Jasper didn't quite get out of the way in time as Appalachia twisted the mass of vines she used for movement together and slammed dozens of the lampreys into the fire at once.

Jasper gave an annoyed squawk as he was tossed up into the air and smacked down into the ashes of the lampreys that had hit the flames. But the annoyed squawk became something else as Jasper's color deepened to red and the scaly legs of the dragon exploded forward. His long neck reared back a moment later, and blue fire joined the spirals of ash of the burning lampreys. Jasper attacked with surgical precision, careful not to burn Vicky as she dove in, wielding dual soulswords and hacking down the lampreys.

I joined her, staying as close as I could while being sure to keep my own soulsword away from her, and hoping she'd keep hers away from me. I'd never actually cut myself with the soulsword before, but I was sure it wouldn't be pleasant.

"Too many," Dominic shouted as he flailed backward, tossing two more the massive lampreys into the fire. "They're just not stopping."

Appalachia scooped up another mass of lampreys and slammed them in the fire. "They are only the beginning. Survive to meet your true foe."

Zola cursed and shouted, "What the hell does that mean, you damned tree!" She whipped her staff around, and a bolt of fire erupted from the end, cutting into the hallway and causing an ear-piercing squeal that cut through all the noise.

The lampreys froze, and those that were still alive retreated into the hall.

We regrouped, sheltering against Appalachia as if she were a mighty oak to shield us from a hailstorm. The rumbling started anew, but it was different this time, more deliberate, less constant. When a scaly hand reached through the doorway pulling a massive shadow behind it, I stared in slack-jawed horror at a creature from the Abyss.

✦ ✦ ✦

I'D NEVER SEEN one so close before. It might have been smaller than the slithering mass I'd seen when walking with Gaia, but this one looked much the same. Gaping maws lined with fangs sat where you would expect the thing's eyes to be. It was bipedal, but it surged and compressed, revealing the fact its body was formed from countless lamprey creatures.

A second arm extended from the writhing monster and pushed on the opposite side of the doorframe until its body spilled forth into the antechamber. Most of us stood there staring.

Drake didn't.

"Take its head!" he shouted. "It's the only way to stop it! The venom triggers hallucinations, and they aren't the pleasant kind."

And with that, the slow moments of horror exploded into the chaos of a pitched battle.

Drake moved with speed and grace. Even Foster fell behind as Drake launched into the air and brought his sword down in a vicious arc. It slashed into the creature's neck, but dozens of the lamprey-like appendages swelled up to meet the sword, sacrificing themselves to save the whole.

Foster tried the same from the other side and met with far more resistance, as if his attack had been anticipated. Even as the creature fended Foster off on one side, it lashed out at Drake and sent the fairy streaking across the room to crash into one of the stone walls. Drake didn't even slow. He charged back at the creature, as the vampires started hacking at the lampreys.

"Burn them," Appalachia roared.

Part of me wondered how wise it was to summon a massive flame in that enclosed space, and another part of me wondered how flammable Appalachia was. I didn't want to injure the forest god, especially not knowing how badly she'd been injured when Falias was dropped into her world, on top of the damage the commoners had inflicted building their cities.

But the forest god stood her ground as Zola extended her cane and summoned a focused needlepoint of power that sliced deep into the arm that was pinning Dominic to the floor. It recoiled, and Jasper crashed into the lampreys, his teeth rending flesh far faster than it could be replaced, and his claws savaging flesh until at last it was not merely the black ooze that spewed from the lampreys at a surface wound, but something rich and blue that flowed onto the stones.

A third appendage erupted from where the thing's mouth should've been. It tightened like a noose around Jasper's neck. The dragon squawked as he was hauled into the writhing mass, a thousand fangs digging into his flesh.

Vicky followed him in, her soulswords snapping out and eviscerating dozens of the fanged heads in seconds.

I cursed, aimed high, and shouted, "*Modus Ignatto!*" The blast wasn't nearly so refined as Zola's, but it certainly drew the creature's attention. Lampreys surged forward, their fanged eyes laser-focused on me as the appendage that was its mouth fell away to be reabsorbed into its writhing body. Vicky exploded out the side of the creature, the furball under one of her arms. The lampreys reached out for them again, but were met with a blast of blue fire from Drake's now full-sized dragon. The arm withered in the heat, just as its head did in the blast from my incantation.

Lampreys surged up over the wounded skeleton, or whatever lay beneath them, but it thinned the layer of lampreys around its neck, showing just how deep Drake's initial cut had gone. Slimy gray flesh spouted a rich blue fluid. Zola focused another blast of the fire on the wound, and the beam lanced out the other side, leaving a smoking hole in the thing's neck. I raised the hilt and lit a soulsword as the towering mass rose up and over me as if it meant to drown me in an avalanche of fangs and snakes and death.

But if that had been the creature's plan, Appalachia fucked it up royally.

The forest god's vines rocketed up from the floor, launching from her trunk-like feet to impale the lampreys. The vines spiraled around the creature's neck, like a noose of their own. I hacked at any lampreys that got too close, but part of my focus remained on the gory spectacle unfolding above me. Blue blood splattered the room as Appalachia roared and her vines shifted violently, jamming thorns and splinters and jagged chunks of bark deep into the neck of the Abyss creature. But something whispered in the back of my mind, something I didn't want to acknowledge that told me I could do more, kill more, if I only called on the power.

A moment later, the creature lost focus on the rest of us and tried to attack Appalachia in earnest. I used the soulsword to cut down as many of the strikes as I could, but still, the lampreys hit their target. Appalachia didn't stop, the rumble didn't stop, and the roar of the furious god deafened us as she throttled the Abyss creature.

I watched in fascination and horror as those vines around the thing's neck seemed to turn into a rotating buzz saw, spinning ever faster, and becoming ever more narrow until at last, with one mighty crunch, the severed head of the creature collapsed onto the stone, and the lampreys fell still.

CHAPTER TWENTY-SEVEN

"WE'RE CLOSE," DRAKE said between rasping breaths. "That thing wouldn't be here if we weren't."

"Close to what?" Vicky asked.

"One of Nudd's prisons," Drake said. "The Mad King used to use those things as torturers. I didn't think there were any left."

"Nudd isn't the Mad King," Aideen said. Her eyes fell to the massive lamprey-like tentacles on the ground around us. She frowned. "But he is clearly mad. Removing the head killed the entire creature."

Drake nodded. "At the end of the Wandering War, there was supposed to be one final attack against Gorias. Hern was to lead an army of these things against the golden walls of the city. But something went wrong when the Mad King tried to bring them through the Abyss. No one knows exactly what happened, but the attack never reached the walls."

"I think I have some idea," I said. "I've seen other things like that in the Abyss. Maybe they've been trapped there since the Wandering War."

Drake looked at me. "Bigger?"

I nodded. "More like the size of a large house. Some were tall, some were a bit more squat. But they were all pretty awful."

Drake blew out a breath. "More awful than you know.

Nudd liked to spread the rumors that these things could spend a century eating a Fae. People used to think that would give them more time to rescue their allies, but they were wrong. More than a day with one of those chewing on you is enough to send most Fae deep into insanity."

"And how does their venom affect vampires?" Dominic asked, holding up his arm to show the gashes from the thing's teeth.

"It's not fatal," Drake said, "but it might slow you down. It will kill most commoners in a few minutes, an hour at most. I wouldn't be surprised if the same went for the necromancers."

A pile of the lampreys moved, and Jasper's head popped out a moment later, covered in gore and his scales showing wounds from the lampreys.

"What about Jasper?" Vicky hurried forward to the dragon, gently touching where some of his scales were missing, and the fangs had obviously torn deep.

"He'll be fine. Don't worry."

The gentleness in Drake's voice caught me off guard. I exchanged a glance with Zola, who tilted her head to the side as if to say, *I don't have any fucking idea either.*

Dominic grumbled before spinning Jonathan around and pulling a bag of blood out of the other vampire's backpack. He bit down on it and drank deeply. He handed the rest to Jonathan. "Drink. I suspect we'll need it."

"Nothing can get through those fire wards," Foster said. "That means nothing sneaking up behind us, but it also means we're not getting through them without taking the wards down."

"So, we backtrack," Aideen said. "Take the corridor this

thing came through."

"That would be the wisest option," Zola said. "If this is truly a guard of the prison as Drake said, then we must assume there are more."

"More would be bad," I said, looking to the shadows. "Hopefully we won't see something worse."

"Always the optimist," Zola said, narrowing her eyes.

"Enough," Appalachia said. The mass of vines and bark shifted and made their way to the door where Appalachia ducked and swept a path that we could all follow through the lampreys. "I will lead the way, should we meet another of these dark things." She glanced back at me, though I couldn't read her expression. "For what you did for Dirge, Damian Vesik. For what you did for Dirge."

"You have a lot of weird friends," Vicky said, readjusting Jasper, who was now just a furball again and cradled in her arms.

"Hey, you're one of my friends, too."

Vicky slowly raised an eyebrow. "I'm pretty sure I qualify as weird."

"I'd go with bizarre," Foster said.

"Hey."

"A man who can survive being Samantha Vesik's brother is a man who has adapted to having some oddities in his life." Jonathan gave me a smile, and I wasn't a hundred percent sure if he was making a joke, or an observation, but I was fairly certain it was Sam who'd had to grow used to oddities in her life because of me. Not the other way around.

My boots slipped in muck as we entered the hall. "I don't even want to know what that was."

"Just be glad you didn't get any in your mouth," Foster said.

Aideen looked at her husband. "Sometimes it's better just to slash, than scream and slash."

The corridor rumbled around us, and it took me a moment before I realized Appalachia was laughing.

✦ ✦ ✦

WE'D ONLY GONE a few hundred feet down the dark corridor before Appalachia paused and pulled her vines back enough that we could see the path leading down a steep set of stairs.

"These stairs were not here before." Appalachia's vines formed into the semblance of a hand, and she ran it along the tops of the stairs. "The slick substance from the lampreys is here. They came this way."

"Then what are we waiting for?" I stepped forward, and Appalachia nodded a moment before she led the way down the stairs.

Aideen eyed the retreating form of the forest god. "So, which was the trap? The room where we fought the Abyss creature? Or this?"

"Both," Jonathan said.

"I agree with the vampire," Drake said. "Be on your guard. We may be far below Nudd's palace, but his machinations are many."

"Ooo, Drake with the fancy words." I blinked at the unbridled sarcasm in my voice.

"Just ignore him," Vicky said. "He gets like this when he's nervous."

"That's true," Zola said.

Drake's gaze lingered on me for only a moment before he

nodded to Vicky.

✦ ✦ ✦

"I STILL THINK it would've been better for the vampire with the flaming sword to lead," I muttered, carefully descending the stairs and letting my *Illuminadda* incantation flow a little bit ahead of me.

"Drake made the right call," Foster said from his perch on my shoulder. "That kind of magic could trigger something down here. At least in the sheath, it's warded, and less likely to be detected. For all we know, that's how the Abyss creature found us."

I wanted to argue more, but I was pretty sure that was my nerves. I let it drop, and focused on what was in front of us. What had started out as a steep staircase hit several landings as it descended. The air thickened with humidity, but the stone walls felt dry.

"Whoa, stop!" Foster snapped. "Damian, stop."

"What is it?"

"That ripple. Something rippled when the light hit it."

Aideen slid up beside us, still in her full-sized form. "Some kind of barrier." She frowned as she studied the apparently empty air from floor-to-ceiling. "It tastes stale. This is old magic, something that survived the trip from Faerie."

"It has to be the prison," Drake said. "What else would they bother warding with magic that strong? We should be able to pass through it, but getting back out could be a problem. I've encountered this kind of barrier before."

Zola ran her fingers across the dry stone. "And Ah'm somewhat concerned where the trail of slime from the lamprey went. It vanished up at the first landing, and we haven't seen it since."

Liam, Lachlan, and Enda could be on the other side of this thing. And if they were, we had to do everything we could to get them out.

"It would be a stupid thing to simply walk right …" Drake started.

Before he could finish his words, I stepped through the barrier with Foster on my shoulder. I'm not sure what I'd expected, perhaps the feeling of twisting and falling like stepping into the Warded Ways. But this was smooth, a mild resistance, and a faint sound like a deep guitar string plucked inside a vast cave.

I was still staring at the awful sight around us before I registered that anyone had come through behind me and Foster. The fairy sat silent on my shoulder, but screams filled the void.

A rotten silo of stone, towering and dripping with slime, sat off to the right. I suspected that's where the Abyss creature had come from, Nudd's prison guard, much as Drake had said.

Beyond that waited a wall of cells. Some were forged from a dark metal, most likely iron. Others appeared to have no enclosure at all, but the creatures inside them, at least those that were still in one piece, were bound by glowing bonds of power. A few appeared to have been fed upon by … something.

A pile of Fae armor rested in the corner, and I had little doubt some of that metal was from our allies. Tortured, slaughtered, or eaten in this place, only their essence left to return to the ley lines.

"Monsters," Aideen said, hurrying to a cell on the other side of the dim room. Inside was a sight I'd seen many times.

The death of a fairy, and the screaming form as it returned to the lines. But this fairy hadn't passed on. Instead, it was trapped in some awful magic, stuck between living and dying in an eternal scream. It was barbaric, and the high-pitched wail never ended.

If Lochlan and his family were there, we might already be too late. Nudd had no reason to keep his word, and most of the commoners wouldn't even know if he executed some other fairy.

The thought filled me with rage. I drew the focus, and a soulsword snapped to life, red fire from my aura licking up through the golden blade. The power in the bars at the front of the cell fell away when I slashed them with the soulsword.

I watched the face of the imprisoned fairy, an aura of pulsing golden light. Its eyes flashed wide and focused on me for only a moment. The blade slid through the glowing bonds and the fairy's eyes closed, the scream grew quieter, and the golden glow slid away, back into the ley lines.

"You should've left him," Drake said. "You don't think they'll notice if you start freeing their pets?"

"I wouldn't leave my worst enemy in something like that."

Vicky laid a hand on the empty armor that sat on the table in the cell. "How long was he trapped?"

"Hard to say," Foster said. "But I'm afraid any length of time would have been an eternity."

"His armor is from the Wandering War," Aideen said. "That's the crown of the Mad King. One of his servants? Surely not."

The mere thought of being trapped in that state of agony for centuries sent a shiver down my spine. It was a level of cruelty I could scarcely imagine.

"Free who you can," I said. "Send them to the Obsidian Inn. They can determine who is friend and foe. Though I suspect we don't have many enemies in this place."

A dark laugh echoed from deeper within the prison. "You have more enemies here than you know, Vesik!"

CHAPTER TWENTY-EIGHT

SHADOWS GAVE WAY to nightmares. A smiling vampire, his face lost in the darkness of a helmet but for his gleaming teeth. Some of the cells opened, and what had at first seemed an empty hall filled with nothing but prisoners revealed itself to be a stronghold, infested with a great many enemies.

Behind us, stone fell in place across the staircase, cutting off our retreat.

"Now, Vesik, I think you'll—"

But the vampire didn't have a chance to finish uninterrupted.

Jonathan roared, and it was a sound not meant for this earth. A cry of frustration and rage and fury that had built over a decade. His flaming sword cut a vicious arc toward the nearest dark-touched, cleaving through the flesh of its thick neck.

"For Alexi!" Jonathan screamed as he booted the collapsing body into its brethren.

Dominic flashed forward, narrowly stopping the incoming claw of another vampire before it took Jonathan's head off. Chaos erupted around us as the shock of Jonathan's attack subsided, and the normally frantic attacks of the dark-touched took on a more deliberate, more terrifying focus.

They didn't come at us in waves. The first who had spoken

flashed hand gestures, and small pods of the vampires scurried at his commands. It took all of five seconds to see what they were doing, but it would take a hell of a lot more than five seconds and a shitload of luck to get through it.

"Boxing us in," Zola said as she stepped closer to me. "They've been waiting for us, boy. They expected it. Expected this. Don't give them what they expect." She held her hand out and gathered a glowing ball of white energy that swirled and flexed until the power itself emitted a high-pitched whine. "Don't. Hold. Back."

"Eyes!" Zola shouted.

I slammed mine shut as half the hall turned toward us, barely enough time to shield myself from the incantation.

"*Magnus Illuminada!*" Zola's voice shook with the strain of it, pooling line energy to magnify even the most powerful of incantations. Light that I thought only Edgar himself could conjure clawed and burned at my eyelids, demanding to be seen, to be witnessed.

The screams and shrieks told me she'd found her mark. She'd blinded at least some of the dark-touched. But vampires healed fast. I didn't know how long we'd have. The light faded, and I opened my eyes on the reeling forces, pale afterimages flickering across my vision. Vicky charged forward and leaped, Jasper's dragon form exploding beneath her, the gouges in his scales still visible from his run-in with the Abyss creature. They streaked toward the cavernous roof above the third floor of the prison.

Appalachia surged into battle, using her vines to haul herself onto the structure of the very cells. From there, she looked like a tree caught in a tornado, lashing out with such speed and fury that Fae died at the impact, and the dark-touched were sent scampering away to reform their ranks. Without her, without that flurry of deadly flails, they would have overwhelmed us in moments.

Zola sagged backward, raising her cane, readying herself for more.

I charged forward, following the path of carnage a half-mad Jonathan had carved. If I'd ever, for a moment, thought he'd recovered from the death of Alexi at Vassili's hands, I'd been wrong. The rage-fueled vampire bathed in the blood of the dark-touched, and what fairies dared to close on him died in pieces.

Foster and Aideen landed on the second floor of the cells to my right, the two fairies fighting in an intricate dance, each strike and parry just one more move in a graceful, deadly series. The prison guard fairies died one after another, their shrieks filling the cavern, only to be drowned out by the roar of dragons.

I lashed out with a soulsword, cutting deep into a dark-touched's forearm. The sword rebounded at the bone, but it was enough to disable one of the thing's claws. I could've used a flaming sword right about then, though I didn't have near the skill and power as Dominic, or the sheer bloodthirst of Jonathan.

Through the carnage, as I faced down fairies and vampires and things I had no name for, the first of the elite dark-touched stood stock still. As if waiting for us to reach him. He didn't bloody his claws beside his soldiers. He simply gestured and sent more to their deaths.

A fairy got through Jonathan's defenses and impaled the

vampire through the gut. I dodged an attack from the right, and glimpsed Jonathan's attacker now in the vampire's jaws. He dropped the fairy and sliced the hilt off the sword in his abdomen with a quick blow from his own blade.

One of the lamprey-like things erupted from another cell, forcing me back against a wall, flashes of tentacles and light and teeth threatening to circumvent my soulsword.

"*Impadda!*" The shield snapped up, and the lampreys sizzled as they tried to bite through it. One got around and cut into my shoulder. I wondered if this one would have the same poison in its maw, but I didn't have time to worry.

I flinched, and saw the cell behind me. Two Utukku stood naked and unarmed with claws extended. A quick bash of the shield forced the lampreys back for the split second I needed. The soulsword made quick work of the wards holding the Utukku in their cell, and its fall sent them into the Abyss creature like a gunshot. Reptilian flesh vanished into the writhing mass as the Utukku started tearing the thing apart with their bare hands.

Drake cursed and slid sideways on his mount as he dove past me, rocketing up toward the cavern's roof in pursuit of Vicky and Jasper. At first, I wondered why. Then I saw the gout of blue flame as Jasper scorched the ceiling.

What had appeared to be stones above us moved, writhing away from the insane heat of the dragon's flame. Drake patted his dragon's neck, and a second blast of fire joined Jasper's. Vicky and Drake strafed the ceiling, sending a shower of flaming *things* to fall from the heights and crunch onto the ground around us.

One smacked down between me and a fairy knight. The

wide black eyes and fanged mouth made it look something like a vampire, but what flesh remained was pale and maggot-like. A being that had not seen the sun in a very long time. If ever.

Dead. Dead for so very long. It called to me, and my aura cried out to it, those creatures who served Nudd. The King of the Dead.

But that which served the Lord of the Dead would serve me. I reached out and touched the thing with my aura, and was greeted with a surge of power unlike any I'd felt before, save one—the electric chaos of touching a gravemaker, of donning the armor of the dead and wearing it like a new face. The mantle of Anubis felt like that, but what did that make these things?

The fairy knight stepped back when I raised my eyes to him. "They are cursed. Do not touch them! Run!" And he fled in earnest, darting back through the blood and gore and charred bodies raining from hell above.

It wasn't a knowing that overcame me. It was something else. A voice, a distant thing that rasped through my connection. "They are coming. They are here."

I tried to pull away, but exhaustion leeched into my bones, as if everything had led to this moment. Vicky, Cara, the Burning Lands, Dirge, the forest, Gaia, had all led back to this point. This doom.

The blackened gums of the dark-touched speaker gleamed as his smile grew mad. He lifted the lip of a large pouch on his hip and slowly raised the reptilian head of an Utukku. "You will all die as they died. Your armory is ours, and now your lives."

I stared at the slack face, the soiled yellow markings beneath her eyes, the clean cut at her neck. The dull black orbs, one half closed, the other smeared with blood. "Hess." The name whispered past my lips, and the spark of anger in my bones chased the exhaustion away. How many did we lose?

Vampires exploded out of a distant cell. Armored, with claws out, shouting commands back and forth as they crashed into our ranks. My heart skipped a beat as a black and white wing was ripped away, sent skyward to flutter to the earth. I couldn't see through the chaos. The screams. I could only focus on what was coming.

What was here.

I exhaled and closed my eyes for a split second, forcing my aura out, calling the centuries of dead things around us. They'd planned their ambush well, shocked us to the point most might have given up, or despaired. But all they'd managed to do so far was piss me the fuck off.

Fingernails cut into my palms when I found them. Not far. Ready to move. Ready to kill. The gravemakers flowed through the earth above, filtering into the air like a cloud of black ash. I flexed my fingers, and the dead below me surged into the hall. A hand large enough to encase a distracted fairy erupted from the prison floor. I felt him resist, felt his bones shatter and his body burst as the Hand of Anubis dragged him into the earth.

Every step was a deliberate thing as I guided the gravemakers, trying to keep them from our allies as I unleashed them onto the dark-touched vampires. But these vampires weren't the brainless killing machines we'd fought in Greenville and Saint Charles. They ran from the slow-moving wraiths, dodging and weaving past the gravemakers, luring them toward my own allies.

Foster and Aideen dove off the third story of the prison,

narrowly evading a dark-touched vampire's strike. Its claws only caught air, but I saw it launch itself into the sky after them, only to be struck down by Appalachia's thorns. The vampires might not have been gifted with flight, but you wouldn't know it from the terrifying leaps they made at their leisure.

Jasper tucked his wings in, diving as Vicky clung to his back with one arm while the other wielded a golden soulsword. A dark-touched met her blade, but instead of cleaving through the armor, the blade rebounded. I wanted to shout a warning, scream, anything! But Vicky had run with the Ghost Pack, she'd battled the dark-touched in the Burning Lands, and she wasn't caught off guard. She used it to her advantage.

In one vicious motion, Jasper's wings unfurled, and Vicky let go. Instead of soaring with the dragon, she wrapped her fingers around the edge of the vampire's helmet and wrenched it upwards. The sloping head of the dark-touched revealed, and the wide black orbs of its eyes widened as the next thing it saw was one of Vicky's soulswords, stabbing deep into it.

The vampire screamed and toppled backward, a flailing arm catching Vicky's leg, but not hard enough to unseat her. Her legs tightened around the thing's neck while she stabbed the vampire over and over until the gray flesh slowed enough that the gravemakers caught it. Vicky hopped away as the dead, bark-like fingers dug into the vampire. Its squeal died as its body was rent to pieces.

Every moment my concentration slipped, the gravemakers would start to wander. Coming too close to our allies, my friends. But I couldn't send them away. Not yet. Not while the dark-touched still prowled this hall.

Instead, I sent them to the cells.

Iron squealed and cracked as long-rotten hinges were torn from their bases. Bars bent, and the few cells protected by shields resisted with a furious shower of sparks. But gravemakers were slow, plodding tanks. Not things to be intimidated by light or pain. The shields fell, and furious Fae poured out of the cells.

But anger can only fuel a being for so long. As intimidating as that flood of potential allies was, they were worn, beaten, and some were broken. I realized my mistake when the first wave broke against the dark-touched and died immediately. Blood and wings rained down across the battlefield as exhausted Fae were torn apart, finally sent to a screaming rest to rejoin the ley lines.

Even at that moment, that pang of regret, I saw Dominic crumble. The vampire that held Hess sent him to the ground, following with the Utukku's head, beating the larger vampire senseless before howling in laughter. I took a deep breath, and time slowed. Vicky bounced from vampire to vampire, managing to score a few good hits, but ultimately retreating to Jasper. They rejoined the battle above with Drake, a whirlwind of fangs and blades and incantations that turned the air into a fine red mist.

Zola burned everything. Whatever creature thought to make short work of a frail old woman met a tortured end. Zola's braids flew with a fury as she spun her cane like a quarterstaff, razor-like blades slicing through flesh and armor alike. The moment a Fae would shriek in pain and double over, an incantation would burst from her staff and end its life. Zola was brilliant. She was always brilliant. The enemies she could strike down died, but those she couldn't easily defeat got blasted back into the core of the fight with explosive bursts of wind and ice.

Jonathan unsheathed his flaming sword from the eye socket of a dark-touched as he howled like a wolf and dove into the heart of the battle once more.

I slowly closed my right hand, feeling the resistance of the gravemakers as if each was a string tied to my fingers. But they obeyed. My soulsword dimmed as the gravemakers vanished into the earth and rushed toward their new target.

The speaker raised his sword to strike Dominic's head from his shoulders. The Hand of Anubis exploded from the earth before him, sending Dominic's limp body spiraling off into the shadows. I smiled at the sting I felt between my fingers as the sword cut into the Hand of Anubis. I tilted my own hand forward, and the mass of dead flesh reached out and snatched the vampire from the ground.

He shouted something, tried to call his allies back to free him. Part of me thought we should interrogate the son of a bitch. That part didn't win.

I closed my hand into a fist and felt the power of the dark-touched struggle to rebuild itself from the pulped mass of flesh that had so recently been his body. The flesh of the gravemakers flowed into the dark-touched vampire's braincase, obliterating it. I absently saw a shadow out of the corner of my eye. Another vampire, another dark-touched, closing on me to bring this battle to an end.

But I didn't care about that as I felt the power surge through my aura. What could one vampire do against a necromancer who contained enough souls to live a thousand years? The dark-touched vampire's fangs drew close, but it didn't much matter what I thought about that.

Jasper's jaws closed around the creature, and the crack of flesh and bone echoed through the cavern beside me. Some part of my mind registered Vicky riding on his back, directing the dragon in who to eat, and who to leave to their own devices. She'd come into her own, that girl. She'd been reborn a warrior, thrown off the mantle of the Destroyer, only to become a destroyer of another sort.

My lips pulled up into a death's-head grin. We'd done that. We'd brought her back, an angel of destruction, of death, whose purpose would topple the empire of a mad Fae king. I raised my right hand to my mouth, coated in blood and death and the stuff of gravemakers. The coppery scent of blood and the stench of long-dead flesh filled my nostrils. I let it crawl over my hand and up my arm until we were one, with one purpose.

I drew my hand away when Foster streaked out of the sky and landed before me. "What are you doing! Damian! Your face … it's … that's Nudd's symbol. The white hand."

"Sometimes it's the history of the man that kills him," I said, somewhat detached from the panic in my friend's voice. "Get everyone back."

"Back where?" Foster shouted as I strode toward the churning wall of destruction that rained down from above, and the scrambling forms below us who rose to meet it.

But they were all dead. Death was all around them, in the walls, in the air. I didn't recognize the laugh that escaped my lips as the floor bubbled forth with the dead flesh of gravemakers, pulling vampires and Fae alike down into the stone, churning their bodies into so much liquid. What I could destroy of the dark-touched vampires, I liquified. The chaff of the gravemakers became what I wanted, what I needed, like a tide of razor blades to slice the flesh from our enemies.

There was joy in this, in the death of creatures meant to kill us. But even as columns of fire raced down through the tide of gravemakers, something called to me in the distance. A vague thought as another Fae exploded into its component parts, and one of the lamprey-like creatures dissolved into a sea of molten power.

"Damian, stop!"

Spears erupted from the field of dead, pinning vampires and knights to the ceiling in one violent explosion.

"Stop!"

I turned my head to that voice. Slowly, as if I were a colossus, and the effort it took to refocus my eyes was a long-forgotten task. The roiling waves of death calmed. The gravemakers that had covered my face reluctantly pulled away, and I stumbled forward, staring at the ruin of what lay before me.

"Damian." Vicky stood behind Jasper. The dragon's head reared back, and a blue spark lit its throat before he deliberately closed his jaws and blinked those massive black orbs at me.

I rubbed at the back of my neck and walked toward the cells, leaning against the nearest bars. "Sorry, kid. Lost track of things for a moment there."

A firm hand grabbed the side of my head. Zola wrenched my right eye open and stared at me. "Are you back? You killed … everything."

I frowned.

Zola glanced over her shoulder. "You've been covered in

gravemakers for ten minutes, Damian."

I flinched, as if her words struck a physical blow. "What?"

"We sent those we rescued back to the Obsidian Inn," Drake said, stepping up beside Vicky. He hesitated before continuing. "I don't mean to sound unappreciative of you saving pretty much all of our asses back there, but Damian?"

I glanced up and met his eyes.

"You've got issues."

Zola barked out a laugh. "You don't know the half of it."

"I saw you destroy the green men on the banks of the Missouri River," Drake said. "I saw the towers you summoned to slay the water witches. This was different. *You* were different. It was a power I've not seen in a great many years."

Foster stepped closer to us, his arm around Aideen.

She looked exhausted, and that was being generous. Even her wings drooped as she leaned into Foster. "I healed who I could. Foster helped, too. It may be enough to get them back to our allies, but I don't know."

I rubbed at my wrist. It felt sore, and a thin line of blood trailed from the base of my thumb. "You did what you could. We can't expect any more."

Drake released a half-mad laugh. "You're *unhinged.*" He gestured wildly around our group. "Vesik's throwing soularts and death magic like they're children's toys, and none of you seem the slightest bit concerned."

"He saved your ass, didn't he?" Vicky asked before blowing out a breath. "Get over yourself. Damian killed Prosperine in the Burning Lands. His powers aren't like anything you've seen before."

"You're wrong, child." Drake wasn't patronizing Vicky. His

words were soft, kind. As if he worried the wrong words would break her.

The fairy perplexed me.

"There is another who wields power over the dead."

"Nudd," Foster said. "We know."

"Yes, the Lord of the Dead." Drake stood up a little straighter.

Zola almost growled.

"Hess," I said, turning slowly to the empty armor and piles of dead vampires. "She's gone." Two shadows stood in the distance, one holding a flickering sword that spewed gouts of flame. The other, larger form held a body.

Dominic let the crumpled form fall to the ground. Dark liquid dripped from his mouth before he reached up and wiped the dark-touched's blood away.

"Did they speak?" Zola asked, raising her voice.

"Yes." Dominic's words were slow, satisfied. "The Fae family was already taken. They'll be executed this evening."

"We missed them." The words felt sour, wrong. I looked to Drake.

"No," he said. "I didn't tell him your precious plans."

Drake turned away and met Dominic halfway down the row of cells. "Where?"

"The gates of Falias," Dominic said. "Same place the media gathered for his little speech."

Drake glanced back at us, a vicious smile cutting through his face. "The Obsidian Inn will devour that gathering. If Liam and his family can be saved, Morrigan will do it."

"How can you be sure?" Zola asked.

"I knew Nudd and Morrigan many years before Nudd

claimed his throne. Morrigan might not have the power to slay the Lord of the Dead, but you can be damned sure she'll go out of her way to upstage him."

"Then we head straight for the nukes," I said. "They can't stay in Nudd's hands. Leave the others to Morrigan."

Drake pursed his lips. "That's what I just said."

"That's not exactly what you just said."

"I'm pretty sure it is."

"*Children*," Zola said. "Save your bickering. We have bombs to steal, and nations to disarm."

I blinked at Zola. She was right. That's the core of what we were doing, and that was insane.

She strode toward the far end of the prison, and we followed.

CHAPTER TWENTY-NINE

I SIGHED AND ran my fingers through my hair. "All I'm saying is maybe I should get out of here and warn the others."

"The risk is too great," Aideen said, echoing Zola's sentiments. "You may be able to step into the Abyss from here, but what if she can't bring you back? You could be stranded above or outside the gates with the Obsidian Inn."

Zola's cane cracked on the stone floor. "We need you here, boy, like Ah said."

But I'd lost time. I didn't feel safe staying here with everyone. Or perhaps it wasn't so much that I didn't feel safe, but I was afraid *they* weren't safe. But what good would leaving with Gaia do me? Abandon my friends, my family, to the jaws of whatever lay ahead? Of all the risks set out before me, that was the least acceptable.

I yelped when Zola thumped my head with her cane.

"Stop it, boy. You lose yourself, Ah'll have your sister out here to cut you down."

The *splendorum mortem*. She could do it. That could stop me. That could stop anything. But it wasn't the kind of thing you nonchalantly wielded when facing an army. To lose a weapon that powerful could be disastrous.

"No," I said. "No one is killing me until I figure out a way to sever the bond of the Devil's Knot."

Vicky snorted. "Oh, come on. It's fantastic motivation for you to not die. You get yourself killed, you get me and Sam killed. So don't get yourself killed."

"You make it sound so easy."

"I'm probably not the best one to ask for advice," she said, turning away as she hid a smile. "I died."

Jonathan took a deep breath, which I tended to notice when a vampire did it. "If I hadn't known all of you for the past several years, I'd have to say this was one seriously fucked up conversation."

"Agreed," Drake said. He ruffled Vicky's hair and followed her into the shadowed pathway on the other side of the bloody hall.

Foster sidled up beside me and said, "I don't trust him."

I crossed my arms. "I rather like his dragon, though."

"Let's just hope we don't have to find out if he fights as well as Jasper."

I raised an eyebrow. "You weren't watching the battle, were you?"

"Actually, I was trying not to die."

"A reasonable goal." I watched the gray shadows slither along the ceiling and drop behind Vicky and Drake. Two dragons, one as deadly as the other. The thought brought me some measure of comfort, but I couldn't silence the voice that whispered in the back of my mind. *What if they aren't on your side?*

Then we're fucked, I whispered back.

Foster was snoring in the hood of Zola's gray cloak by the time we reached the next hall. The yellow stone of Falias gave way to rock with veins of magrasnetto running through it. I worried they could be warded, ready to tear us apart with one wrong move. But despite my nerves being on edge, and nearly jumping out of my shoes at every random sound, no attack came.

"It's quiet," Jonathan said.

"Hmm …" Zola started. "If he says 'too quiet,' Ah'm going to slap him."

Jonathan glanced back and flashed a toothy grin at Zola. It looked sincere, and it was one of the few smiles I'd seen on the vampire's face since he'd resurfaced.

Aideen ripped a thunderous snore from her perch on Vicky's shoulder, loud enough to startle herself awake.

"Foster would be so proud," I said.

She narrowed her eyes and gave me a look that could have killed a commoner. "Remind me to heal you last."

I froze when Dominic pulled up short, and Jonathan drew his flaming sword.

"This is it."

At first, I didn't understand what Jonathan was talking about, or why he'd drawn his sword. But when the vampire stepped forward, the smooth stone wall was plain to see in the light of the sword.

"That's the bunker?" I asked. My gaze trailed toward the ceiling as I stepped out of the passage we'd been walking through. It stretched at least a hundred feet into the air, apparently nestled in a massive cavern. And that's just what I could see of it.

Dominic felt along the wall before punching it. A tiny chip of stone dust fell to the ground. Whatever it was, it was sturdy as hell. "This is going to take a year to punch through."

"Then we find a door," Drake said, his dragon expanding to fill the void in front of the wall.

"Oh, Ah'm *so* happy we have such a brilliant strategist with us," Zola muttered. She summoned a light and sent it racing from one end of the cavern to the other, the dull white glow highlighting every inch of unforgiving rock. "Only there isn't a door."

"Then we burn through it," Vicky said.

"Burn through the rock?" I said with a half-hearted chuckle. "I don't think that's going to—"

But by the time I finished speaking, Jasper exploded into his dragon form, hip checking Drake's dragon to the side before he reared back and unleashed a torrent of bright blue fire.

"Whoa!" I shouted. "Turn down the fireworks! There are *nukes* on the other side of that thing!"

"Nuclear weapons are actually highly resistant to fire," Jonathan said, his voice so calm and teacher-like that I didn't think he'd really thought the situation through. "You could theoretically drop one into a volcano and the warhead wouldn't go off."

"Oh sure," I muttered before raising my voice into a near-hysterical scream. "But what about the rocket fuel?"

Jonathan's eyes widened before he joined me in shouting, "There are nukes on the other side of that wall!"

Jasper slowly relaxed, his neck curling back as the flames died out. In the sudden darkness, I could just barely make out the massive head of the dragon turning his eyes on me.

"Thanks for not blowing us up."

The dragon chuffed and started collapsing into himself. A moment later, only the dust bunny remained, a ball of fur with huge black eyes and teeth like a demon in the shadows.

Zola stepped closer to the hole before raising her left arm and cursing. "That's hot enough to boil your ass right there." She grimaced, raised her cane, and said, "*Modus Glaciatto.*"

A whirlwind of ice showered the red-hot doorway Jasper had melted into the stone. The moment I thought the incantation was dying out, Zola leaned into it, forcing more line energy into the ice storm. The clash of frozen precipitation and molten stone sent a geyser of steam up toward the ceiling, until it crashed against the rock and billowed back down toward us.

For a moment, it felt as though we'd stepped into a sauna, but that gave way to a cool breeze, and finally a bone-deep chill from Zola's incantation. The molten red stone solidified into a gray mass, and the mist cleared.

I stared into the cavern, a place filled from wall to distant wall with man's own ruin, and said the only words that could encompass the sight of endless death. "Fuck. Me."

Acres of bombs, if not more, stacked end to end but for narrow aisles and unstable-looking catwalks stretched so far into the distance that our lights could not reach it. Staring at those vessels, those metal shells that held the end of all mankind, a tiny thought took hold inside my mind. We could never return these to the military. We could never let the hands of political adversaries hover over shiny red buttons. Egos could not be allowed to end us all.

"We have to destroy them," I said.

"What?" Zola said. "And what do you hope to gain from that, Damian? The governments of the world will only make more. It's one of the few things Nudd seems to understand."

The thought curdled my blood. That humanity could build

its own extinction on a scale that was scarcely imaginable. And then escalate it.

For a time, we stared in silence at the mass of warheads and rockets laid out before us. I'd seen pictures of bombs before. I'd thought I knew what to expect, but some of them were so small, not much taller than I was. And yet every single thing in that place was born for such destruction. Others were what I imagined to be hidden in the silos of Kansas and the plains, massive rockets capable of reaching out and annihilating cultures on the other side of the world.

More than the soldiers, more than the jets, tanks, or ships. This was the core of our military. The deterrent that should anyone be foolish enough to attack us, we could wipe them from the face of the earth. Did Park understand it? Casper? I shook my head. They had to know what they served.

They had to know the blood our country had on its hands. But did they understand how much more it could bleed?

We walked deeper into the bunker, thoughts of Liam and his family being choked out by the limitless destruction that flanked our every step.

"What can we do against this?" Foster asked.

"This isn't for us," Aideen said. "The commoners have always been particularly good at murdering themselves. And whatever darkness falls, we can always retreat to Faerie."

"Where? Gorias? That city is a shit town. Whatever glory it once had is long dead."

"You judge too harshly, my love. Gorias has a great deal of life left to give."

"This is insane," Drake said, turning in place and raising his arms to gesture around us as we stepped into a small clearing that wasn't choked by massive metal cylinders and sleek warheads. "His mind is gone." The old fairy turned to Foster and Aideen. "You know who he is, don't you? You have to know."

Aideen frowned. "Gwynn Ap Nudd, the Lord of the Dead. King of Faerie, Betrayer of—"

Drake gave a violent twist of his wrist. "No."

I stared at the fairy, his words from the sparring ring coming back to me. *Nudd, a Fae who is truly mad.* "The simplest answer is most often the truth. That's what you said …" The pieces slammed together in my mind, the hand, the Lord of the Dead, the fairy who slayed the Mad King, only … "Nudd *is* the Mad King."

"What?" Foster hissed. He glanced at me before stepping toward Drake. "That's … not possible."

"Isn't it?" Drake asked, leaning toward Foster. "How could *I* bear the mantle of Demon Sword while its power still flows through you? The answer is simple, no matter how much you wish it wasn't."

"Nudd killed the Mad King," Aideen said. "That's common knowledge."

"Of course it is," Drake said, "because he wanted it to be."

Aideen narrowed her eyes. "We're already enemies of the king. What do you think this will accomplish?"

"Tear through his glamour and see the truth for yourself. Let the world see the twisted thing he's become, the Eldritch magic that keeps him alive." His eyes grew distant, focusing on a point only he could see in his mind. "You'll never forget it. He's not … he's something else now."

"What do you mean?" Aideen asked, some of the conviction of her earlier words bleeding away.

"He's not of the Fae. That's how he's still alive. Only a Fae can sit on that throne."

"Apparently not," Foster muttered. "He's been on the throne for centuries. And why would we still have our powers if he wasn't a Fae anymore?"

Drake focused on Foster, opened his mouth as if to speak, but said nothing for a time. "I don't know. That's old magic, older than any of us. Older than him."

Aideen laid a hand on Foster's shoulder. "Cara always thought the mantle was tied to the throne itself more than the king. The king simply … guided it to the next bearer."

"Ah don't think …" Zola started, but she trailed off. "What in the seven hells is that?"

At first, I saw nothing, just the endless pit of bombs that could end life as we knew it. But I frowned as the shadows in the distance grew. Subtle at first, the ambient light and reflections were almost being devoured as something moved through the bunker.

Metal screamed as Appalachia shifted one of the warheads so she could more easily join us.

I cursed. "Whatever the hell it is, it's big. Make ready."

"Make ready?" Vicky said. "You sound like Carter."

I glanced at Vicky. "Really?"

She frowned. "That wasn't a compliment. You just sounded old. Like, older than you are."

Zola let out a humorless laugh as she stepped between us and joined Foster and Drake. Aideen gave one violent flap of her wings and shot toward the ceiling of the bunker. She came down again a moment later, lines etched into her forehead.

"Bad?" Zola asked.

"It couldn't be much worse."

"Dark-touched?" Drake asked.

Aideen grimaced. "I'm afraid Hern didn't come alone. The Wild Hunt is here."

CHAPTER THIRTY

"THERE'S NO FOREST here!" Foster shouted. "No oak! He can't summon the Hunt without oak!"

"Things change," Vicky said, so matter of fact all Foster did in response was blink. "What are they?"

"The Hunt?" Drake asked. "More like, who are they? Any Fae caught up in the spell can be pulled into the Hunt. They'll do Hern's bidding, and your own mother would murder you on his command."

"She does that every night when she cooks for me," Vicky muttered, patting Jasper on the head. She made a quick hand motion, and the furball exploded into the dragon. Drake's mount followed suit, and it lent me some modicum of comfort, being wedged between the two massive reptiles.

Except, of course, there were still nukes all around us. I shivered, drew the focus, and summoned a soulsword.

Drake stared at the blade. "Be wary. They'll have magic, in force, and some of them may be able to meet your blade."

The distant shadows spread out and irregular patterns formed in the murk. The sight chilled me to the bone, and that was before I saw the faces. Cara had told us stories of the Wild Hunt, a lost tradition that only Hern had domain over until Nudd took the throne. The Hunt had once been a celebration, a yearly gathering when the Fae would walk among the humans and partake of their offerings: fresh game, cider, and mead.

But the darkness before me was something else. I'd come to think of many of the Fae as tranquil when they weren't actively trying to kill me, but the faces in the shadows here were pierced by anger. Eyes glazed over, glowing a dull white while the fairies closed on us. The cloud was power, Hern's power, and it spread like a black web across all of those caught up in the hunt.

The wings of the Fae vanished into a rolling bank of power that reminded me of a thunderstorm crashing down on the cabin in the woods of Missouri. What I wouldn't have given to be back there, on familiar turf, instead of underground, surrounded by world-killers.

A sloping, skeletal hand erupted through the mist. I vaguely heard Drake shouting orders for Vicky to take to the air a moment before the dragons raced away. My eyes were all for the skeleton. It had less flesh than the wights we'd fought along the rivers and old battlefields, and it wore much the same armor. But the eyes … the eyes glowed with sickening green light, unlike any power I'd seen before.

Hern rode out of the mist behind the creature, a broad smile on his face as he sat astride a horned monstrosity the Wild Hunt had brought him. The antlers of his helmet glowed until they became one with the Fae, both majestic and deadly.

"Crush them!" These were the only words Hern spoke, and they were the only words the skeletons erupting from the mist needed.

A sound rose, like the keening of a dying animal trapped in the darkness. The shadows around Hern flared and fluttered, reminding me of a cape in a strong wind. The creatures came as one.

I stepped backward as Hern's power brought forth the likes of which I couldn't comprehend. A few Fae retained a normal appearance, aside from their glowing white eyes. But the other things—the lamprey-like creatures and the skeletons mounted upon steeds of bone and blood—were the stuff of legends.

"For the Sanatio!" Foster howled as he sprinted toward that oncoming wall of death. His wings flared and fires as bright as the sun surged around the hilt of his sword.

Zola ran her tongue over her teeth and spat. "Seen worse."

"Oh really?" I asked, adjusting my grip on the focus. "Where was that?"

"In the hands of men. But they all die, Damian. Everything dies." Her voice changed, and I didn't understand the words she muttered as she dropped the carcass of some long-dead thing onto the stone floor at her feet. Old blood stained Zola's fingers. Old blood from a young body, I realized when I recognized the form of an Owl Knight's mount.

"Zola?"

But Zola wasn't there anymore. She'd stepped away, her posture straightening, the power of the ley lines arcing up as if it meant to embrace a long-forgotten lover.

Ritual magic. Death magic, performed on the body of a Fae creature.

The cloud of darkness reached us, and hell came once more to burn upon the earth.

✦ ✦ ✦

THE FIRST OF the skeletal horsemen closed on Zola. It was taller than I'd thought, as if the skeleton of a Titan, one of Gaia's siblings, had been stripped of its flesh and animated by Hern's madness. My master took no heed of the thing.

I didn't know what magic she was working. Some ritual spells could last hours, though she'd never try something like that here. But wrapped in that kind of power, you could lose yourself. Lose awareness of your surroundings. Lose awareness of the blade angled to strike your head from your shoulders.

The soulsword raging from the focus in my hands met the strike of Zola's mounted assailant, and the vibration of the impact sent me down to one knee, my entire body shaking. But my attack hadn't been without effect. The horseman spiraled as he hit the stone floor, a massive clang echoing around the chaos as he crashed into one of the nukes.

I raised the sword and struck out at his mount. The horse-like creature screeched as the bones in its neck shattered, and for a moment the dismounted rider's eyes flashed like the glowing orbs of a dullahan. The horse stumbled, once, twice, and then fell to pieces. They could be destroyed. That was good.

Six more of the riders slipped from Hern's darkness.

That was bad.

Aideen swooped down in front of me, raised a hand to the rising skeleton I'd knocked down, and shouted, "*Inimicus Sanation!*"

White healing light flowed across the animated undead. Flesh crept onto its ribs for only a moment, but that one flash of power, of life was enough to break whatever hold Hern's magic had on it. The skeleton collapsed into a pool of bone and bloody new flesh.

I reached out to it, curiosity warring with common sense,

but it was just death now. It was *mine* now.

A flicker of fiery blades cut into the shadows. Dominic and Jonathan, side by side as they worked to whittle down Hern's forces as quickly as possible. Every blow from the vampires sent another enemy to the ground like straw men, cutting through another layer of Hern's shroud, but that shroud was thick, and hid an unending army.

I brought the horseman back to his feet, the flash of knowing somewhat dulled by the roar of souls welling up in my head so that I could scarcely follow which vision was his. The field of wildflowers with the young girl? The bloody alley that died away in a storm of light? No, it was the screaming warrior, the family cut down by Nudd's gambit a thousand years before. A lightbringer, a warrior of Gorias.

"Well, now's your chance to raise a little hell," I muttered as I pointed the skeleton and its reanimated, reassembled mount at the nearest of the Abyss creatures. The horseman surged forward, plunging into the tangled mass of tentacles and teeth.

Drake's dragon unhinged its jaws and swooped down, obliterating the shadows for a moment in a storm of blue fire. Something lashed out and scored a hit along the dragon's flank, so fast I could scarcely comprehend anything had moved.

"I see you," Zola said, raising her voice loud enough to startle me half to death. She opened her eyes, and looked out at the field before us, her pupils glowing like angry red suns. She raised her hand, fingers curled like a fist with two knuckles standing higher than the rest.

She struck out at the air, a vicious lunge that wouldn't have done much of anything on a normal day. But today, a sickening black and red sludge burst from the body of the dead owl. It surged forward as though it had a life of its own, its wings too rubbery, too red, too wrong.

But the effect when it met the darkness was unmistakable. Something screeched in the shadows as Zola's zombie owl barreled into the ultimate battle of its short life. It brushed up against one of the fairies, and the result was horrifying. Black and red lines shot up the Fae's legs while Zola's clumsy creature continued on.

I stared in awful fascination as a webwork of red and black raced up the fairy's legs and spiraled around his head. The knight tried to cut it away, cutting so deep as to remove half his own face before the red tendrils flashed brightly, and the fairy collapsed.

Hern backed away from whatever Zola had conjured as it sprinted through his ranks and closed on the antlered form itself, leaving a trail of self-mutilated, dying Fae behind it.

With every step, Zola's creature changed, morphed into something different with each Fae it touched, with each Fae that died screaming when the bloody gelatin mold brushed it. It was bigger by the time it reached Hern, more sure of its footing as it plunged through an unwary mass of lampreys. The tangled figure collapsed, dead.

Hern was not such easy prey. He gestured at the creature, and pale yellow light exploded from his fingers, cutting through Zola's summoning. Steam rose and hissed from the split body as it still tried to flop its way to Hern. The Fae lord grimaced as he drew his ax. The strike was swift, and the creature moved no more.

But the damage had been done. The veil of darkness that had been stretched across the bunker had decidedly bright spots now. The dragons had burned through the edges of Hern's power even as Zola's creature had slaughtered its way into the heart of Nudd's army.

There were still too many left. Another skeleton struck down the horseman at my command. Though I still had control of it, the rider could no longer support its own weight. It crumbled to the ground as a dark-touched vampire flickered through Hern's ranks, crushing the horse's skeleton beside its fallen rider.

Dominic and Jonathan pounced, engaging the dark-touched vampire as it laughed and deflected the blows from their swords. They moved faster and faster until little more than the violent arcs of their flaming blades were clear in the chaos.

Jasper dove toward us. Vicky raised a soulsword in her right hand as the dragon cleared my head by inches. I spun to follow them, realizing then that the veil had surrounded us, the edges having seeped through the bunker and filled the space behind us, cutting us off from Appalachia. And with the veil came … things.

This isn't Hern's magic. A tangle of tentacles writhed and flopped its way forward into the bunker.

"The veil is a doorway," Zola said, drawing my attention back to her. She brushed her braids back from a haggard face, took a deep breath, and straightened her back. Whatever the summoning was that she'd done, it had taken a great deal of energy.

"Since when can Hern summon something from the Abyss?"

Aideen hit the ground beside us, hard. She grunted, rolled

over, and came up to one knee. "Never." Another healing spell flashed from her fingers, cutting down a horseman as it trampled the armor of its fallen comrades. "Nudd's done something to his power. I'm sure of it."

The closest of the tentacles lashed out, reaching for Zola, but Drake had seen what came through the gateway. He dove in Vicky's wake, his dragon unhinging its jaws as the leviathan came fully into our realm. A torrent of blue flame engulfed the end of the tentacle. It curled back, blackened and cracked and oozing as the undamaged tentacles spread out, revealing a gaping maw of three beaks within the slimy flesh.

I'd seen Jasper beat a leviathan before, but here, in the bunker I feared what would happen if the dragons tried to incinerate the creature in earnest. The nukes might not go off, but I was guessing it wouldn't be a good thing to be in the same room if the radioactive material in those warheads was exposed. Plus, rockets.

I cursed. "Zola! They didn't just choose this bunker for the warheads. They're limiting our strongest allies."

"Ah know, boy. Ah know. Now get over it and *fight!*" Light and death burst from Zola's knobby old cane, a laser-focused fire incantation that punched through flesh and armor alike. Fae fell in the path of that power, but it wasn't the kind of thing Zola could keep using. She was already slowing from her summoning, and the more powerful incantations would exhaust anyone in short order.

They'd handicapped all of us in the bunker. I couldn't conjure the pillars of the dead to spear Hern's army. If I pulled too hard on the structure around us, I could kill everyone. That would have been a neat trick if we weren't locked inside with

Hern's hellish forces. If it came to it … I could do it. I could bring the bunker down. But that was a last resort.

Instead, I called on the gravemakers to rise. With care and patience and more caution than I normally exerted, I let the dead flow from the earth beneath my feet. The blackened bark-like flesh rolled up my legs, caressing my torso as it slid over my chest and down my arms. I could feel the desire in the gravemakers. The urge to kill, the urge to smother the one who dared order them. But we shared an enemy, and whatever animated Hern's army drew the ire of the gravemakers.

We moved as one, though I had to expend a great deal of focus to keep the gravemakers away from my face. Whatever had happened when we battled the dark-touched in the prison, I didn't want it happening here.

Swords clanged, and metal slurped greedily at the blood left behind by rent flesh. For a time, the world around us vanished. There was only the enemy, and the world of the commoners we were fighting to preserve. Hern sent wave after wave to crash against us. They all died. But they did damage of their own.

The vampire, Jonathan, lay unmoving on the ground behind Dominic. Drake's dragon bled liquid metal from its tail. But still the beast hammered away at the leviathan, beating back a foe that would otherwise have long ago crushed us beneath its massive tentacles.

The shadows of the bunker still flowed from Hern's back like some damned cloak, spewing horsemen, lampreys, and more of the possessed Fae. The chaos of the battle echoed through the giant room, making it sound like things were right beside you when they were far away, and far away when something was about to slit your throat.

I didn't dare risk summoning the pillars of the dead, but the Hand of Anubis did well enough for my needs. Two of the Fae lay flattened to the stone, their bodies screaming as they disintegrated, never knowing what had come from the earth to crush them. But for Jonathan, I took a softer touch, more concentration. Instead of the jagged and cracked bark, a sleek obsidian hand slipped through the fractures of the stone, dragging the vampire back toward Zola and Aideen until he rested at the healer's feet.

"I can't heal him!" Aideen shouted. "He's not like Sam!"

"Just feed something to him," I barked back, my voice gruff and changed by the layer of gravemakers flowing around me.

Zola laughed as Aideen grumbled, spearing the nearest Fae and slamming it down on top of Jonathan. I worried he wasn't conscious, or at least not aware enough of his surroundings, but his arms closed around the fairy like a bear trap. Blood sprayed. I didn't watch the rest.

I stalked forward, grabbing, crushing, and hurling our foes into the jaws of the leviathan. Hern hadn't expected that. I grinned, madness at the edges of my mind as Nudd's right hand backed away.

The voices came to me as I teetered on the brink. Seductive things, whispering to me. "*Give in to the power. Be consumed by it so that you might consume our enemy.* I could silence them most times, even when the world was quiet, but this was different. The souls from Gettysburg knew who Hern was, sensed the exhaustion in my bones, understood Hern's tie to Nudd, and they screamed for the death of the old hunter.

I stumbled as I crushed one of the horsemen in a Hand of Anubis. I couldn't stop fighting. If any one of us stopped now, every one of us died.

Foster spun toward me after Hern turned away another attack. The fairy's eyes widened, and he shouted, "Nudd's balls!"

I swatted a pile of bones away and turned to see Jasper, wings flexing and Vicky riding upon his back, hauling the leviathan into what limited airspace he had to work with. The dragon spun, and the churning mass of tentacles and beaks sailed into the oncoming line of dark-touched vampires.

Whatever the leviathans were, they were no friend of the dark-touched. Two of the vampires vanished into the leviathan's maw before they could so much as react. I half expected them to tear out the sides of the writhing mass, but it didn't happen. The leviathan had devoured them.

Unfortunately, the mass of tentacles and beaks didn't seem to care that several dark-touched had escaped. Instead, it was content to smash through the lines of skeletons, almost as if it was making for Hern. But the illusion was shattered when one of those tentacles snatched Drake from the back of his dragon.

The fairy shouted. And I didn't have to imagine why. I'd seen the tentacles of the leviathans up close before. Inside each was a savage hook, and I had little doubt that some of them had found purchase in Drake's armor, and others anchored themselves in his flesh. A smaller, faster tentacle wrapped around the dragon like a noose, dragging both the shouting fairy and the bellowing reptile closer to the beak-filled maw.

I moved toward Drake, the flesh of the gravemakers slowing every stride. Another of the dark-touched angled to intercept me. I almost yearned for the vampires we'd fought in Greenville. For these were smarter, and while they may not have been faster, that intelligence allowed them to avoid the deadliest of our attacks.

A Hand of Anubis missed one of the vampires, but I managed to let it fall backward and knock another away. All the time, Drake was getting pulled closer to the beak of the leviathan. At first, I thought he was still fighting, trying to throw spell. But now I could see the leviathan had wrapped another tentacle around Drake's head, and the fairy could do little more than writhe.

Vicky dove for the writhing ball of tentacles. I watched helplessly as she vanished into the deadly mass. Awe swept over me as her hand reached up and grabbed Jasper's tail, and the dragon became a blazing blue sword. Fire rippled and licked out in deep hues, and the blade made short work of the leviathan's tentacles.

I was close enough to call a Hand of Anubis up between the beaks and Drake. I curled the hand gently over the fairy, stumping the leviathan for a moment. But a moment was all Vicky needed. She spun like a whirlwind through blood and ichor. With each slash of the dragon-born blade, another piece of tentacle fell. Another part of the leviathan died. Until finally she hurled that flaming blue mass at the giant black orb of the leviathan's eye.

A giant gray lid closed as the light reached it, and the leviathan turned away just enough to preserve its eye. As the sword bounced away, Jasper exploded into his dragon form once more. The leviathan's attention was fully on the dragon now, giving Vicky time to drag Drake back to the relative safety of our party.

The distraction allowed Drake's dragon to free himself. It

lashed out, its tail denting the core of the leviathan before it fled, and the dragon followed Vicky back to us.

"I can fight!" Dominic snapped, pushing Jonathan away from him. I could see a flash of white bone in Dominic's left arm. He wasn't moving well.

"You're no good to us dead," Jonathan shouted before plunging back into a ferocious exchange with a dark-touched vampire.

"We're only holding the line," Zola said, standing on top of the gravemaker flesh that oozed out of the earth around me. "We have to change the tide."

"Come on!" Vicky said, igniting another soulsword as she sprinted past us. Jasper followed her, and the metallic blood and scars on his tail perhaps told me more about how much shit we were in than anything else had. I'd never seen the dragon go more than a minute or two without healing himself. The fact he hadn't couldn't be good.

Pain, white hot and merciless, lanced through my right side. I folded, almost crumpling in half as I stared in confusion at the feathers sticking out of my side. They glowed like the eyes of the possessed Fae. I looked up in time to see the next volley, a line of archers behind Hern. The bastard wore a smug smile. He wasn't worried at all. He was toying with us.

"*Impadda!*" I growled as the incantation snapped up around me. Sparks and electric blue light exploded as the arrows shattered and bounced off in various directions. Lightning gathered above one of the arches, lancing down to meet his bow.

Zola snarled, stepped around the shield, and raised her staff. "*Tyranno Eversiotto!*" A lightning storm of her own making carved a deadly path through the stone floor, cutting a rocket in half before obliterating the arch. Electric blue light vanished as a fireball erupted from the severed rocket.

I shouted the first incantation that came to mind, even if it wasn't the smartest. "*Magnus Glaciatto!*"

A hailstorm of water, frozen into dagger-like projectiles, stormed across the battlefield. It cut through the fireball, and Fae screamed as they were cut down, or burned up. The orange and red smoke billowed out along the ceiling of the bunker and cast an unsettling light on everything around us.

"Enough!" Hern's voice broke through the shadows, and his power split the flames as he strode toward us. "Surrender now so that you may hear Nudd's offer!"

I gritted my teeth and snapped the arrow off where it stuck out from my back. The pain was unlike anything I'd felt before, and the flesh of the gravemakers burned against the open wounds like a brick of salt. I jerked my hand into a fist, and a spike of gravemaker flesh erupted from the ground in front of Hern. It wasn't as lethal as the pillars, but it could do some damage.

The antlered god stared down at his torso, now impaled on a spike nearly half a foot in diameter. He studied it for a moment, before simply walking forward and snapping the spike off. The gravemakers reeled, and I staggered backward a step at their pain. I'd never been connected to them when something managed to injure them. It was a thousand fingernails on a blackboard that tore through my mind at once. A screaming pain from something that should feel nothing, a vicious burn that inflicted more torment in a single moment than getting shot with that damned arrow had. It was all I could do to stay on my feet, but I had no illusions that I looked wobbly as hell.

Whatever Hern was, he was more of a threat than I'd given him credit for.

"Surrender yourselves and be spared." Hern's words were steady and clear. I didn't sense irony in them, or the deception I was sure waited within. "It would be senseless to waste such fine soldiers."

Foster righted himself as he drew his sword from the gut of a wounded Fae. A quick slash to the throat, and the fairy disintegrated in a horrible wailing scream. Foster held his sword firm in his right hand and stared defiantly at Hern. His voice raged, torn between absolute anger and something far closer to despair. "You've betrayed *everything* you are! Millenia spent serving the Mad King, masking the truth of who he is, of *what he's done!* It is better to die free than serve as a vessel for the rot that lives inside your *king.*"

Jonathan stood beside Foster, his own sword's flame surging, as if reaching out for the blood of Hern.

"Will none of you join us?" Hern said. "None will join the new glory of the Wild Hunt? A glory I have rebuilt, made better, made great once more?"

We stood silent. Jonathan sneered at the old Fae god and spat upon the stone.

"Then you die." Hern's sword was suddenly through Jonathan's chest. Blood poured from the vampire's mouth as he tried to free himself.

"No!" Dominic screamed.

Jonathan looked up, eyes wide, the surprise plain on his face. He reached for Dominic before he slumped to the side.

The last garbled words on his lips were "Kill Vassili … Alexi …"

"Now," Hern started, but a screaming ball of brilliant rage slammed into him a second later. Vicky, stabbing, slicing, and spinning as her soulswords cut a gory path into the Fae's chest. Hern stumbled backward, the shock on his face so profound it would have been comical in almost any other situation.

A shadow of darkness flowed from Hern's shoulder, tried to surround Vicky, but the air around her ignited into blue flame as Jasper exploded off her shoulder. The dragon chewed away the darkness, burned it, tore it, until the magic died, and all that was left was an ancient tattered cloak on the bloody stone floor.

Vicky's breath came slow and hard as she rebounded off Hern and stalked toward him once more.

"Get back!" Drake cried out, leaping onto his dragon as they made for Hern.

I thought it had been a warning that he was about to burn Hern off the face of the earth, but Hern spread his arms wide, and a skeletal deer charged out of the shadows. Its antlers were like daggers, sharpened and gleaming on their broad rack as the deer lowered its head.

Jasper dove toward Vicky, but more shadows swarmed the dragon. He screeched as one of the leviathan's tentacles managed to snatch him from the air. A shower of blue fire erupted behind a missile, casting the choking clouds and smoke into a sickening blue and orange light.

"You are magnificent, child," Hern's shaky voice announced. "But you are too great a threat to live."

Drake's sword lashed out at the air in front of him. A red wound opened in reality before snapping closed, devouring him and his dragon.

I called a Hand of Anubis, raising it between Vicky and the stag, but the antlers pierced the gravemakers, scattering them to the four winds with one vicious toss of the stag's head. I barely recognized the agonized shout that rose from my throat at both the pain of being struck, and the realization of how helpless we were in that place.

Another of Drake's portals opened, and a ball of fire preceded the return of his dragon. Drake followed, directly in front of Vicky. The dragon crashed into the stag, claws and antlers slicing and gouging. They both bled, but the stag didn't stop. It scored a hit on the dragon's rear flank, and the reptilian leg collapsed as whatever muscles were in that form took the brunt of the hit.

The antler tore free of the dragon as Drake raised a shield. An explosion of blue light blinded us all as the crash of the impact of those two powers threatened to deafen us. Drake leaned into the shield, fires licking up around the edges.

Drake cried out between gritted teeth. "The neck, behind the skull!"

I didn't know who he was talking to until Foster and Aideen flashed into their Proelium forms, and their swords cut deep into the massive stag.

The beast whined for a second before it collapsed to earth, dead.

"You dare!" Hern cried.

Drake tried to stand up, and that's when I realized he'd been hit. He'd placed himself in front of one of the most powerful of Nudd's allies to protect Vicky. He had to know he was putting his life at risk. It wasn't until that moment that I truly trusted the fairy, the ancient Demon Sword whose power rivaled Foster's own.

Vicky leaped to the fairies' defense, soulswords still blazing.

Hern stepped toward the child, and the rage of a million souls screamed inside my head.

"Damian, no," Zola croaked from beside me. "We cannot win this fight without Morrigan and Edgar. This was a mistake." Fear showed on my master's face. A fear I didn't understand. Until I called a soulsword and realized it was black as pitch.

"Damian …" It was almost a plea, but the note of loss in her voice was unmistakable.

I'd crossed a line. A line I hadn't realized I was so close to. That's why I'd felt the pain of the gravemakers. I'd let them in too deep. The mantle closed over my head, and the power of an ancient god settled into my bones.

Hern pulled his arm back to strike Vicky down, and my body exploded into motion. Between one moment and the next, the gravemakers surged with me. Not the slow, unstoppable crawl I was so used to seeing from them on the battlefield, but a whip-like response that put me in the path of Hern's blade.

My black soulsword met his strike with a thunderclap. Powers that were never meant to collide exploded into lightning and thunder. My mind warred with itself, and the screaming voices that escaped my throat were not my own. This Fae, this creature, had helped shatter thousands of families, murder innocents, and defile ancient grounds that had been fertile with the blood of our ancestors.

I felt my hand close around Hern's throat even as his sword

ripped through my gut. If we were going to die, we'd take that fucking bastard with us. Vicky roared as she leaped onto the old Fae, the rage at a loss I would never comprehend, one that fueled her in every battle. Brilliant soulswords cut through Hern's armor, and I relished the scream of pain as the Old God fell to a knee.

It was the simplest thing … to squeeze, extending claws until the lifeblood of a god flowed over my hand. Vicky's soulsword stabbed deep into Hern's eye. He twitched twice before I felt the body start disintegrating beneath my grasp.

But something changed. A knowing … unlike any I'd felt before. Memories of grand cities and lavish dwellings built in harmony with the natural world around them. This vision spoke to me. I could feel it in every beat of my heart. Memories that were not my own flooded my mind. *Remember what we lost.*

The rise of man and the wars in Faerie that followed. Hern's memories … but mine … but … the line between what I'd lived and what he'd lived blurred. At once, I was myself, but I was a fledging Owl Knight in the ranks of the Mad King. Something was wrong, but the light was fading. But maybe that was ok. Maybe the price of our lives for peace was a price we could pay.

Darkness rolled in on the edge of my vision even as I tried to fight it back. I *couldn't* let this be the end, I couldn't let Vicky and Sam down … couldn't let them die because of me. But even as Hern's allies fled, and his power fell apart around us, all I could feel was the need to fight. But it grew into a need to kill. To punish. To devour.

CHAPTER THIRTY-ONE

JASPER SCREECHED IN pain as he pulled away from the writhing mass of the leviathan. Someone shouted a name, I think it had once been mine, but I didn't turn to look at them. They weren't the thing that needed to be killed. They were insects, worthy only of my mercy to allow them to exist. Worthy only to serve. The leviathan wasn't. It didn't belong here.

I raised my arm, and the sword of light appeared within its grasp. I'd once called it a scepter, but I understood better now. It was a soulsword without a hilt, without a focus. An unstoppable weapon that could bring the end to any enemy.

The leviathan raised one of its largest tentacles, revealing an eye. Without hesitation, I lunged for it. For all its power, the leviathan's eye was too large for it to easily defend. The soulsword cut deep until my entire arm was encased in the screaming mass of my enemy. I clenched my fist, and the soulsword lanced out like a spear, deep into the creature's brain. A quick twist of the blade ended the beast.

I stepped back, satisfied, as the slimy gray tentacles fell still.

"Damian!" a small human said, standing atop the corpse of my enemy. "Come back to me!"

A strange thing for a mortal to say, for she spoke to me, an old power, and an ancient being.

My voice filled the cavern. "I am always here. I have always been here, and always shall be."

"What's wrong with him?" one of the knights of the Court asked.

I studied another of the fairies as he stepped up beside the first. I could see the red glow of the mantle of the Demon Sword, but it was split between them so that neither wielded its full power. An odd thing for a king to do.

But these beings did not demand extermination. No, I could feel the corruption above us. It felt like my old city, Falias, but wrong. We weren't in Faerie, but I could sense its power in the ley lines. Fragments of the Hunt surged around me, but they weren't right. Something had changed them. No matter. They'd follow their master.

More banter from the mortals followed me as I stepped toward the wall, a wall I knew hid an ancient stone ramp. Once used for transporting ballistae and green men, now it was reduced to a loading dock for the mortal weapons.

I raised my hand and pictured the old wards in my mind. They glowed yellow in my memory, but as they appeared on the wall, they were tainted with darkness.

Stone fractured and shattered and fell away in an avalanche of rubble. I made my way out of the shadows and up into the light of the old city.

✦ ✦ ✦

ONE OF THE mortals screamed the name Damian again, but that was a question I could ponder later, after I'd removed the scourge from the walls of the sacred city. Words came to my mind as I stepped into the sunlight. Words I didn't recall knowing the last time I had walked upon the earth. The mortal weapons, those they called tanks, surrounded a gathering of Fae.

The old gates of the city stood broken before me, but the mortals did not seem to be battling the Fae here. Fairies and mortals alike screamed as I entered the gathering. Most were quick to leave my path, but a few tainted ones gave a satisfying crunch beneath my powers. I wasn't here for them, I was here for the darkness pulsing through what was once the golden city of Faerie. But now there was poison and shadows where there should have been light and obedience.

The armor of the dead gave protection to most creatures and magicks foolish enough to attack, but the first of the mortal tanks to fire sent me stumbling into one of the great towers of Falias. It held firm, having been built by one of the most skilled Fae architects of the last several millennia, but the mortals had caused pain. For that, there would be consequences.

A quick flick of a wrist and power surged through my fingertips. The earth roiled with the dead, and a wave of blackness powered through the soil, swallowing the tanks in a heartbeat.

The mortals continued shouting, "Dig them out! Dig them out!" But none were foolish enough to try my patience again. Even after all this time, with all their modern weaponry, they still knew how to obey their gods.

A gray blur darted in front of me before hovering not twenty feet before my face. Almost within reach. One of the ancient dragons, and atop it a mortal who had once been human. Something forgotten stirred deep inside a memory. I had an attachment to this being somehow.

"This isn't you!"

"Of course it is," I said, my voice twisted into a growl by the armor of the dead. "There is none but I who wields the blade."

The mortal, little more than a child, lit a soulsword from the back of her mount.

Fragments of memory wormed through the edges of my mind. I'd walked through the forests of the Burning Lands, side by side with a cu sith. I'd battled through the armies of fire and crossed the Sea of Souls. The Destroyer …

"Don't leave me."

"Find shelter, little one. I have no quarrel with you and yours. But all who impede the glory of Falias shall be struck down."

Her voice snapped with anger. "*What's wrong with you!*"

"Nothing, child. I am reborn. As it is written, so it shall be."

"Then save that family!" she shouted. "If you're so great, prove it. No one here remembers you!"

That was a ridiculous sentiment. I'd been a fixture of Faerie for millenia … the Wild Hunt … the … I shook my head, as other memories crawled into my mind. Not my own, but hundreds of minds, thousands, that had died at the hand of the King.

"Fool!" I shouted as the memories played out, relentless. "To begin a war with the mortals? At a time such as this? Fool!" Nudd had always been unstable, always teetering on the edge of madness. He'd never been fit to be the Lord of the Dead. It should have been me … Hern … Vesik … what was my name?

I shook my head, and the blade in my hand flared. Regardless, I'd seen the memory of his declaration. I'd seen the family of Fae he meant to execute. That I could stop, but the dark ones were all around us. Once this battle began in earnest, too many would die.

But it was a price someone had to pay.

The small mortal released a string of curses fit for a soldier in the fight of their lives. Something in the child spoke to me, struck a chord of fondness I did not fully understand. The rider and her dragon swooped back into the clouds of the Wild Hunt now billowing up behind me as the great cloak, not the corrupted thing my enemy had conjured.

The masses had taken notice of us now. Those who knew, fled. Those who were our enemy stood their ground.

I leveled the blazing fires of the soulsword at the nearest of Nudd's men. He'd gone back to days long forgotten, marking his soldiers with a white hand. A hand that for many represented the iron rule of a Mad King.

"Release them." My voice boomed across the field. The three Fae, strapped to pikes as though they were meant to be burned alive, looked up at me with something like hope on their faces. It was possible they'd be more useful as martyrs, but the moment that thought crossed my mind, another voice rose up to shout it down, telling me they were allies, disgusted at the mere thought.

But thought did not indicate action. The thinking of an atrocity did not make it so.

The ranks of dark-touched filth Nudd had welcomed into his forces didn't move. A smile crawled across my face, fracturing the blackened flesh that formed my helmet. I rolled my shoulders and let the antlers rise into the sky. Confusion lit the nearest vampire's expression before I dropped the soulsword, and a wave of dead carried our enemies into oblivion.

The thunder of hooves echoed through the mists of the Wild Hunt, and my power rose.

✦ ✦ ✦

LONG AGO, IN the time of the Wandering War, the Mad King had sought to make a pact with the dark-touched vampires. It hadn't ended well, their betrayal leaving scores of our knights dead, their blood on the hands of the Mad King. There is much for which I was able to forgive the old king, but the alliance with creatures that should have been our mortal enemies was not one of them.

Some of the Fae in the audience were drawn into the Hunt, and as they matched the step of those shadowy apparitions, the silver armor of the Hunt materialized on each of them in turn. The Mad King would have called it blasphemy, visages of his victories replaced with the fauna and antlers of my own. But the dark-touched had harrowed this world long enough. While Gwynn Ap Nudd might have been willing to sacrifice much to reach his final goal, I found myself still loyal to Faerie. Still loyal to the families that had raised Gorias and Falias into the empires they had been.

"Destroy them," I growled.

The Hunt didn't need more guidance than that. It was old magic, and understood intention better than most. That was also what made it dangerous. It's why the thoughts of those atrocities could bear fruit, but I'd been in control of the Hunt long enough to understand the difference between a stray thought, and a death sentence.

The front line barreled into the streets and alleys as the dark-touched descended in force. They came from the windows and the doorways, seeming to melt out of the shadows. A grin lifted the corners of my mouth as I realized some of them were old enough to know what was happening. Toward the back of the ranks, as the boldest dark-touched were pulled down into the surging clouds of the Wild Hunt, a few turned and fled. Perhaps they meant to report back to their generals, their strategists, but to me, it did not matter. Send more, send them all. The Hunt would harvest them like a dullahan seeking its prey.

A series of thunderclaps sounded across the field of battle. It was something I'd never heard on this world until nearly a century past, humans and their weapons. Shells exploded inside the shadows of the Hunt. Fiery balls of light showed the death of innocent Fae, and some of the humans' own people. I'd fought many wars over the millennia, but no creatures fought among themselves quite so often as the humans.

Something spoke to me, a voice from the shadows, that the ground we stood on had been some of the bloodiest seen on this side of the world. But that mattered little.

Another round fired from the commoners' tanks. One of them caught me in the chest, blasting a hole through the black armor of the mantle. I fell to a knee, catching the charred flesh of the gravemakers as it tumbled away from me. I frowned at the sight. The mantle of Anubis was not mine. It was a necromancer's, Vesik. Enemy to the throne, but … confusion swept through me. Two lives, one a short span—mortal, violent, and dark—and the other the gleaming beacon of the Hunter, a life of millennia and violence, but more peace than the mortal would have imagined.

I turned my attention back to the tanks. A quick sweep of

my hand and a line of gravemakers exploded from the earth, sending one of the tanks into a cartwheel. A glimmer of satisfaction lit in my gut, at the same moment a stark sense of horror crawled through my brain. But they'd threatened me, injured me, and it was my place to strike them back. Of that, the voices could agree.

Another tank swiveled to take aim at the crowds, but one of the Demon Swords, the dragon rider, dove into it. The barrel collapsed under a fiery strike, and the Fae shouted something into the mass of steel and gears.

Whatever he'd said, one at a time the tanks ceased their attack. as the communication made its way through the ranks. They began to retreat.

I felt certain they would need to be punished, made to understand why no one could interfere with the Hunt. But for now, my prey waited in Falias.

✦ ✦ ✦

THE CITY HAD changed. I recognized many of the streets and towers, but their position no longer matched the ley lines in Faerie. For a moment, I wondered if they had been changed to match those in the world of the commoners, but it was easy to see that the line energy here was diluted, and only a few massive trunks of power flowed through the city. It would be enough to fuel Gwynn Ap Nudd, but I didn't think it would be enough to restore Falias to the glory it once had in Faerie.

And maybe that's because you let Nudd murder millions.

I frowned at the whisper in the back of my mind. That hadn't been true. Ezekiel and the old necromancer, that had been their doing.

The fucking hell it had.

The voices in the shadows grew quieter as we stormed through the city, carving up dark-touched, obliterating whatever Fae decided to stand against us, but even though the voices grew quiet, I could not silence them entirely. Some insisted on speaking, apparently never having learned the appropriate time for quiet and concentration skills they would've learned in the army of Falias. I could scarcely imagine an Owl Knight prattling on in the midst of combat. They would confuse their birds, and likely leave nothing but their armor behind.

"Damian, turn back!"

The other dragon rider had returned, hovering precariously close to the edges of the shadows. What a prize she'd make, a warrior with control of the beasts, not so unlike the Demon Sword.

From one step to the next, I found my body hesitating. One of the voices sent up a scream of rage, and I had to focus to bring silence once more. A flick of my wrist sent another wave of the fairies crashing into the nearest tower, surging up the side and striking down every vampire they found. It would take time to clear the city, but time I had. I smiled beneath the dead flesh of the gravemakers.

CHAPTER THIRTY-TWO

DARKNESS. EVERYTHING IS darkness. I am aware, somewhat, of Vicky's voice and others in the darkness. At times the shadows become light, and I can see the scarred streets of Falias before me, the billowing shadows and night. But I know something is wrong. I know I am not in control of myself. Something happened with Hern, and the gravemakers absorbed some piece of his personality. They've corrupted the Hunt, and I fear what is happening. I can only watch as the scene unfolds around me. Only listen as Vicky cries out to me in the shadows. I try to move, to stop the destruction before me. But I have no control. The light fades out once more, and only the echo of a terrified girl follows me down.

CHAPTER THIRTY-THREE

"TAKE US IN!" Vicky shouted as she steered Jasper too close to the dark-touched. But whatever was happening to Damian, whatever the fear and power was she felt through her tie to him, the monster before her did not lash out.

Jasper unleashed a torrent of blue flame. It sent two of Hern's Owl Knights to the ground as little more than ash. But one of their mounts evaded the fires and circled back, the massive bird of prey darting toward them, claws extended.

The dragon tried to veer to the side, even as Vicky drew a soulsword, but they were both too late. The claws were already in Jasper's hide, the beak inside their defenses.

An ungodly screech sounded above them as Vicky drove her blade into the owl's foot. A moment later a ball of black feathers hurtled into the owl, knocking it toward the ground. Jasper didn't hesitate. Another burst of blue fire consumed the oversized bird.

"Child!" the crow shouted.

"Morrigan?" Vicky asked, frowning at the bird as it matched Jasper's pace.

"Yes, you must retreat! Whatever that thing is, it's not Damian."

"Yes, it is! I can still feel him." Vicky felt as though the bird was scowling at her, and perhaps Morrigan was, but the unblinking eyes of the crow didn't leave her own. "He's scared."

Morrigan closed her eyes for a moment and then surveyed the battle around them. "You'll only complicate matters. He must be subdued before all of Falias is lost. Hern's drive has consumed him, child. Get away."

"If he dies, I die," Vicky said, her hands clenching the spiky scales of Jasper's neck. "Sam dies."

"Then it is true. The magic used to break your bond to the Destroyer bound you to a different master."

Morrigan's words infuriated Vicky, but the realization that the crow had succeeded in leading her away from the fight was far more irritating. "He's my friend. So is Sam. I won't let you kill him."

"Find peace in your time, child, for we all must die."

"I already did," Vicky said. "I didn't enjoy it very much, and I don't plan to do it again for a long time."

She pulled to the right on one of the spikes protruding from Jasper's back. She'd come to think of it as a steering column, and the dragon had grown quick to respond. Jasper soared right, ducking beneath the Morrigan. But even as she closed once more on the massive jackal-shaped colossus that had once been Damian, the Morrigan's words crept into the back of her mind.

She couldn't stop them. Not like this. Not alone. But there might be one who could.

✦ ✦ ✦

THE SOLDIER STARED down at his hands, and the long rifle clutched between them. He didn't know how long he'd been in the old field, or the city that had overtaken it, but he certainly didn't remember the bizarre towers climbing into the heavens. Or the monster storming its gates. He remembered a battle, a gunshot as a Confederate cut him down.

He'd heard they were winning, but it didn't stop his friends from dying. Didn't stop brothers and fathers from being turned into lifeless chunks of meat, strewn across the ground. The sight had been madness, until there was only pain, and then nothing. Then he stood, stock still, staring as the carnage in the field slowly overtook everything. He remembered the shadows of the things that came for the men, and the shadows that the men became. But he hadn't been able to speak in those silent days. Hadn't been able to move. Only watch in horror at what men could do.

But now his feet moved freely. He could feel the air on his face, and smell the blood and the soil. The creatures around him might have been bizarre, but he'd seen worse. And he knew an aggressor when one made itself known. The beings that fled past him looked like fairies from children's stories, but they were large, and armed, and many of them screamed the wail of a banshee as they died.

And that was what had happened to him so long ago. He had died, too. But it hadn't been here. For a moment he thought he would report back to his sergeant. The man had a head for common sense, would have some idea of what to do. But he only saw a few other ghosts in the area. A few other soldiers. Most of them had an odd glow, much like the rifle in his hands. If the battle had been won, the war should have been over. So, what was happening now? He shook his head, trying to remember, instead giving in to his instincts to make for the tree line.

He'd be safer from the armies there, and whatever other monsters lurked on the battlefield. As he slid into a copse of trees, he saw the massive gray wings of what could only be a dragon from the storybooks. A shadow rose before him, and he knew the end had come. One of the corrupted men, creatures that seemed to be made of bark and rot, reached a hand out and grabbed him by the arm. Cold bled into him, but a frisson of excitement ran down the soldier's back. He could feel, he could touch, and without thinking of what he was doing, he planted the barrel of his rifle firmly into the neck of the creature and pulled the trigger.

The boom was thunderous, and the satisfaction was undeniable as chunks of the creature exploded out the back of its head. Milky white eyes widened before the thing collapsed and seeped into the earth.

Monsters they might be, but now he could hurt them. He moved through the chaos, searching out his brothers, and avoiding the dying fragments of those wounded so long ago. Memories surged into his mind with every step, as if telling him to follow the colossus into the city and strike down the creatures for the white hand.

The soldier fought the compulsion for a time, but in the end, the dead obeyed their lord.

To be continued in the Books of the Dead novellas.

Coming in 2019.

Note from Eric R. Asher

Thank you for spending time with the misfits! I'm blown away by the fantastic reader response to this series, and am so grateful to you all.

If you'd like an email when each new book releases, sign up for my mailing list (www.ericrasher.com). Emails only go out about once per month and your information is closely guarded by hungry cu siths.

Also, follow me on BookBub (bookbub.com/authors/eric-r-asher), and you'll always get an email for special sales.

Thanks for reading!
Eric

Also by Eric R. Asher

Keep track of Eric's new releases by receiving an email on release day. It's fast and easy to sign up for Eric's mailing list, and you'll also get an ebook copy of the subscriber exclusive anthology, *Whispers of War*.

Go here to get started: www.ericrasher.com

The Steamborn Trilogy:

Steamborn
Steamforged
Steamsworn

The Vesik Series:

(Recommended for Ages 17+)

Days Gone Bad
Wolves and the River of Stone
Winter's Demon
This Broken World
Destroyer Rising
Rattle the Bones
Witch Queen's War
Forgotten Ghosts
Book of the Ghost*

*Want to receive an email on the day this book releases? Sign up for Eric's mailing list.

www.ericrasher.com

Mason Dixon – Monster Hunter:

Episode One

Episode Two

Episode Three – coming soon*

*Want to receive an email on the day this book releases? Sign up for Eric's mailing list.

www.ericrasher.com

About the Author

Eric is a former bookseller, cellist, and comic seller currently living in Saint Louis, Missouri. A lifelong enthusiast of books, music, toys, and games, he discovered a love for the written word after being dragged to the library by his parents at a young age. When he is not writing, you can usually find him reading, gaming, or buried beneath a small avalanche of Transformers. For more about Eric, see: www.ericrasher.com

Enjoy this book? You can make a big difference.

Reviews are the most powerful tools I have when it comes to getting attention for my books. I don't have a huge marketing budget like some New York publishers, but I have something even better.

A committed and loyal bunch of readers.

Honest reviews help bring my books to the attention of other readers.

If you've enjoyed this book, I would be very grateful if you could take a minute to leave a review on the platform of your choice. It can be as short as you like. Thank you for spending time with Damian and the misfits.

Connect with Eric R. Asher Online:

Twitter: @ericrasher

Instagram: @ericrasher

Facebook: EricRAsher

www.ericrasher.com

eric@ericrasher.com

Made in the USA
Middletown, DE
12 February 2020